CAPTAIN BLACKWELL'S PRIZE

Captain Blackwell's Prize

by

V.E. Ulett

www.oldsaltpress.com

ISBN: 978-0-9882360-6-6

BISAC Subject Headings:
FIC027050 FICTION / Romance / Historical
FIC047000FICTION / Sea Stories
FIC032000FICTION / War & Military

Cover design by Julie K. Rose & Rick Spilman

Publisher's Note:

This is a work of historical fiction. Certain characters and their actions may have been inspired by historical individuals and events. The characters in the novel, however, represent the work of the author's imagination. Any resemblance to actual persons, living or dead, is entirely coincidental.

1.0

Chapter 1

The battle started the moment the English captain clapped his hat back on his head after raising it in salute to Captain de Leon y Castillo, who stood on the quarterdeck of His Most Catholic Majesty King Carlos IV's 42 gun frigate *La Trinidad.*

"Serve the brute out," Captain de Leon y Castillo called to his officers; to a man, their faces expressed surprise at the temerity of a mere sloop of war approaching to engage them.

La Trinidad's broadside roared out at her captain's command. Her ill-aimed guns sent shot flying through the sails of the English ship and clear over her, the cannonballs' shrieking progress ending in the tossing sea. The English captain pressed on and brought his ship within three cable lengths of *La Trinidad,* maneuvered into position and opened fire directly into his opponent's lower gun deck, then hauled his wind, dropping astern of *La Trinidad,* and raked her with grapeshot and chain.

The deck of *La Trinidad* erupted into a cloud of wreckage. Splintered wood from the width of needles to sharpened stakes flew wildly through the air. The devastation aboard *La Trinidad* was tremendous: gun ports knocked into jagged, gaping holes, cannons dismounted and more lethal on the heaving deck than the enemy. The English vessel wore and sent in another rolling broadside, killing nearly all *La Trinidad's* officers on the upper deck.

Captain de Leon y Castillo was unharmed on the quarterdeck, protected in part by the splinter netting. He rallied the men to fight the previously disengaged side of the ship where the British vessel was ranging into position. *La Trinidad*'s twenty-four pound smashers spoke out, dismounting two of the Englishman's carronades. The enemy's fire became unremitting and men were cut down around Captain de Leon y Castillo. The wind of one of the Englishman's shot took off his hat as it passed and killed the entire gun's crew serving the larboard quarterdeck carronade. His ship and her people were cruelly mauled. Her broadside had not been heard since the raking fire across her stern, her fore and main topsail yards were down on the caps, and *La Trinidad*'s hull had been breached many times. Captain de Leon y Castillo ordered the carpenter to rig slings over the side to reach the holes, but the slings were shot away. Moments later the ship's rudder was disabled, leaving *La Trinidad* helpless in the rising swell.

The British ship of 28 guns edged down before the wind and lay on *La Trinidad*'s quarter, the intention quite clear. The Englishmen would board. The British captain's shouted orders were heard as the ships neared. Captain de Leon y Castillo was knocked to the deck by the collision of the two ships, and he was struggling to his feet when the boarding hooks were tossed to *La Trinidad* and the Englishmen began lashing the ships together. The sight spurred Captain de Leon y Castillo, who sprang up drawing his sword. He almost injured a youngster in midshipman's dress, scrambling to his side beneath the splinter netting.

"All hands to repel boarders!" Captain de Leon y Castillo called.

The pale and blackened faces of Englishmen came screaming up the Spaniard's side, calling out the name of their ship and slashing with boarding axes. The pop and ping of pistol and musket shot filled the air, and the clash of sword on pike, cutlass, and axe. Captain de Leon y Castillo met one enemy after another.

The young person fighting beside Captain de Leon y Castillo was aware the men of *La Trinidad* were giving way before the furious English assault. The majority of the Spanish crew were natives pressed into service in America, and without their officers to urge them to die for a king and a land they had never yet seen, they didn't fight with the spirit the Englishmen brought to the contest.

On the quarterdeck they were being overrun. Captain de Leon y Castillo, who had never yet lost a duel, laid about him the first rush of attackers. But he was a middle-aged commander, far from well, and when the fighting on the quarterdeck was in a close packed crowd his elegant swordplay counted for little. The Spanish captain's young companion witnessed a well-favored lieutenant of the Royal Navy hammer so effectively at Captain de Leon y Castillo that he dropped his guard in weariness, and the Englishman thrust his sword under the captain's ribs and ran him through the vitals. The lieutenant withdrew his bloody sword, crouched and sprang, throwing the youngster into the binnacle.

The cap she wore flew off from the tremendous knock, revealing long, dark hair; Mercedes pushed herself to her knees and crawled back to Captain de Leon y Castillo. She dragged his head and shoulders onto her lap.

"Mercedes, John Bull over there is a gentleman. You must go below and put on a gown. Tell him you are my wife, my daughter, whatever you wish. Carry my letter to Maria Angel. Make haste now, and promise me you will send the letter, and my weapons to my sons."

Mercedes held Captain de Leon y Castillo's hand. Never had she heard him speak so mildly of an Englishman, always before they were dogs or whoresons. The hell-scene of fighting had shifted to the break of the quarterdeck. *La Trinidad*'s men were fleeing the British, trying to gain shelter below and turned back by the soldiers. The captain recalled her, squeezing her hand.

"I swear it, Captain. God's blessing on you," Mercedes said.

She eased him to the deck and rose. The captain, with the last of his strength, called out to the sailing master, "Señor Martinez, lower the flag. Marines there, lift that grating for Doña Mercedes."

In his cabin below she changed the stained midshipman's attire for a gown selected as most resembling those worn by Englishwomen, but she hadn't traded the boots for slippers when she heard the commotion outside. There was no time for the captain's effects. She tied the sash in which were sewn her mother's jewels around her waist, and secured a letter and her slippers under the belt, then she opened the cabin door.

The same handsome officer who had murdered Captain de Leon y Castillo was pulling his sword from the sentry's stomach. Mercedes ran for the companion ladder and began to climb, but paused in her ascent when the sentry cried out, "God go with you, Doña Mercedes!" She turned and found the British lieutenant behind her on the ladder, his face level with her backside, and she saw him raise his arm and discharge his pistol. The ball caught the sentry, the second son of a good Barcelona family, in the face. Mercedes flew up the ladder, stumbled over the coaming of the hatchway and gained the deck.

Chapter 2

Captain Blackwell heard the single pistol shot and saw the woman stagger out of the hatchway and run to a Spanish seaman by the taffrail, who immediately put her behind him. He continued giving orders to his carpenter to report on the captured vessel's condition, and wasn't surprised when his second lieutenant came up the companion ladder in the woman's wake.

"What was that shot below, Mr. Sprague?" Captain Blackwell called out.

"Resistance from the sentry at the captain's door, sir."

"His papers?" Captain Blackwell said. Mr. Sprague answered with a blush and a mumbled excuse.

Captain Blackwell turned away to attend to his third lieutenant who, with a party of seamen, was coming up from the main gun deck with more prisoners under guard. He heard Mr. Sprague's comment, "Ain't it just like the Dons to bring a woman along of them," before receiving Mr. Verson's report. The two lieutenants were similar in their backgrounds. Neither came of an influential family. Captain Blackwell judged them as he did all naval officers, first as seamen and then as men. He thought the one capable and honest, and the other a lubberly, wicked brute.

While he listened to Mr. Verson's report, he stared at the blood covering the lieutenant's shoes. Staining his white stockings, it looked as though he had waded in it. Mr. Verson had been in a party sent round the disengaged side of *La Trinidad* when the firing ceased, boarding through her entry port to subdue her main deck gun crews.

"There was not much fight in them when we arrived, sir, with no less than three eighteen pounders loose and causing bloody murder. We secured them, sir, and bring up thirty prisoners."

"Well done, Mr. Verson. Where's Mr. Whittemore?" Captain Blackwell's first lieutenant had led Mr. Verson's boarding party.

"Dead, sir. Copped it as we were boarding. Some bugger slammed him with a handspike."

"Oh! He shall be sadly missed. Who's bringing up the rest of the prisoners?"

"That's all there is, sir, all the men able to walk." Mr. Verson came closer to his captain and lowered his voice. "There are many dead, sir, many, many dead and wounded."

"Mr. Bransford," called Captain Blackwell in a voice strong enough to reach the midshipman in charge on his quarterdeck. The ships had parted the lashings and drifted apart. "Send the doctor across. Take possession, Mr. Verson, if you please, and send a party immediately to bring up Mr. Whittemore and any of ours. Mr. Sprague, count off twenty men from the prisoners to man the pumps and the rest to *Inconstant*."

Captain Blackwell called for his gig and was at his station on the weather side of the quarterdeck in time to watch the Spanish woman come aboard *Inconstant*. She judged the swell, looking over her shoulder, and sprang for the ship on the rise. And then she came up the side like a right sailor, with the man who had shielded her on board *La Trinidad* behind her, ready to place her feet should she slip. Captain Blackwell wondered how many of the men looking on envied that seaman. He certainly did, yet he strove to appear disinterested.

He saw the attentive gazes of his officers and the younger hands. There were wry looks from some of the older men, the man-of-war's men, who believed women brought ill fortune to a vessel. Captain Blackwell didn't credit nonsense about women being able to control the wind and bring on storms, but as a man subject to the vagaries of war and the elements, he reserved judgment on the sources of fortune, ill or otherwise. His opinion of a woman on a ship of war was it might certainly be a bad stroke of luck for the woman.

"Mr. Sprague, assemble the prisoners aft. I wish to address them."

When the prisoners were there, several score of disconsolate faces turned toward him, Captain Blackwell ordered the word to be passed for his brother. Mr. Blackwell came on deck a few moments later, a younger, slighter version of the captain, stepped to his brother's side and, with a bowed head, listened to his instructions.

"Men of *La Trinidad,* you are prisoners of His Britannic Majesty's ship *Inconstant,*" boomed out Captain Blackwell, followed by his brother's translation at lower volume in Spanish. "You will be taken below and set down to be exchanged at the nearest port, if you cooperate. If you do not, you will be killed and put over the side." Bodies in fact, were already going over the side of *La Trinidad.* "If any of you rated able seamen, any skilled men, wish to join His Britannic Majesty's service, you will be set to work." Captain Blackwell turned to his new first lieutenant. "Prisoners below, if you please, Mr. Sprague. We shall work out a schedule to give them air and exercise at a later time."

"Aye, aye, sir."

"Not the lady! Put her in my cabin," Captain Blackwell said, perhaps a shade too loudly. Conscious of a misstep, Captain Blackwell muttered, "The fucking brute," under his breath to his brother beside him.

Francis Blackwell merely pursed his lips. They were the only offspring of a country parson, but Captain Blackwell had been from home since the age of twelve and was more the product of the Royal Navy than a genteel upbringing.

"Go below and speak to her, won't you Frank? Discover the Spaniard's cargo and her sailing plans."

"Certainly," Francis said.

"I shall join you directly. We're to have dirty weather, the glass falls steady, and we need to move everything out of that tub before it sets in to blow."

Some time later, Captain Blackwell came into his cabin. Having forgotten the presence of the woman aboard, he walked in pulling his shirt over his head until he saw both his brother and the lady jump to their feet.

"Allow me to present Doña Mercedes de Aragon," Francis said. "Doña Mercedes, Captain Blackwell, of His Britannic Majesty's ship *Inconstant.*"

"Mercy!" Captain Blackwell said. It must have been fatigue or a reaction to that bloody little action just past, and he immediately felt a fool. The Spanish lady, a young woman, was curtseying to him, and both she and his brother started at his outburst. "Forgive me. I won't be a minute."

He dodged into his sleeping cabin, followed by his steward catching up his discarded clothes, and the ship's surgeon.

"It's someone else's blood, goddamn it, as I've told you," Captain Blackwell said. "You have your hands full, doctor, with those poor men from *La Trinidad.* I suggest you return to them."

His steward poured water and Captain Blackwell washed away the worst of the battle's dirt and emerged a moment later, having exchanged his bloodied finery for working clothes. He found Francis and the lady still standing. The doctor and McMurtry, Captain Blackwell's ugly, toad-like steward, slipped out of the cabin.

"Please sit down. My brother has made himself known to you, ma'am? He serves the King as well, in the diplomatic service." Captain Blackwell paused and looked at Francis, awaiting his translation.

"Miss Mercedes speaks English, sir."

Captain Blackwell turned to her. "Ah, indeed. How's that?"

"I boarded Captain de Leon y Castillo's ship in Alta California, sir. I am not from Spain."

"de Leon y Castillo ... that was her captain. And she was coming from the Spanish Main?"

"Yes, sir. Captain de Leon y Castillo brought *La Trinidad* from the Pacific waters, round Cape Horn, and we were two days out of Funchal when ..." Mercedes paused, clasped her hands tighter in her lap, and hurried on. "She carries 35,000 gold *escudos*, and she has some fine instruments in her cabin. A Berthoud's chronometer."

Captain Blackwell regarded Mercedes with appreciation; thirty-five thousand gold pieces, and this handsome woman had survived the passage round the Horn, and understood the value to a ship's captain of a well-made chronometer.

Whatever her loyalties to Spain, Mercedes no doubt felt extremely the uncertainty of her present situation. Captain Blackwell noted her troubled expression as she looked from his face to Francis's, and then turned her gaze out the stern windows near which she was seated. Mercedes gave a little shriek, her hands held together over her breast. Captain Blackwell came near her and saw floating face down a body dressed in the uniform of Spain. It was a smallish man in an officer's coat.

Captain Blackwell knew a strong desire to comfort her in her distress. "And what is your relation to Captain de Leon y Castillo, ma'am?"

Mercedes had sprung up and Francis stood also. Captain Blackwell strode to the door of the little closet knocked out of his own living space where his brother slept and flung it open. "In here, ma'am, if you please." He bowed to Mercedes as she ran in, and he closed the door.

"You shall have to change your quarters, Frank," Captain Blackwell said. "You may have the first lieutenant's berth. Mr. Sprague must remain where he is."

"But she hasn't even a maid to loan her countenance," Francis said.

"This is not a yacht, sir. What would you have me do? Put her in the gunroom with my officers, on the lower deck where any man may get at her? There are men in this ship straight from His Majesty's prisons."

"I ... I was not thinking."

"No, indeed, and you a diplomatic cove. Allow me to arrange matters in my own ship. Only McMurtry comes in here without my permission, and I shall answer for McMurtry. Now, we must knot and splice."

Captain Blackwell hastened out of the great cabin, leaving Francis behind distracted and bemused.

Chapter 3

Inside the tiny cabin, Mercedes sat on the cot, shaking. She wrapped a rough blanket she found there around her shoulders. She hadn't had time in those last moments in Captain de Leon y Castillo's cabin to put up her hair, and she had been ashamed to have it down around her shoulders in view of all those strange men. They were so large, with a ruddy colored, half burnt skin. Yet Mr. Blackwell, and to a lesser extent his brother the captain, seemed gentlemen.

She closed her eyes and put her face in her cupped hands, but the images were there in her mind of the British lieutenant murdering Captain de Leon y Castillo, and Private Alcarez, the Marine sentry outside the captain's door. In battle, men were killed, but she had seen the eager pleasure in the face of the officer as he did the killings, and she trembled still.

She had been in the cockpit with *La Trinidad's* surgeon during the first part of the battle and done her utmost to assist with the wounded. But though she'd seen many horrible sights, floggings of slaves and Indians in California and wounds from shipboard accidents, she was overwhelmed when the numbers of wounded being brought down increased and showed no sign of stopping. Then a cannonball came through the side of the ship into the orlop deck and took off the head of the surgeon.

Mercedes ran away, stumbling and slipping to the captain's cabin. She tore one of his disused swords from the rack on the bulkhead, went up the companion ladder, and crawled under the fallen splinter netting until she reached the quarterdeck. This was just before the Englishmen boarded and she had felt if she were to die, she would far rather die on the quarterdeck in the open air than in the charnel house below. On deck, she might at least fight for survival.

Mercedes had frequently to brace herself into the area of the cot as the ship thrashed on the heavy swell. She had been Captain de Leon y Castillo's consort, not his wife or his daughter. It was the price she'd paid; for she found the true cost of the passage her mother arranged with Captain de Leon y Castillo to carry Mercedes to Spain after her death, was that she should sleep with him all the passage. But it hadn't been a bad bargain, and Captain de Leon y Castillo's death grieved Mercedes. He had been a cultured man, fifty-six years old, with grown sons and a wife in Barcelona. A *hidalgo* of the old school, Captain de Leon y Castillo had brought vast experience to his amorous relations with Mercedes. His attentions, never those of a hot-blooded youth, had fallen off as the voyage progressed, apace with Captain de Leon y Castillo's malady. Indeed, Captain de Leon y Castillo might never have reached Spain, whether the English had attacked or not.

She was a prisoner of war in effect, though she really had no country, and as a woman, no legal existence. Mercedes brooded on the answer she should make the Englishmen respecting her relation to the late captain, and which of the English brothers might further her hopes. When she heard the striking of six bells in the afternoon watch Mercedes rose to prepare for supper.

After months aboard ship Mercedes knew a ship's routine, at least that of *La Trinidad*. She knew where to draw water, and she went out of the sleeping cabin. The sentry at the door, having received no orders regarding the lady, let her pass. The seamen she met looked carefully away from her until she was returning with her bucket, and McMurtry startled her by popping up at her side.

"Oh, no, Miss, no. You mustn't fetch your own water. The Captain would stripe my back. You just tell me how much you want and when, and I'll bring it to you."

Mercedes yielded her bucket to McMurtry and followed him into the cabin. She knew better than to ask this ill-favored man what sort of character his captain had. She had enough experience of naval life to comprehend the strict hierarchy of these small communities, and McMurtry, if he were any kind of seaman, would never comment upon his captain to a mere passenger.

"Won't be any supper this evening, Miss, Captain's that busy. He'll take a bite on deck, and I'll bring your vittles in here."

It wasn't a restful evening. In her sleeping cabin after supper Mercedes wore herself out with worry. The strain of the day and the fatigue of bracing herself in her cot ended in sleep early in the morning hours.

On deck, and everywhere in the ship, they were furiously busy, with boats plying between *La Trinidad* and *Inconstant* until Captain Blackwell judged it too dark and the sea too high to continue. The hold had to be rearranged to accommodate the prisoners and create a secure stowage for the gold. There were repairs to effect to both ships, and what concerned Captain Blackwell beyond all else, he had to make ready for the gale every seaman aboard knew was approaching. They had taken this Spanish ship of superior weight of guns, bearing New World treasure to her ally Napoleon, but it would be to no avail if she were to sink with her astonishing fortune. This was to say nothing of *La Trinidad's* wounded, of her fine chronometer and other instruments Mercedes had so obligingly described. A worse apprehension, one Captain Blackwell wouldn't permit to form in his mind, was that he might lose both the Spaniard and his own good sea-boat were he ill-prepared to meet heavy weather.

He drove his men hard through the afternoon and evening watches, eating his bread and meat on deck, though he had the crew piped to supper at the usual hour. At the start of the middle watch, with Mr. Verson on deck, Captain Blackwell finally went below to his cabin, and without a thought for the woman so close, threw himself on his cot and slept.

Yet he thought of her when he rose just before dawn and splashed water on his face before going on deck to give his first orders of the day. He thought of her as he came below again, washed properly and shaved, and waited for the appearance of his brother. Captain Blackwell had invited Francis to breakfast in the great cabin, and he was debating whether to ask him to take all his meals there just as previously. It would give the situation with his lady prisoner some countenance. But he remained undecided after Francis had walked in, and when Mercedes came out of her sleeping cabin, Captain Blackwell's intentions were thrown into confusion.

He did not know how she managed to look so fresh and lovely. She had tied her hair up with a clever use of strips of cloth, and her dress, the same she had on yesterday, wasn't frowsy and slept in. The thought of her removing it to sleep roused Captain Blackwell, and he hastened to cover how much she moved him by throwing himself into the role of the good host.

Captain Blackwell held a chair for her, but took no liberties of touching her shoulder. He pressed the dishes brought in upon her. "May I help you to another chop, ma'am," and behaved as though they were attending a country house party. But even before the meal had reached its end, Captain Blackwell's mind had turned to the innumerable tasks of the day before him. A sudden lurch of the ship caused the coffee urn to jump, and Mercedes clapped both her hands over it.

"May I beg a favor, sir?" Mercedes said. "May I have my chest, with my clothes and my things, from *La Trinidad*?"

"Certainly, ma'am, I'll give the order."

Captain Blackwell rose, but Mercedes made a movement toward him, and it was clear she hadn't done speaking.

"May I also have Captain de Leon y Castillo's weapons, sir? He desired me to return them and a letter to his wife and his sons. I can show you the locker where they are kept. He was an *espadachin*. I don't know how to say it in English." She looked to Francis.

"Swordsman."

"Thank you, of course. He was a swordsman, and these are his finest weapons. He didn't use them yesterday. But he extracted this promise of me before he died, sir. I am charged to carry this news to his family. I'm sure it shall be as little welcome as I."

Captain Blackwell glanced at his brother, and the look Francis returned revealed his awareness of what Mercedes communicated. She wasn't Captain de Leon y Castillo's wife, nor his daughter, and might in fact have been to him what his family would despise.

"I'll find a moment to take you across myself, and we shall collect your things, and his," Captain Blackwell said. "I don't believe I said so before, ma'am, I am sorry for the loss of your – "

"You are very kind, sir, and I am obliged to you. Might I impose on your kindness a little further? I should like to visit *La Trinidad's* men in the sick berth, and in the hold if you'll permit it."

Captain Blackwell opened the door to his cabin. "Pass the word for Captain Christensen."

When the captain of Marines came in, Captain Blackwell said, "Mr. Christensen, you're to escort Miss Mercedes to visit her former shipmates in the hold. She may touch no one and no one may touch her. Then you'll take her to the sick berth. She may spend as much time there as she wishes."

"Aye, aye, sir."

"If you will join me, ma'am, on the quarterdeck afterward, I will have you rowed across."

Mercedes was curtseying to him, thanking him in gentle tones. Captain Blackwell turned back to her before quitting the cabin. "Be so kind as to repeat my offer to your shipmates, Miss Mercedes, of joining the Royal Navy. I shall be particularly pleased if *La Trinidad's* carpenter or his mates were agreeable."

Mercedes was in the hold conversing with Severino Martinez, the seaman to whom she'd run on the deck of *La Trinidad*. Before they parted the day previous, he for the ship's hold, and she for the Englishman's cabin, he had advised her, "Be forthcoming with the captain, you owe nothing to Spain." She asked what he had had to eat and drink, and he told her the prisoners had been given water and ship's biscuit. Mercedes hung her head, shamed by the comfort of meat, eggs, and coffee in her stomach from breakfast in the cabin.

"Tell the Captain I wish to speak to him," Mr. Martinez said. "I will take his offer to join."

"Oh, no! Would not it be better to be put ashore? We're not far from Spain."

"We're not headed to Spain, girl. He'll take us into Port Mahon or Gibraltar. What waits me there is prison. Listen, Mercedes, you can discover where we're bound. Use what the Captain taught you of navigation."

Mercedes cast a quick glance at the captain of Marines. It did not appear he understood their Spanish conversation, but she was cautious and unwilling to assume ignorance in others. She did not reply, though she bowed her head in acquiescence to Mr. Martinez's suggestion.

"What ails Juanito? Was he wounded?" Mercedes asked. "He should be in the sick berth." She moved toward a boy, one of Captain de Leon y Castillo's servants, curled on his side and facing the bulkhead.

Mr. Martinez and Captain Christensen stepped forward together to prevent Mercedes reaching the boy.

"Remember the Captain's orders, Miss."

Mercedes halted and clasped her hands in front of her.

Mr. Martinez gave her a severe look. "We will care for the boy, don't worry yourself. And don't come here again, do you hear? This is no place for a gentlewoman. I will volunteer and look to these men."

"He said he would welcome a carpenter," Mercedes said.

She followed Captain Christensen up out of the stench of bilge in the hold, through the press of men on the berth deck, and along to just outside the sick berth where they encountered the first lieutenant, Mr. Sprague. Mercedes dropped her gaze and listened to the men exchange greetings. They did not use Christian names.

Mercedes kept close to Captain Christensen, passing around the canvas curtain forming the door of the sick berth. She encountered a tall, white haired man straightening from beside a hammock. Captain Christensen presented Doctor VanArsdel to Mercedes and made the surgeon aware of Captain Blackwell's orders concerning her.

"I'm afraid we cause you much work, Doctor, and so I come to offer my help, little though it may be."

"Not at all, ma'am," Doctor VanArsdel said. "I'm sure it will cheer the men to see you. Come, you may attend my rounds."

Mercedes knew most of *La Trinidad*'s men by sight, even the majority of their names, saving the natives whose names were impossible to pronounce. She went round with the doctor, speaking with each man in gracious, formal Spanish, tying bandages and doing as the doctor bid her.

"Did your surgeon survive, ma'am?" Doctor VanArsdel asked when they had completed the circuit of *La Trinidad*'s wounded.

"Oh, no, I saw him die, may God bless him. His name was Roberto Sepulveda." They both bowed their heads for a moment. Mercedes continued, "He was from Barcelona, as was Captain de Leon y Castillo, and my people also."

"That's where you were bound?"

"To Cadiz first, yes, then to Barcelona."

"I am sure you shall see your home once more, Miss Mercedes."

"I have never yet seen Barcelona, Doctor. My mother's brother and his family live there, to whom I'm sent. I expect I shall be nursemaid to my uncle's children."

"Then they shall be the most fortunate of youngsters, ma'am," Doctor VanArsdel said. "Your English is remarkable. Besides the Spanish, do you speak other languages?"

"You are kind, sir, only French. My mother called it the language of civilized people."

"Ah! What said she of English?"

"Why, that it's the language of trade and our modern times, and she took particular pains I should learn it."

The doctor smiled at Mercedes, with a mature man's appreciation of intelligence and self-possession in a young woman.

His opinion of her qualities could only have risen further still when she said, "I don't wish to suggest anything out of the way, Doctor, but would it be permitted to visit the English wounded as well? They've been looking at me very curious this last little while."

Doctor VanArsdel escorted her round his patients, who had indeed been staring at the Spanish lady. But they hadn't a hope she would put her hands on them the way she'd done with her countrymen, the lucky sods. The wounded British seamen were sure the Spaniards never deserved such fine attentions.

"May I beg you to look in on one of the prisoners, Doctor?" Mercedes said. "His name is Juan Luis Montelongo, one of Captain de Leon y Castillo's servants. He is fourteen, active and lively, but he seemed quite ill when I saw the prisoners earlier. He wasn't wounded in the battle or he would have been brought here. I fear it may be the flux."

"I certainly shall, ma'am." Doctor VanArsdel bowed to her. "And may I say, Miss Mercedes, should you ever need anything in the medical line, I'm at your service. Please don't hesitate to come to me."

Mercedes curtsied to the doctor and took her leave. It was not lost on her what the doctor had left unsaid. Then he could not very well say, "If ever you are too much raped, ma'am, you may come to me."

She was escorted on deck, where what seemed to her furious activity involving a great number of seamen was going forward. She tried to make herself small as she wove through the crowd of men parted by Captain Christensen. The men only looked at her covertly and would no sooner have lifted a hand to her than to one of their officers. For there stood Captain Blackwell on the quarterdeck with his eye upon everything, not unlike the Almighty.

"Well, ma'am, and how did you find your shipmates?" Captain Blackwell asked.

"Tolerably well, sir, I thank you. Doctor VanArsdel is very kind," Mercedes said.

"He's hard pressed at the moment. Thank you, Captain Christensen, you may return to your duties. Call away my gig!" Captain Blackwell shouted to the officer of the watch.

Mercedes watched the efficient operation of the seamen swaying up the captain's gig and lowering it away smartly over the side. Never had she seen the launching of a boat performed with this level of professionalism aboard *La Trinidad.* She did not wonder they had been taken. The officers and crew of *Inconstant* saw nothing remarkable in the scene other than herself, and they loitered about to watch her descend into the boat, with the unrelenting wind whipping her skirts tight against her legs.

It wasn't just the woman going over the side with the same agile grace of the day before that won Captain Blackwell's notice and approval, but Mercedes knowing as a person of no rank whatever she must be the first into the boat. He would have felt it a severe trial if his lady prisoner had been one of those vaporous, fainting women. Captain Blackwell had no use for such females; no, for when it came to the ultimate favor a woman could bestow, he doubted delicate creatures could bear his weight.

Captain Blackwell watched as she held on with strong, shapely arms while looking down into the gig. He didn't see her anxious expression, nor hear his coxswain Narhilla coach her, "Now, Miss, cast off!" He only saw her drop into the boat as it and the ship came together. Narhilla, one of the captain's followers, held Mercedes' elbow until he'd seated her in the stern sheets, then the rest of the gig's crew dropped in, followed last by Captain Blackwell.

Captain Blackwell took his seat alongside Mercedes. She leaned away from him, pressing herself to the gunwale as though he required an extra wide berth.

"Give way!" he ordered. "It will be a wet pull, ma'am."

And in the reverse order, with the captain leaving the boat first and climbing *La Trinidad*'s side to the sound of the pipes of the bosun's mate, they ascended wet indeed from the short crossing. When Mercedes gained the deck, the last up save for the coxswain, Mr. Bransford stepped forward and offered her a boat-cloak.

"Welcome aboard, sir," Mr. Verson said. "Mr. Bell shall be up directly, sir."

Captain Blackwell's first concern was hearing the carpenter's report. "Thank you, Mr. Verson. Bring him to the cabin if you please. I'm taking the lady below."

Mercedes preceded the men, Captain Blackwell, Narhilla and McMurtry, into the great cabin. On the deck was strewn broken glass from the shattered stern windows, but it was still an elegant apartment; even in its present ruined state it was far more so than the cabin of *Inconstant*. Mercedes led them to Captain de Leon y Castillo's sleeping place where she pointed out her chest. Captain Blackwell gave the order, and McMurtry and Narhilla heaved the chest up and carried it out of the cabin.

Captain Blackwell remained, watching Mercedes from the doorway of the sleeping cabin as she knelt and pulled open a locker underneath the bed box. It was a fixed berth, a cot wide enough for two people. Mercedes withdrew a long, finely finished wooden box from the locker, placed it on the cot and opened it. She stood aside so he might inspect the contents.

"I'm no judge, ma'am, but they certainly seem fine weapons. Elegant, indeed."

He didn't touch the edged weapons of Toledo steel: a pair of rapiers, a broadsword, a stiletto and a dagger, finely crafted with silver and gold inlaid in delicate patterns on the hilts. Captain Blackwell was afraid to offend some unknown Spanish sensibility by handling the late captain's property, though they were quite alone in the intimate space. He met Mercedes' dark, frank gaze as he regarded first one of the Spanish captain's treasures, then the other. She put out her hand at the same time as he to close the lid on the swords, and his hand covered hers. A knock came at the cabin door.

"Come in." Captain Blackwell stepped back with the box under his arm. "These will be stowed in the hold, ma'am, until we make port."

Captain Blackwell met Mr. Verson, midshipman Bransford, and the carpenter, Mr. Bell, in the great cabin. Mercedes sat on the cot in the sleeping cabin while their conference went forward, graciously relieving them of the burden of a lady's presence.

Inconstant's carpenter, a tall, lean man who had to stoop even in the great cabin of a 42 gun ship, reported, “It's no go, sir. She's hulled in more near a dozen places, with five foot of water in the well and rising. The rudder shot away and no spare, sir, and my mate and crew copped it in the late action. And I can't get at them holes in this here sea, sir.”

“Thank you, Mr. Bell. Mr. Verson, let us inspect the remaining...” Captain Blackwell had an odd aversion to saying “gold” and he went on, “cargo. All the wounded are got over?”

“Yes, sir, completed in the forenoon watch. Come this way, sir. I should think we may complete the cargo in the afternoon watch, sir.”

“Excellent, Mr. Verson. Lead the way. Oh!” He leaned his head in the door of the sleeping cabin. “Beg pardon, ma'am, I shall return directly.”

“Mr. Bransford. What marines on board?” Captain Blackwell said.

“Lieutenant Hoffinger, and a half dozen men, sir.”

“Is that Hoffinger the fat one?” Captain Blackwell knew every man Jack of his crew by name and watch, but the marines were not his province.

“Aye, sir, the fat one.”

“Pass the word for Mr. Hoffinger, Mr. Bransford, and he's to station a man outside the cabin door. Mr. Verson, Mr. Bell.”

He left the cabin and went to *La Trinidad*'s strong room where in the passage outside a line of marines and seamen passed bags of gold coin, bars of gold ingot, and finished pieces in chests of various sizes. Captain Blackwell caught the somber air of the men handling the treasure, but underneath it he perceived a keen excitement.

“I agree with you, Jack,” Captain Blackwell said, slipping into use of Christian names in his preoccupation. He stood in the room with the remaining treasure where his clerk had catalogued the room's contents and was carefully checking off each item as it was borne away. “We should complete the transfer by eight bells. God send the gale don't worsen.”

"Amen," Mr. Bell said. "Sir!"

Captain Blackwell went all throughout *La Trinidad* with his second lieutenant and carpenter, and in the well they found the carpenter's newly appointed mates in water to their armpits. Climbing up behind Mr. Verson and Mr. Bell, Captain Blackwell gained the upper deck.

"We shall scuttle her, Mr. Verson, once the cargo is complete on board *Inconstant.*"

He went to the great cabin and collected Mercedes. She was standing next to the desk with Captain de Leon y Castillo's letter clasped in her hands. When he came in, calling his orders to the sentry, Mercedes faced him and expressed her readiness to leave *La Trinidad* with him.

Captain Blackwell was piped aboard *Inconstant*, and even before Mercedes with Narhilla behind her came up the side, he felt the tension on deck. The officers on duty, excepting Mr. Sprague, didn't look him in the eye, as though something shameful had just occurred, and many of the men had sullen faces. He had left *Inconstant* a tremendously busy, but he believed happily working ship, and returned to find the men cursing and running afoul of one another. He shouted several sharp orders to bring the hands to their duty and wondered if the cause of the disagreeable atmosphere on deck sprang from the usual circumstance, Mr. Sprague and his chief follower, the bosun Mr. Peakes, starting the men.

Captain Blackwell had forbidden beating with knotted ropes or rattan canes since the action. His crew had behaved well and willing, and he thought the men would work hard enough without being beaten. Even the simplest among them knew *La Trinidad* was a Spanish treasure ship, a lawful capture as an enemy of England, and what that meant in prize money. But while he was out of *Inconstant,* the first lieutenant was in command, and Captain Blackwell couldn't call Mr. Sprague to task for cruelty, to the detriment of discipline. As a commander he knew this, but as a man he was appalled at the number of times he'd seen, during his career in the Royal Navy, how brutal officers never lacked company.

Captain Christensen approached and saluted. "One of the prisoners desires a word, sir, if you please. Wishes to volunteer."

"Bring him below, Captain. Pass the word for Mr. Blackwell. Miss, I must beg you to walk below to your cabin."

Severino Martinez was escorted into the great cabin and to Captain Blackwell's inquiry of his position aboard *La Trinidad*, put to him by Francis in Spanish, Mr. Martinez replied he'd been her sailing master.

Captain Blackwell stared. "I've no need of a master, nor master mates."

The man must be daft to offer his services. No captain in his right mind would allow an enemy volunteer to act as sailing master.

"I was a carpenter by land, sir, in the building and repair of ships," Mr. Martinez said.

When Francis translated this, it gave Captain Blackwell pause.

"The lady calls him uncle," Francis said.

"Ask him about that."

"She's no relation of mine, sir," Mr. Martinez replied. "I'm merely an uncle in affection, known to the young lady and her mother, to whom I made promises to keep my eye upon the girl."

Captain Blackwell paced up and down the cabin. He badly needed more skilled men; Mr. Bell's new mates were not trained carpenters, but he did not need another complication.

"May I say something, Captain?" Mr. Martinez said. "About the lady."

Receiving a curt nod from Captain Blackwell, and a scowl that let Mr. Martinez know he should not speak until spoken to, the former sailing master said, "Captain de Leon y Castillo had peculiar ideas. He was a philosophical gentleman. He set Doña Mercedes to work with the sail maker's crew. She is a fine hand with a needle. And he taught her to navigate and to use the sword. She fought in the late action, on the quarterdeck by his side."

The remark about the lady being taught navigation had caused Captain Blackwell to pause in his pacing and give Mr. Martinez his full attention. But upon hearing his statement about her fighting on *La Trinidad*'s deck, Captain Blackwell emitted a sound of disbelief and vexation.

"I'll grant you a trial, Mr., Mr...."

"Martinez," Francis said.

"I'll give you a trial, Mr. Martinez," Captain Blackwell said. "*La Trinidad* is to be scuttled, and you shall direct us. Show my men the best place to lay charges and assist in carrying out the explosions."

It was a cruel assignment. *La Trinidad* had been Severino Martinez' and Mercedes' home, and there was no seaman who didn't respect and value his ship.

Mr. Martinez hesitated only a moment before responding, "Aye, aye, sir."

Captain Blackwell shouted for the midshipman on duty, and when a little squeaker named Knight came in, he desired Mr. Knight to send Mr. Martinez in the next boat across to *La Trinidad* in company with his coxswain. Mr. Verson was to put Mr. Martinez to work in the carpenter's crew. He would follow shortly and relieve Mr. Verson to return to *Inconstant*. Mr. Martinez passed out of the cabin, responding to the midshipman's piping inquiries in halting English he must have picked up from the Americans trading in Alta California.

"Well, Frank, now I must beg a service of you. With so many prisoners aboard I can't spare my Marines to guard the lady. I don't wish her about the ship unescorted nor to deny her the deck, so I would be much obliged if you were to attend her."

"Why certainly, with pleasure."

Captain Blackwell stared at his brother a moment. "Don't overdo it. You are a diplomat, it would seem somewhat in your line our dealings with the Dons, if you take my meaning."

Francis bowed his head, in an attempt to hide his grin. Captain Blackwell made to leave the cabin.

"A moment, James. What do you make of that fellow Martinez' claims?"

"Miss Mercedes, we require your presence, if you please," Captain Blackwell called.

Mercedes stepped out of the sleeping cabin and stood between them.

"What was *La Trinidad*'s position yesterday noon?"

"35° 38' North 18° 54' West, sir. But we had not a decent noon observation since one day before yesterday, when we parted from the squadron." Mercedes looked a trifle confused.

There was no confusion in Captain Blackwell's face. "There you have your answer, Frank, part of it. I'm leaving you in my brother's charge, ma'am, as I'm sure you are aware." Captain Blackwell bowed and left the cabin.

"I meant to call on you in any case, Miss Mercedes," Francis said. "I must beg leave to shift my books and other belongings out of your cabin. The Captain tells me your trunk cannot be stored until I do."

"Of course, sir, please." Mercedes stood aside to let Francis pass into the little compartment, where he began gathering books, and was soon passing them out to her. "What a great many you have, Mr. Blackwell. I should be obliged for a loan of one of your English volumes."

"You're a great reader, ma'am, besides your other accomplishments?"

Mercedes didn't blush, but smiled, for she was a great reader, and delighted to talk of books.

"In Alta California I was fortunate to be permitted the Governor's library. He had a handsome collection, but most of the volumes were in Spanish. Some few were in French and other languages, German, Italian, and English. And my mother was a great novel reader. She preferred the French novels."

"If you enjoy novels, this is one everyone reads in English," Francis said, handing her *Clarissa: or the History of a Young Lady*.

"How kind. Thank you. Here is what I read last night." Mercedes stepped inside the sleeping cabin and handed the last number of the *Naval Chronicle* to Francis. "I took it up yesterday evening, at supper here alone."

Francis regarded her with renewed interest; Mercedes knew how she appeared, a purported Spanish woman, speaking excellent English, and reading the British Admiralty's latest intelligence in the *Naval Chronicle*.

"I find it's written in a way I can understand. I am afraid this," she held in her hand Richardson's tome, "may be quite beyond me."

"Tell me, Miss Mercedes, did Captain de Leon y Castillo instruct you in navigation and in the arts of war? What sort of man was he? Or forgive me, it must pain you to speak of him."

"It couldn't pain me to speak of a man for whom I hold a tremendous respect and admiration. But he taught me those things, not from any desire to fly in the face of convention. He wished to prove he was so accomplished in those skills he could teach even a woman to gain some facility in them."

This was the most speech Mercedes had yet had with Francis, and they looked at one another with astonishment and unfeigned interest. Then Captain Blackwell's heavy tread was heard over their heads and the shouted order, "All hands! All hands about ship!"

Chapter 4

The men at the helm had to be relieved every half glass from the tremendous physical labor of keeping the ship on her course before the shrieking wind, with a gigantic sea following, and a bare scrap of canvas forward which Captain Blackwell couldn't keep from anxiously regarding. He'd been lashed to a stanchion on his quarterdeck since the end of the second dog watch, and at present, past one o'clock in the morning, he was weary and wet through to the skin. The officers and men on deck were also sodden, and nearly all his officers were on deck, even Mr. Sprague.

Captain Blackwell remembered gales lasting three days and more off the coasts of Spain and France. Yet this was a sea such as he had never experienced in over twenty years of naval service, a sea with the white foam boiling over great expanses of it and blown in dense ribbons at their stern. They were going to find out whether his preparations were sufficient or lacking. If they were found wanting, the toil with the treasure would be for naught, and he'd chosen the removal of gold from *La Trinidad* over making all fast for this storm and cost them their lives.

In the midst of these miserable reflections, Captain Blackwell's exhausted mind turned to his brother and the young woman below. He cast off his lashings, bellowing to the officer of the watch that he meant to go below while he might. Conditions were worsening, with the waves crashing down with shocking force. He staggered into his cabin after negotiating the companion ladder. Mercedes appeared at her cabin door on hearing him enter.

He stood just outside her door, water forming in a puddle around him.

"Where's McMurtry?"

"Lashed to his cot, sir," Mercedes said. "He had an accident with the spirit stove, burned one arm quite severely and received a blow to the head."

Captain Blackwell looked at her in astonishment, which increased when she presented him with a jar of coffee and a biscuit.

"The coffee is cold, sir. Its making was the cause of your steward's misfortune."

"And how do you keep, ma'am?"

He could see how she did: remarkably well under the circumstances, neither sick, nor hysterical, offering him refreshment. She handed him a towel, so he could wipe his face dry. He forestalled her reply. "How is it one of my prime hands is so knocked about, yet you're not even the least sea sick?"

"I was sick, Captain, but got it over before you came down. And as to the other, I cannot say." She bowed her head. If anything she looked grieved, apprehensive; Captain Blackwell didn't wonder she should feel so, alone at sea with two hundred forty men. "Perhaps it's because I was born on a ship," Mercedes said. "Shall I fetch you a dry shirt, sir?"

"No, no, leave it. It's no use at all." Captain Blackwell reached out and grasped Mercedes' arm as she tried to pass him on her way to his cabin for dry linen. She'd apparently determined to do her part while McMurtry was on the sick list.

The ship was descending the crest of the next enormous wave, and Mercedes was flung against Captain Blackwell. He looked down at the top of her head and smelt the flowery scent of her hair. How did she manage such a thing in a ship? The passing thought unexpectedly made his heart ache for the possibility he might never live to know.

"Put on your warmest clothes now, Miss. I shall wait and lash you into your cot."

He turned his head and when he turned back to her, Mercedes was braced in her cot in a midshipman's jacket and breeches, with a cloak over all.

He made her fast in her cot with seven neat turns, trying not to gape at her, and though he took no more than a few moments to do so he still wet her liberally from his own dripping person. "You shall be able to get free, Miss, but won't wear yourself out so in keeping in."

"God preserve us then, Captain."

"Amen," said Captain Blackwell, leaving the cabin.

He made his way forward to descend to the gunroom, but met Narhilla coming aft. By mutual accord they halted next to the gun named *Sudden Death.*

"Begging your pardon, sir." Narhilla brought his hand to his forehead. "I just come from your honor's brother. He gave up his good salt horse and Madeira wine took with supper, but other than that, sir, he's brave. Lashed him to his cot, sir."

"Thank you, Narhilla. Did you hear McMurtry took a tumble?"

"Aye, sir, carried him to the sick berth myself. He'll not soon be allowed to forget it, sir, oh no! Cracking his pate while that little Miss sits there cool as a ship's cat. Oh, oh! Beg pardon, sir."

Captain Blackwell couldn't help grinning at the scene Narhilla described, as he and the coxswain battled their way back onto the deck. When they gained it, the momentary human glow of happiness was completely wiped from Captain Blackwell's mind by the spectacle nature presented him. Over there astern was a wave stretching away to the horizon, a wave like a straight wall of water, neither curving nor with a crest, but having a line of white foam running its length.

He was strapped once more to his stanchion on the quarterdeck when the shock of that wave hit *Inconstant,* exploding on her deck, pressing her down. But the ship righted, the water streaming from her scuppers, and she ran up the next sea with sickening speed. Captain Blackwell had no choice but to continue to run down sea, with blocks and spars, even the ship's cutter and jolly boat plucked from *Inconstant* and whirled away out of sight.

"*Santisima Madre de Dios*!"

Captain Blackwell heard the prayer and turned to see Mr. Martinez, one of three men at the wheel, just before there was a splitting, tearing noise distinct from the shrieking wind and the crashing sea, and the foremast came down upon the deck and canted half over the side. Captain Blackwell cast off his lashings, roaring "Axes! Axes!" and ran forward, leading a party to clear the wreckage and try to get another sail on her before she broached to and was pooped by the next enormous wave.

Below in her sleeping cabin, Mercedes endured the racing climb and violent descents as the ship struggled in the storm. She couldn't imagine how it was for Captain Blackwell and the men on deck. She heard Captain Blackwell's heavy tread and shouted orders, some of which were intelligible to her, some reaching her only just perceptible as human speech, and she felt the tremendous concussion when the foremast went by the boards.

Mercedes was lying on the port bulkhead, the ship heeling well over. She was kept from flying about the cabin by the ropes bruising her. The ship lay over and groaned, and Mercedes couldn't keep the image from her mind of the masts under water; then *Inconstant*'s head came up into the wind. Even with the roar of the wind and sea, Mercedes heard the men forward cheering. They were once more running before the gale.

Dawn brought a second crisis. Mercedes must have slept, despite the shocking high sea, for she came awake to a cry of "Breakers! Breakers, there! Helm hard a larboard! All hands to wear ship!" It was Captain Blackwell's voice, a desperate and violent bellow.

She heard the shrilling of the bosun's pipe, followed by the drum beat calling the men to their stations and the sound of near two hundred men racing about the ship. Mercedes slipped under the ropes Captain Blackwell had made fast the evening before and out the end of the cot. She hadn't been told her station; she supposed it must be in the cockpit, the area of the ship dedicated to care of the wounded, as it had been in *La Trinidad*.

Just outside the cabin she met Mr. Martinez with the carpenter's crew, and as soon as he saw her he jerked his head toward Mr. Bell.

"Mr. Bell, sir, will you permit Mr. Martinez to escort me to the surgeon?" Mercedes said.

Mr. Bell looked sharp round at the sound of a feminine voice and stared at Mercedes in her Spanish midshipman's garb. "Aye, Miss. See you step back lively, mate," he called to Mr. Martinez. "Because we're all going to have to tally on to turn this here barky, that's why."

Mr. Martinez took Mercedes' arm, and they hastened forward.

"He is as brave as a lion," Mr. Martinez told Mercedes as they ran along. "Saved us all last night when the foremast went. John Bull is a prodigious seaman whatever else he may be."

They entered the screened off sick berth and found Doctor VanArsdel tending the casualties of the gale, broken bones, contusions, and one serious fractured skull.

"God keep you, girl," Mr. Martinez said. "Stay here until the Captain sends for you." He leaned forward as though he would kiss Mercedes' cheek.

Mercedes' head came up in a proud, sharp gesture, and Mr. Martinez backed away and took his leave with a resigned look.

Their exchange wasn't lost on the doctor, though he attended to the patient under his hands. After Mercedes had assisted him in his round and they were sitting a moment on the lockers set up for operating, listening to the shouting and furious activity of the ship, Doctor VanArsdel commented, "Your friend has volunteered, ma'am."

"Yes, sir, he would not go to prison."

She fell silent, contemplating how she felt about the English doctor referring to Mr. Martinez as her friend. A man her mother never would avow, even while accepting the roof he put over her head and the food for her table. Mr. Martinez was no more than a working man, while the de Aragons claimed relation to the renowned Spanish poet, playwright and wit, Francisco de Quevado.

They heard the powerful voice of Captain Blackwell calling for silence on deck, then a series of orders and the stamping of hundreds of feet, and the groaning of the ship. Neither Mercedes nor Doctor VanArsdel knew what was taking place over their heads, but they felt the tension of the seamen and the collective relief when the ship went about, then settled on the new tack.

Later in the same watch the captain's coxswain Narhilla came into the cockpit to visit his mate McMurtry.

Narhilla gave the steward his understated account of the emergency on deck. "Captain had both watches tally on, and we wore her right round. Barely clawed the barky off that lee shore, mate. Shaved it right close, we did. Speaking of which, My Beauty," — in the singular way of seamen, McMurtry, surely among the most ill-favored men in creation, was called either My Beauty or McBeauty — "you look precious strange with one part your head shaved. Mind you don't scare the Captain's little Miss now!"

"Mind your own gob, Narhilla. That's her yonder in them breeches. So you just clap a stopper over it." And then, in a low, confidential tone, McMurtry said, "Captain knows as how I'm good with the ladies, see? So he sets me to look after her, like."

"If washing petticoats along with the Captain's shirts pleases you, why, it makes no mind to me."

McMurtry scowled at Narhilla's management of the last salvo, and looking about him, he struggled out of the hammock, propelling himself with his one good arm. "If you was wishing to return to the cabin, Miss, I'll be pleased to take you."

"Lay down, McMurtry. Your head has been concussed," Doctor VanArsdel said. "You're not fit for duty. I'll take the lady back to the cabin. They have beat the retreat, have they not?"

When the two men nodded, glum faced, Doctor VanArsdel offered Mercedes his arm. "Come, ma'am, I'm sure you'll be more comfortable in the cabin."

"May I have a private word, first, Doctor?"

Doctor VanArsdel nodded, took her arm, and brought her to the dispensary, a little closet where the surgeon's medical stores were kept.

"I found, Doctor, after looking over the contents of my sea chest, when the Captain was kind enough to allow me it, I did not bring away any vinegar, sir. So I must beg some of you."

The doctor's head was necessarily bowed in the small apartment, hiding the expression of his face. After Mercedes made her request Doctor VanArsdel showed her a professional, non-committal countenance, and moved without a word to draw off a pint bottle from the stores at hand.

"Here you are, ma'am, and please to let me know when you require more."

He led Mercedes out through the lower deck to the upper, past where the Spanish prisoners were working the pumps. They called respectful greetings to Mercedes as she walked aft to the captain's cabin. She had given the doctor further evidence of her maturity, for vinegar was used against conception.

The gale had abated in the morning watch, allowing *Inconstant*'s narrow escape from wrecking on a lee shore, on the ironbound coast of Spain none had seen until the first gray light came creeping into the sky. The tremendous seas of the night before had pushed *Inconstant* far east and north, until in the morning they found themselves almost upon Cape Finisterre.

Blackwell cursed himself for how close to destruction he had allowed his ship to come. He knew the coast of Europe intimately well and he should have smelled the land, he certainly did now even as they struggled to windward. He was exhausted, but after the effort of wearing ship, with both watches on deck and near one hundred men hauling the mainsail, he was another ten hours about the ship overseeing repairs. *Inconstant* had lost her foremast, her mizzen and main topmasts, and all of her boats saving the barge, launch and gig. In the first dogwatch, just before the master Mr. Hammerly took the deck, Blackwell passed the word for Mr. Sprague.

"Repairs are going forward very well. The people have behaved splendidly." Blackwell gazed over the ship's side at the sea. A high swell, nothing more, was left of the shattering storm, and removing his coat and waistcoat he let them fall where he stood.

"And I believe we shall complete the jury masts by the setting of the first watch. Then we shape our course for Gibraltar, and I must beg you to stand a watch from this time forward. I'll move up one of the youngsters but until I have time to consider, you must stand a watch, Mr. Sprague."

"Aye, aye, sir," Mr. Sprague said, a disobliging look on his face.

Blackwell flung off his shirt and breeches, stepped up on the taffrail, and jumped into the sea below.

In the cabin the large body flying past the stern windows caught Mercedes' attention. She hastened forward and dropped to her knees behind the lockers. The area was a little stockade from which she peered out at the form in the water.

Blackwell had plunged deep and kicked his way back up, breaking the surface with water darkening his hair. He took a few strokes up and back, then flung himself at the stern ladder and hauled out. She had a fine view of his nakedness as he did. Those powerful thighs gave her pause. Captain de Leon y Castillo had been a much smaller man, frail even, and she imagined enduring his feeble thrusts would be as nothing compared to what the act would be with this man.

On deck, the sight of *Inconstant's* captain striding naked to his cabin wasn't cause for notice. The captain frequently plunged into the sea or caused the pump used in washing the decks to be turned on him, and no one was bold enough to remind him there was a lady in his cabin.

Blackwell yanked open the cabin door and went straight into his sleeping cabin without glancing right or left, his mind occupied with moving one of the midshipmen up to acting third lieutenant. Then they could make up three watches and give his officers more than four hours sleep at a stretch. It was like Mr. Sprague to act as though it were beneath his dignity as the new first lieutenant to stand a watch and oblige Blackwell to order him to it. Yet bitter thoughts didn't linger in Blackwell's mind as he lay down on his cot. He was too gratified to have brought his ship through the terrible gale, and he sunk into unconsciousness with something like happiness in his heart.

Captain Blackwell woke smiling, for he had been dreaming of pressing Mercedes in his arms. He smelled coffee and breakfast making in the galley, and realized he'd slept through four watches and missed his habitual appearance before dawn on the quarterdeck.

He didn't linger over washing and shaving and paused a bare moment, choosing between his uniform and working clothes. He knew he looked well enough in his Naval coat, white breeches, and Hessian boots, but he abhorred anything like showing away. Captain Blackwell put on duck trousers and a disreputable Guersney frock, and walked out into the great cabin. He hadn't preceded Mercedes, for there she sat at the table and the dishes were already being carried in.

She looked more the Spanish lady now she had her store of clothing. Mercedes wore the white blouse and colored skirt one thinks of as the costume of country women, with little slippers on her feet. Her hair was neatly done up and she wore no cap, the lack of which she would have been anxious to remedy, had she known this set her apart from Englishwomen in the eyes of the ship's crew and her captain.

"You have no appetite, ma'am," Captain Blackwell said, after Mercedes refused a second bloody chop. "Were you very cruelly flung about?"

"No, Captain, it's not that. If I worked as hard as you, I dare say I would have a great appetite, too." He sat before her chewing his fourth chop. "But as it was, I had merely to cling to my cot, then sit with Doctor VanArsdel quite at our ease. I believe I must thank you for bringing us through the dreadful storm. It was more severe, indeed, than anything I experienced rounding Cape Horn."

Few men could have resisted the pleasurable feeling such words provoked, and spoken by such a woman, and Captain Blackwell wasn't among them. Then, too, there was that sense of camaraderie for those with whom one has survived a crisis. He was enchanted with Mercedes, but at a loss how to respond with anything like sang-froid. A knock came at the door.

"Come in," Captain Blackwell bellowed. Mercedes gave a little start.

Francis walked in, his face pale and drawn. There were dark patches beneath his eyes, and he seemed to have grown thinner.

Captain Blackwell leaped to his feet. "Oh, Frank! Dear Frank, do sit down. How pasty you look to be sure!"

He redeemed his bluff remark with a tender regard for his brother's health, calling out to McMurtry to light along porridge and toast for Mr. Blackwell.

"Eh? How's that?" Captain Blackwell asked Mercedes, after a hint she gave him regarding his steward. "Oh, yes. Cracked his nut at the start of the excitement."

"Never trouble yourself, brother," Francis said. "There's more than enough here that I shan't be able to eat to satisfy, believe me. I could do with tea, a little tea."

Mercedes rose, and immediately so did Captain Blackwell and Francis. She looked at them in confusion, brought up by the fact she couldn't simply leave the cabin to fetch tea for Mr. Blackwell.

"Pass the word for the steward's mate!" Captain Blackwell roared toward the door. They were then able to sit down again companionably.

Captain Blackwell left them when the tea was brought in, and shortly after his strong voice could be heard, full of authority, directing the work on deck.

Mercedes and Francis knew to stay off the holy quarterdeck when the captain was there, so they planned to walk along the gangway, and perhaps on the forecastle in the afternoon watch. But in the event, upon reaching the forecastle, they found a sail-maker's party sewing dead men into their hammocks.

The body of a boy was lying in an open canvas before them, and Mercedes cried, "Oh, it's not Juanito!" and knelt beside the boy. She looked around at the seamen, who were mutely regarding her. "I thought for a moment he was a boy who waited on the

Captain's table, but he is not, the poor soul. May I?" She reached for the needle and yarn a man was bringing, and the seaman gave the implements over to her.

Francis stood with his hands clasped behind his back near Mercedes as she joined in the task of readying the dead for burial. They were for the most part *La Trinidad*'s men, carried off by wounds received in the late action.

Mercedes was a fine hand with a needle, just as Mr. Martinez had observed; not that this particular task required elegant stitching. She worked efficiently, deliberately unmindful of the smell of blood and worse around her, and had sown in two bodies when the sail-maker's mate in charge approached Francis.

"Begging your pardon, your honor, but I've a notion the Captain might not be best pleased to see Miss working alongside of us."

"I am sure Captain Blackwell could not object to her attending her countrymen," Francis said. "But if her presence distresses you, I shall certainly make her come away. Though she was to have an hour's airing on deck, those were the Captain's orders."

The sail-maker touched his cap and walked off, muttering as how "country gents don't know a fucking thing about the Navy."

A short while later Mr. Bransford came forward along the gangway and waited upon Francis. "Captain's compliments, sir, and would you and Miss join him when you are at leisure?" And both Francis and Mercedes, lubbers though they might be in the eyes of the seamen, knew such a request was more a command. Mercedes, overhearing Mr. Bransford's remark, immediately rose and gave her needle into the hand of the nearest man, murmuring, "Thank you for permitting me."

Francis hastened to make the introduction of Mr. Midshipman Bransford, the most aristocratic of *Inconstant*'s officers, to Miss Mercedes de Aragon. Mr. Bransford bowed over Mercedes' hand.

"Yet Mr. Bransford," she said, as they made their way aft. "Your uniform is that of a lieutenant."

"How very kind in you to notice, ma'am. I'm made acting third lieutenant this very day. This is Mr. Whittemore's uniform, God rest him."

"I wish you joy of your promotion, indeed, Mr. Bransford," said Francis, casting a curious look at Mercedes.

Her knowledge of the differences in British naval uniform, after so short an acquaintance with them, was better than Francis's own.

They reached the quarterdeck, three smiling, carefree seeming young people, Mercedes having offered to tailor the uniform jacket should Mr. Bransford wish it, and confronted Captain Blackwell, whose countenance was less than pleased.

"Thank you, Mr. Bransford." He dismissed the lieutenant. "I wish to have a word with Miss Mercedes, if you please, Frank."

Naturally Francis bowed and left the deck.

Captain Blackwell found he had nothing to say to her once she was walking with him at his invitation on the quarterdeck. He had seen her over there amidst the sail-makers' party, and immediately sent for her. Initially it had offended him, seeing this lovely woman working next to the foremast jacks, sitting on the deck in their midst with the slippers she wore peeking out from under her skirt. Then as he reflected, he realized he couldn't chastise her for any of it, though he had at first in mind a lecture of the sort he might give a midshipman, on the importance of maintaining distance between officers and seamen.

Those were mainly her people, dead on the forecastle. Men he might have helped murder, and far from feeling the stern commander, Captain Blackwell began to steal anxious glances at the woman beside him. He was wondering if Mercedes, under these circumstances, could ever be brought to bed of him quite by her own will.

He could compel her, but he wasn't a violent man, in spite of his profession. Neither was he a man of much formal education, having run away from the private school his reverend father had placed him into at the age of twelve. He'd begged to be allowed to join the Royal Navy; as a boy he'd reasoned if he were to be beaten he had rather it be toward some tangible end. But Captain Blackwell was a man of parts nonetheless, and he had an excellent memory. He recalled the lines from Tobin's play:

The man that lays his hand upon a woman,
Save in the way of kindness, is a wretch
Whom 't were gross flattery to name a coward.

Captain Blackwell agreed wholeheartedly. No, there would be no violence in the case. He was a gentleman, though he had seen and participated in brutality. He had other means at his disposal. Yet in regarding Mercedes now, Captain Blackwell fairly burned with the desire to put his arm round her waist and draw her close against him.

He was saved by the ship's routine. The sand ran out, the glass was turned. Mr. Knight, the midshipman of the watch, reported to his captain, after heaving the log; "Five and a half knots, if you please, sir."

"Pipe the hands to supper, Mr. Bransford. Come, ma'am, we may wait our supper below. And before quarters, I do assure you, we'll say a prayer over your countrymen before we commit them to the deep."

Seven days passed before the weather cleared, and they anticipated their first decent noon observation in ten days. Captain Blackwell had sent the midshipman of the watch, Mr. Bowles, three times into the cabin to check the reading of the Berthoud chronometer, which he was comparing against his own watch. The fourth time through the routine of Mr. Bowles's knock, followed by Mercedes' permission to enter, she said, "Tell the Captain, Mr. Bowles, with my compliments, if he will call out *Time*, I shall mark it down. I can hear his voice perfectly from here."

So they proceeded, and when noon had been struck on the ship's bell, Captain Blackwell came into the cabin to look at

Mercedes' notations, and to show her his observation. "Work out our position, if you please, Miss Mercedes," he said. He was a conscientious captain where his midshipmen were concerned, instructing them himself in navigation and mathematics. He considered *Inconstant*'s sailing master, Mr. Hammerly, somewhat past his prime in his usefulness as an instructor of the young. With days of blue water sailing in front of them, he was curious about the extent of Mercedes' abilities.

He suspected the man Martinez had been her instructor, not Captain de Leon y Castillo as he'd been led to believe. Captain Blackwell came to this after observing Mr. Martinez working aboard the ship. A prime seaman, he had already earned Mr. Bell's approval of his carpentry skills, and Captain Blackwell did not doubt Mr. Martinez had been an equally competent sailing-master.

After dinner, Captain Blackwell compared the midshipmen's and Mercedes' calculations to his own. "Was you one of my mids, ma'am, I would say you weren't the greatest blockhead among them by far."

Mercedes appeared confused by his remark, and his brother chagrined.

Captain Blackwell went to the cabin door and spoke to the sentry. "Pass the word for Mr. Bell and his mates."

When *Inconstant*'s carpenter was admitted, followed by a man named Bohan and Mr. Martinez, Captain Blackwell led them into his sleeping cabin. "I want a double berth, a fixed bed box, Mr. Bell. Ample room for two, lockers beneath."

"Aye, aye, sir, double berth, lockers below."

Francis rose from his seat at table, his expression having changed from chagrin to outright dismay. "Shall we take the air now, ma'am?"

"Hold a moment, Frank, if you please. She'll join you on deck after I have a word." Captain Blackwell backed out of his sleeping cabin where the carpenter and his mates were making their measurements.

His brother passed out of the cabin with his head bowed, and Captain Blackwell led Mercedes aft to the stern windows.

"I'll require bedding for that berth, ma'am, and it occurs to me you might oblige me." He glanced significantly at another of Mr. Bransford's coats. It lay on the stern lockers where Mercedes had put it down before dinner.

"If you will desire the sail maker to come to me, I'll get the material of him," Mercedes said. "Finest sailcloth number seven should answer nicely."

Captain Blackwell looked directly into her determined eyes, smiled, gave her his arm, and led her on deck.

She was kneeling over the canvas next day, completing the mattress by attaching the cover that could be unbuttoned from the top and laundered, when Francis knocked on the cabin door and walked in. Mercedes rose from the deck, straightened, and stretched her back.

"Do you know what I should very much like, Mr. Blackwell?" Francis had stepped in to take her to walk on the deck. "If it were not frowned upon, I should very much like a turn or two with those." Mercedes pointed with the needle in her hand to the rapiers grouped with swords and other weapons in racks on the bulkhead.

Francis told her he didn't believe it would be considered irregular, for the Marines and young gentlemen practiced the sword daily, and they were, after all, quite alone in the cabin, if they might just move the furnishings. Mercedes hastened to her sleeping cabin, emerging in the Spanish midshipman's dress. Francis looked astonished as he handed her a rapier, hilt foremost, but he said nothing. They took up their positions, looked one another in the eye, a slight nod, and commenced.

Captain Blackwell paused with his hand on the latch of the cabin door, his head jerking up at the sound of the clash of steel on steel. Casting a scowling glance at the sentry he stepped inside. He found his brother and Mercedes in the midst of parry and thrust.

They stepped apart, sword points down immediately at his entrance.

"No, no," Captain Blackwell said. "Please to continue with these." He took from the bulkhead two swords of the light cavalry type officers wear.

He was surprised at how well Mercedes handled the heavier sword. A master must indeed have taught her. Captain Blackwell knew the fencing master had been Captain de Leon y Castillo. The thought of her with that other man, and the sight of her in men's attire, revealing the strength of her arms and more especially her legs, stirred him tremendously. An image of being clasped by those limbs rose up in his mind, and without thinking, his heart beating hard, Captain Blackwell called out, "Sword!" to his brother. And when Francis gave the sword into his hand, he attacked her hard.

She gave way before him, stepping back and back, unable to parry his heavy blows.

"Peace, peace, Captain!" she cried.

"Never think you can best a man, Miss. Never!"

He handed the sword back to Francis and turned on his heel to the cabin door.

"I don't think it, sir!" she called at his retreating back. "I merely wanted the exercise. Don't blame Mr. Blackwell!"

Francis rushed after him up the companion ladder. "Captain. Sir, a word if you please."

In a low impassioned voice, when he'd been invited to walk on the quarterdeck, Francis said, "How can you treat her so chuff? Ordering her to make the bed she is to lie with you in. And such an ungentleman-like display below!"

Captain Blackwell stopped in his pacing and turned to face his brother with furious indignation on his countenance, but self-righteousness quickly died away. He had no sooner done those things Francis brought him up for, than he had accused himself in the same way. His behavior was ungentlemanly, coarse, that of a common sailor.

"I beg your pardon, Frank. I quite lost my head when I saw the two of you. And she in those clothes."

"You should beg hers."

"I shall, tonight."

Francis paced in silence at his side, and Captain Blackwell felt certain his brother was carefully formulating what he desired to say. He was a well-bred man and a diplomat.

"You told me, I believe, we'll make port in three days?" Francis said.

"Yes, I expect to sight the Rock tomorrow evening and put into Gib in the morning."

"Would it not be the wisest course to wait until we're in port before proceeding any farther down this path? Men think they might trifle with women with immunity. They believe, quite wrongly, the consequences to be on the woman's side. Don't trifle with her, James. Doing so might bring about what you cannot foresee."

Captain Blackwell understood Francis's intimation about their proximity to port. He need only wait three days to satisfy his lust with some willing woman. Yet he resented his younger brother's lecture, and he couldn't explain in any case how much he desired her. Not just a woman, though that was true enough too, but her, Mercedes.

He watched her walking on deck with Francis, in his cabin with her head bent sewing or reading, and pacing the quarterdeck in the evenings at his side, and he absolutely burned for her. His sense was becoming swamped by his need, and, with the quick decision years and years at sea had taught him, Captain Blackwell had set on a course of action from which he couldn't easily be turned.

"I'll consider what you say, Frank. But I must beg you, tonight, to take your supper in the gunroom."

Francis was turning away, with a face expressive of having done all he could, when suddenly he cried out, "Why must you have her?"

"Because she'll have me."

"Of course she'll have you, for the same reason she likely accepted the Spanish captain. Is that what we're come to?"

"You forget yourself, Frank."

"Indeed. Good night to you, sir."

Francis left Captain Blackwell on the quarterdeck, with *Inconstant's* officers standing in a cluster a discreet ways off, either turning their backs or gazing purposefully out to sea.

Mercedes had taken up the task of completing the mattress once the men quit the cabin, though her hands were unsteady after the unfortunate business with the swords. She strained to catch the discussion carrying on above her head, making out a word or two as the brothers came to the skylight in their round of pacing. They'd halted in their circuit next the skylight and exchanged those last, low pitched and vehement words. Mercedes heard them all.

Next moment the drum was beating to quarters, and the ship came alive with the sound of men hurrying to their battle stations. Captain Blackwell was simulating some emergency or preparing to exercise the great guns, just as he had the afternoon before, and every day since the taking of *La Trinidad*.

Mr. Bell and his mates came into the cabin to knock down the bulkheads and screens. McMurtry followed the carpenter's crew to store the captain's personal effects below and Mercedes intercepted him before running for the cockpit.

"This is finished." She touched the mattress. "Please to take it."

"Right, Miss, mattress to be stuffed and returned. Here's Mr. Hoffinger to bring you to the cockpit, Miss."

One of the mates of the hold, as they were stowing plate, candlesticks, and the mattress below made so bold as to remark, "So Captain's to board and take the little Spaniard in comfort, now."

McMurtry, by way of rejoinder, kicked the man in the backside. The foremast jacks, and a great number of the officers, believed Captain Blackwell had been punishing Mercedes since the day he ordered her into his cabin.

Another man murmured, from the comparative safety of the darkness, “Officers got all the luck, mate.”

Chapter 5

Mercedes was back in the cabin, having paid her visit to Doctor VanArsdel and the sick-berth patients. The drum had long since beat the retreat, the captain's furniture was once again exactly in order, and Mercedes was mending the trousers of her midshipman's costume. She put them hastily aside when she heard Captain Blackwell's voice booming down the companionway, she had no wish to annoy him with such enterprise. He came into the cabin and startled her by striding straight up to her, and dropping on one knee before her.

"Forgive me, Miss Mercedes, for my behavior earlier. At times I act the common sailor, and I deeply regret the offence I gave you. You might practice the sword whenever you desire with my brother. Never with me, however; a captain cannot indulge in such competition. I should not have done it."

Mercedes saw the open, honest look of his face, felt the rough pressure of his hand over both hers. The warmth of his touch stirred inside her, and she had to drop her gaze to hide it from them both. She returned the clasp of his hand. Supper was carried in and Captain Blackwell rose to his feet, presenting his back, standing before her, to the men bringing in the meal.

They ate and conversed over supper and drank between them an excellent bottle of Hermitage. Captain Blackwell gave Mercedes his arm and brought her on the quarterdeck after the meal. It was full dark and the world seemed composed of the dome of the sky with its infinite space and glory of stars, and the one tiny ship. The remembered fear of the vast ocean she'd confronted at the start of her sea voyaging struck Mercedes anew, intermingled now with more earthly apprehensions. She chose, with a conscious effort, to concentrate on the beauty of the night and responding to Captain Blackwell. He spoke of taking a celestial sighting next evening, and led her back down to the cabin.

McMurtry and Narhilla were going out at the cabin door, leaving the mattress stuffed with wool, cotton and the odd handful of oakum. When the door closed behind them, Mercedes glanced at Captain Blackwell and walked into his sleeping cabin. She had no notion of making him wait, none at all, and she began taking off her clothes.

He followed her, shut the door of the sleeping cabin, then slumped there, stunned by the sight of her. Mercedes had taken off her blouse and was unfastening and dropping her skirt to the deck. Underneath she wore a corset and a shift that didn't quite cover her buttocks. The shift was a delicate little garment Blackwell would have loved to take off her himself. But he would not have frightened her for the world.

He hadn't risen to post rank in the Royal Navy by being the type of fellow that long stays open mouthed and gaping. He threw off his own clothes and had her in his arms when she removed the shift and turned around. Mercedes' hands had come up in a defensive way between her breasts and his chest. She moved her hands by small degrees to grasp his arms, so their bodies were pressed together.

"Are you cold, sweetheart?" Blackwell asked, feeling her shiver in his arms.

"It's not that, Captain. I am anxious. I have never been with a man of your bulk. Forgive me, for I mean no offence, but I confess I am afraid to bear your weight."

"Why, sweetheart, you need not. Come, there are other ways." He fairly chuckled, turning her around, lying upon the cot and pulling her on top of him. "You need not do any more than you wish."

He began to caress her, stroking and kissing her body, and running his calloused hands over her thighs and buttocks and concentrating gentle strokes between her legs. He had endured a great deal of privation in his career in the service. Blackwell had withstood cold, hunger, fatigue, battle and injury, and he brought those powers of endurance to bear now. For being a man, he longed to dominate, to hold Mercedes down and to press and thrust, but he forbore. The greater number of his sensual encounters had been hurried affairs, performed with the removal of the barest amount of clothing, and there was suddenly nothing more important to Blackwell than she come willingly to lie with him again and again. The best inducement was to give her pleasure.

He could hear her rapid respiration in the dark of the cabin as she lowered her body over his, and putting her hand between them, guided him into her. She took him in slowly, Blackwell gritting his teeth against the exquisite pain both of the feel of her and of keeping still. Her movement atop him became urgent and little cries were escaping her. He felt her trembling and clasped her hard against him. “Don’t cry out sweetheart,” he whispered. Mercedes nodded and buried her face in his shoulder. He did thrust into her then, reaching his climax just after her, and sagged back into the cot, still clasping her tightly to him.

Mercedes waited a scant few moments before easing away from him. She could not lie down beside him, for though it was a double berth it could not accommodate a man of Captain Blackwell’s size and a whole other person. She had to lie on her side and half over him.

“Excuse me, Captain. I need to ... I must ...” She scooted out of the cot, bent and felt around for the dressing gown she’d tossed into the cabin earlier. Mercedes rose, draping it around her shoulders.

Blackwell put out his hand and grasped her arm. “Will you come back?”

“Yes, of course. If you wish it.”

She went out of his cabin and into her own. And while she washed his seed from her body with a mixture of vinegar and water, she reflected on the experience: the sexual act. It was not what she’d imagined it would be with Captain Blackwell. No pain, or very little, just at the beginning, the tender touch of his hands, his intimate whispering to her when before she'd heard only the loud tones of the captain. Then quite unexpectedly she'd experienced surging pleasure. She shook a few drops from her last bottle of Otto of Roses on a moistened handkerchief and rubbed the cloth over herself. Mercedes used the scented water to wipe the salt from her skin and hair after bathing in seawater.

She crept back to Captain Blackwell's quarters and found him with his arms and legs flung out, snoring in his cot. Mercedes smiled and covered his nakedness with the bedclothes and retired somewhat relieved to her own sleeping cabin.

Blackwell awoke in the pre-dawn darkness and put his hand out to the narrow, empty space beside him. There was no warm, consenting woman in his cot. He swung his legs out of the berth, rose, washed, and dressed for the changing of the watch.

The master Mr. Hammerly was turning the deck over to second lieutenant Mr. Verson.

"Here you have her, topsails, foresail, jibs and staysail. Course east, north east."

"Very well, Mr. Hammerly, topsails, foresail, jibs and staysail. Course east, north east."

"Mr. Bowles, Mr. Bowles! Mind yourself, Mr. Bowles," cried the master. The midshipman, Mr. Bowles, staggered up the companion ladder, frowsy and malodorous, his hair uncombed. "A bucket of water over Mr. Bowles to waken him!"

Standing near the binnacle, Blackwell was ready to cry, "Belay that!" when he saw Mr. Hammerly jested, and was slumping below to his own cot. He was in charity with all mankind this morning, and he might have thought he'd dreamed the encounter with Mercedes the evening before except the wonderful ease in his body spoke differently. He was on the point of ordering topgallant sails when he checked himself. He didn't particularly desire to run into port as fast as ever he might.

"Good morning, Jack," he said instead to Mr. Verson. "Keep her very well thus."

"Good morning, sir. Aye, aye, sir."

Below Blackwell paused to listen outside Mercedes' sleeping cabin. He could hear nothing of the woman asleep within. He wanted her, but he didn't believe he had the right to wake her at this hour of the morning. He walked into his own cabin and was delighted when he saw the feminine form in his cot. Mercedes had her back to him, lying on her side facing the bulkhead, her curves revealed by the rise and fall of the rough blanket covering her. Blackwell stripped off his clothes and lay down in back of her, kissing her shoulder.

"Shall I tell you something, Captain?"

"Please do." He put his arm over her waist and brought her up against him.

She turned under his arm and faced him. "I'm no longer afraid to bear your weight."

Blackwell didn't need any further invitation. He pushed her gently back on the cot and raised himself on one elbow. He leaned over her and kissed the hollow at the base of her throat. Then he kissed a line down between her breasts and taking first one in his hand, and then the other, he sucked at each nipple, gratified by her sharp intact of breath. His hand trailed down over Mercedes stomach, rested on her womb, then he pushed her legs apart and covered her sex with his fingers. Blackwell thought of this intimate part of her like a flower. A sweet bud he could make open and accept him. He stroked her and kissed and suckled until she pulled at his shoulders with both her hands, and insinuated her body beneath his. He rose over her, grasping one of her legs and clamping it above his hip where he wanted it, and then she did yield to him. But she also took of him, raising her hips to meet his thrusts. "Oh, Captain," he heard her murmur.

"Call me by my Christian name. James." He gasped. "Jim."

Mercedes could indeed clasp him warmly with her strong limbs. She moved with him and strained against him, and he had the great satisfaction of hearing her breath, "Oh, James, oh, Jim!" at the height of her pleasure. Yet when the fog of passion lifted from Blackwell's brain, his first concern was whether he had pressed her too hard. He looked down at her. Her face was still turned into his arm, where he did recall her smothering her cries. Then he became aware Mercedes was running one smooth, shapely leg over the irregular, lumpy scars on his buttock and the back of his left leg. Her other leg the poor woman could not move, it was pinned between his bulk and the bulkhead. He eased his weight off of her.

"It's an ignoble wound. A grenade, when I was third of the *Etrusco*."

She trailed her fingers over the scar running from his right breast to his navel.

"Midshipman," he said. "Battle of the Dogger Bank."

It was a litany of his career as Mercedes ran her fingers over his scars and Blackwell recounted the ships, his rank, or the action in which he had received the wound. When she came to the scars on his face, he caught her hand and brought it to his lips.

"Listen, Mercy, sweetheart. I know I'm a heavy man. If ever I do anything you don't care for you need only say, 'Belay that, Jim,' and I shall." He kissed her hand.

Mercedes leaned her forehead against his chest and smiled.

"Will you not allow a heavy man, a large man might please a woman?" She gave him an intimate caress that made Blackwell clutch her convulsively.

"Lord bless you, sweetheart. You do please me, you surely do."

They breakfasted together and when Captain Blackwell held Mercedes' chair he did run a hand over her shoulder. Mercedes observed he had an odd sense of propriety. He wouldn't touch her when others were present, and during the entirety of their intimacy he hadn't kissed her mouth.

After the meal Mercedes went into her own sleeping cabin, staying out of his way so he might use the quarter gallery before going on deck. She heard Captain Blackwell say, "Mr. Verson, what are you about Mr. Verson? What do you here?" in that gentle tone she had first heard only the evening before. There must have been an answer but she did not hear it because her pulse was pounding in her ears. Did he mean to share her with his officers? Was that what his tenderness amounted to? Mercedes yanked open the door to her cabin. She would not stand it. She saw Captain Blackwell taking his leave, and smiling at her over his shoulder.

Before her stood a little boy of four or five years, trying to stand with his hands clasped behind his back in the characteristic manner of sea officers. His composure lapsed and he stuck his thumb in his mouth and stared past her at the table where the remains of the captain's breakfast were spread.

McMurtry came in to clear the table.

"I'm breakfasting yet, McMurtry, if you please." She led the boy to the table, filled her own plate with the food still on it, and sat him down with the plate before him.

"Why, young Goodman Jack, your governor will be main displeased when he finds you come in here," McMurtry told the boy.

"Captain let me in."

"Captain let you in, is it?"

McMurtry left, muttering, "Is it a man-o'-war or a fucking nursery?"

"What am I to call you, Miss?" the little boy said.

"On the ship *La Trinidad*, they called me Doña Mercedes. It means Lady Mercedes, I think, in English. I suppose I have not deserved that," she said, more to herself than the boy. "The Captain and his brother call me Miss Mercedes."

The boy had ploughed through the food on the plate and was casting longing glances at the pot of marmalade.

"Just this bit, it is the Captain's favorite." She lay a spoonful of the jam onto his plate. "How many years have you?"

The boy didn't answer, and Mercedes reconsidered. "How old are you, *chico*?"

Now it was the boy who turned thoughtful. Then he brightened. "My Pa says I'm old enough not to play the goddamn fool."

Half a glass later the boy's Pa knocked on the cabin door and was admitted. Mr. Verson found his son seated beside Mercedes, who held a book on her lap from which she read to him. Mercedes rose when Mr. Verson walked in, prodding the boy to do likewise. When he saw it was his father entering the cabin, the boy shot to his feet and saluted. Mr. Verson and Mercedes could not help but smile.

"I do beg your pardon, ma'am." Mr. Verson beckoned to the boy, and when he came near laid his hand on him not unkindly. "Jack, you know you are not permitted in the captain's cabin. Why are you here?"

"Captain let me in, sir, and Miss gave me vittles and told me a story."

"Thank you kindly, ma'am, he will not intrude on you again," Mr. Verson said. With his hand on his son's shoulder, he was urging him toward the cabin door.

"Mr. Verson, sir," Mercedes said, taking a step forward. "I could teach him to read. He does not know how, and he ought to begin, at his age." She knew she was bold, perhaps overstepping the bounds of propriety. The blush on Mr. Verson's face was all the confirmation she needed.

"I am obliged to you, ma'am, deeply obliged. But I could never give you so much trouble."

"It will be a simple task with Mr. Blackwell's books." Mercedes turned the book so Mr. Verson could read the title, it was the *Arabian Nights*. "Everyone on this ship has occupation, sir, except perhaps young Mr. Verson and I. You would oblige me if you allowed him to spend an hour with me each day. A young man cannot learn navigation, you are aware, sir, until he learns to read."

She had hit upon the right tack with this last. There was nothing more important to a sea-officer, or a man who hoped to make an officer of his son, than early acquisition of the skills of his profession. Mercedes' argument allowed Mr. Verson to assent to her scheme with equanimity.

"May I just have a word with your son, before you take your leave?" Mercedes said.

Mr. Verson bowed to her and pushed the boy forward. Mercedes took Jack Verson by the hand and led him back to the stern windows, where she sat down and turned a serious gaze upon him.

"Should you like to come visit me again? Your father has consented to it."

"I should like it of all things, Miss, 'specially if there is jam in the case."

"Well, you may then. But listen to me, my fine young friend, you must wash first before you come to call. Your father there," Mercedes nodded at Mr. Verson, who was standing sideways to the cabin door, his head bowed and his cocked hat under his arm. "Your father is a gentleman and so must you be. Gentlemen wash every day, sir."

The boy stared at her, his fist creeping toward his mouth.

"Jack!" Mr. Verson called sharply. "Repeat your orders!"

"Wash every day, sir ... Miss!" The boy snapped to attention. "Then come eat vittles!" He skipped over to his father.

At the door, Mr. Verson turned and touched his hand to his forehead with a smile and a bow in Mercedes' direction.

"I would not have thought a man as young as Mr. Verson to have a son of five, sir." Mercedes was standing next to Captain Blackwell on the quarterdeck. They had taken the celestial observation, a merely academic observation with the ship hove to within sight of Gibraltar and Spain.

"We sailors do not make the best husbands, ma'am, you want a banker or some intellectual cove like dear Frank for that," Captain Blackwell said. "You are right, Mr. Verson is no more than four and twenty. He came off the West Indies station to find his missus bolted. Left that poor wight Jack with the landlady, who paid him no more heed than to let him grub the floor with the dogs. Mr. Verson brought him aboard. What else could he do?"

"And the men call him young Goodman Jack?"

"Yes." Captain Blackwell hung his head, smiling. "The young because we have two Mr. Jack Versons aboard. And as to the other, one day when we put into Plymouth to refit, young Mr. Verson was getting into the jolly boat to go ashore. He missed his footing and fell between the boat and the ship, and the men, as is usual in such a case, sat still and gaped. When up comes young Jack spluttering the vilest oaths. Narhilla leaned over the boat's gunwale and fished the boy out. 'You tell them, my good man,' he said. 'Give them hell, young Goodman Jack!'"

Captain Blackwell laughed, a heartening sound that brought a smile to the faces of the men within hearing, all saving Mr. Sprague.

But Captain Blackwell was pleased on many levels. He had spent much of the day writing his report to the Admiralty in anticipation of running into Gibraltar, consulting the ship's logbook and his own journal and log. His report contained the usual forms, "...honor to inform your Lordships of the successful engagement of the enemy ... 35,000 gold escudos, 27 gold bars and 22 chests of gems and finished gold and gemstone pieces ... Spanish casualties 55 killed, 85 wounded ... *Inconstant* suffered 2 fatalities, one first officer Lieutenant William S. Whittemore ... and 15 wounded ..."

He'd been able to look up and see Mercedes sitting near, mending his shirts or stockings or reading the Naval Chronicle. She was not a chatty woman, which suited Captain Blackwell, yet he found her cheerful and obliging. His brother came in at the hour when he and Mercedes walked on deck, and after looking earnestly into Mercedes' face, and spending no more than three minutes in her company, he led her away with a satisfied expression replacing his earlier one of concern. Captain Blackwell wondered if this affair of Mercedes teaching young Mr. Verson to read signified she meant to stick by him.

Spain was some four leagues away, and if, once in Gibraltar, Mercedes desired him to put her into a conveyance for Cadiz or Barcelona, he would not refuse. Yet what Captain Blackwell hoped was tomorrow he would run into Gibraltar, unload the treasure and the hundred odd Spanish prisoners, repair and provision *Inconstant*, and quit the port replete with an advance on his prize money from *La Trinidad*. A happy smile touched Captain

Blackwell's face as he imagined this scheme going forward, and then putting to sea again with both his brother and his mistress under his lee.

Chapter 6

Inconstant rounded Cape Carnero next morning, opening the full view of the great Rock. She proceeded past the New Mole and came to anchor between King's Bastion and the Old Mole. The weather could not have been finer yet the anchorage was crowded with ships, and coming in before the eyes of even a small portion of the Mediterranean Fleet was an anxious time for Captain Blackwell and his officers. They became aware of the savaged appearance of their ship as heads turned on the decks of other men-of-war as they glided by. When at last the ship swung to her cables some wag in the frigate *Elephant* anchored nearest called out, "*Incontinent*, ahoy! Wipe your arse, you need to wipe your arse!"

The signal broke out aboard *Royal George*, 'Captain repair aboard flag'. Captain Blackwell called for his gig, and sweating in his best uniform jacket he went over the side, landing with a prodigious thump in the boat. He called out "Give way!" and was rowed smartly to the flagship, where the commander of the Mediterranean Fleet awaited.

Never did a man receive a reception less like what he had imagined it would be than Captain Blackwell found in the great cabin of *Royal George*. It was a noble apartment with gleaming brass and wood paneling, which Captain Blackwell had plenty of time to admire as Admiral Gambier did not acknowledge him. The Admiral continued his business with his secretary; a response to a minister of the Grand Porte who'd complained of the scurrilous behavior of the British envoy – a man who did not even speak the language of the Empire; letters to two Beys of Barbary states, begging their indulgence in allowing His Majesty's ships to continue to wood and water in their ports after incidents taken as slights to the Beys' dignity perpetrated by certain froward British captains. Finally there was a communication to a British commissioner in Malta, urging him not to relax his vigilance in reporting the activities of the French.

During this long interval Captain Blackwell had not been invited to a chair, and resentment began to build in his heart. Even an admiral had seldom treated him with this level of disregard. Captain Blackwell had supposed the thumping great treasure he'd brought in, that would not now reach French coffers, should have at least earned him precedence over the sins of the King's other servants.

Admiral Gambier at last looked up from his correspondence with a gaze of weariness and displeasure. "You are come in at last, Captain Blackwell."

Captain Blackwell, after handing his report to the admiral's clerk, settled himself with one hand behind his back, his cocked hat under his arm, and a look of conscientious neutrality on his face.

"But stay! I know what has detained you. What you don't know, sir, is that it's peace. Peace signed at Amiens on the 12th of March, and the Dons have been raising a hue and cry about *La Trinidad*. Parted company with her squadron in heavy weather and fallen upon by a British sloop of war. That is what they said, sir, a British sloop of war!" The Admiral paused and the two Englishmen hung their heads over the ignorance of the Spaniards, to call a twenty-eight gun ship, a sixth rate, a sloop of war. "Demanding her cargo returned. Whitehall shall be wrangling with the Dons for years. No prize money, Captain Blackwell. No, nothing — droits of the Crown for the moment."

Admiral Gambier finally relented and waved Captain Blackwell to a chair, allowing the servant in with a tray.

"Joy of your capture, Captain." Admiral Gambier raised his glass.

In spite of the ill-natured company in which he took the refreshment, it was a grateful glass of Madeira Captain Blackwell tipped down his throat.

"Of all circumstances, sir, I believe this is the one I least looked for," Captain Blackwell said.

"Did you not notice the levity of the men as you came to anchor? The utterly altered appearance of the Fleet, this sluttish disregard for what is due the Service?"

"No, sir." Captain Blackwell struggled to keep incredulity from his face as he returned Admiral Gambier's fierce gaze.

The Admiral's once handsome and now venerable white head shook a little as he raised his glass to his lips, glaring out the noble sweep of stern windows at the ships at anchor. In trying to adjust his views to accommodate this news of peace, this unlooked for peace, Captain Blackwell was not assisted by the unaccountable temper of Admiral Gambier.

"I am not one of those money getting fellows, Captain Blackwell. I am a good Christian. Here, take that."

He pushed a pamphlet across his desk, which Captain Blackwell retrieved with a "Thank you, sir," and put into his coat pocket.

"No, the Bible says money is evil. This taking of treasure carries no weight with me, now that one way and another Bonaparte shall not receive it," Admiral Gambier said. "But the taking of a forty-two gun ship by a twenty-eight? Well done, sir. But do you not know, in a single ship action you must board and carry. Not sink the other fellow and come off so clawed you might come to grief yourself."

"The damage to *Inconstant* was a result of the weather following the action, sir, not the battle itself," Captain Blackwell said. "It is in my statement of condition, sir."

The Admiral glared him down. "Unload your prisoners and the gold without loss of a moment. Refit *Inconstant*. I shall give you chits for the ordnance. Mr. Land!" The Admiral turned to his secretary. "Mr. Land, chits for Captain Blackwell for canvas, spars, rigging. Boats, is it, sir? Boats? Should you like anything else, new paint and gold-leaf perhaps!" Admiral Gambier had worked himself into a fine passion. "And then complete your commission, sir! Mr. Blackwell to Ceuta without loss of a minute, and no more arsing about with Spanish galleons."

Captain Blackwell did notice, as he was rowed back to *Inconstant*, the holiday atmosphere spoken of by Admiral Gambier in the many boats plying between ships and shore. He saw it on the decks of the fleet among his brother officers as ship visiting took place; their laughter and exclamations reached him as his gig passed by.

And women, women getting in and out of boats tied up to men-of-war. The sight recalled Admiral Gambier's ranting indignation. Captain Blackwell wondered if Gambier was the sort who could not abide women, or just the class whose occupation he had flung out about during their interview. But then Captain Blackwell's own ire rose when approaching *Inconstant* he saw just such a boatload of women in the act of latching the main chains of his ship.

"Belay that!" Captain Blackwell bellowed. "Boat ahoy. Stand off."

The gig was brought up smartly to the ship's side. Captain Blackwell threw the briefest glance at the boat full of women making the usual chatter and stir, before going up the side to the cries of the bosun's pipe and the clash and stamp of Marines. He returned the salutes of the quarterdeck and glared about. Captain Blackwell didn't like to admit there could be truth in Admiral Gambier's tirade, but indeed his ship had something of the look of a slut. Both off watches on deck, the idlers in the waist, even young Mr. Verson, who the hands usually made an effort to keep out of sight in port, he gave their barky a decidedly unwarlike appearance with his thumb in his mouth, was standing there by the taffrail spitting over the side.

"Mr. Peakes, Mr. Peakes, there! Call the men aft," Captain Blackwell ordered.

When the faces of the men were turned attentively to him, Captain Blackwell addressed them.

"You have heard no doubt that there is peace, and that is true." There might have been a huzzah but for the stern set of his face. "We should be grateful for the blessings of peace. But France and her allies are not our country's only concern, and *Inconstant* still has a job of work to do before we see England. You will do well to remember this ain't no goddamn yacht. This is a ship of the King's Navy! There will be no shore liberty, no wives allowed aboard," Captain Blackwell turned pointedly to the boat of women backing and filling alongside, "until we have safely landed every last prisoner and wounded man. Back to your stations! Mr. Peakes, out boats. Mr. Bowles, pass the word for Captain Christensen. And desire my brother, with my compliments, to step into my cabin when he is at liberty. Mr. Sprague, Mr. Verson, in my cabin if you please."

He gave orders to Mr. Sprague and Mr. Verson for the unloading of the treasure, a file of Marines to line the dock on the quay, and to the Marine captain and Mr. Bransford for the disembarking of the prisoners. "No more than fifteen on the deck at one time, Captain Christensen, and take Mr. Martinez below with you to explain to those men what will take place. Mr. Bransford, pull across to *Elephant* and give my compliments to Captain Digby, and I should be obliged for the loan of his jolly boat and cutter."

A short while later Captain Blackwell stood in conversation with his brother. "Lord, Frank, I never was so much taken aback. Peace! And the men to have no prize money, droits of the Crown, so says the Admiral." He was absorbed with the unexpected issues this brought forth: the great disappointment of his crew, their possible disaffection and their desire to be homeward bound now there was no enemy to pursue. He felt *Inconstant*'s people had behaved well and did not like to see them denied reward. "A most unaccountable sort, Admiral Gambier. One moment breathing hell and damnation and the next giving me that." He took out of his pocket the evangelical tract Admiral Gambier had put into his hand, and tossed it on the table. "And we do not go home, as you well know. Provision, repair and put to sea." Captain Blackwell cast a meaning glance at Mercedes' door. "But, however, first the prisoners and *La Trinidad*'s cargo. Miss Mercedes?"

"Sir?" Her response came immediately.

Captain Blackwell could not help but be gratified she had never yet failed to call him that when others were by. "If you wish to see your shipmates disembark you had better come now."

Mercedes issued from her door, and he and Francis bowed to her.

"I must beg to be excused while I prepare to call on shore," Francis said. "You will accompany me to Government House, Captain?"

"Yes, Frank, certainly."

Once on deck Captain Blackwell could not play host, and Mercedes, leaning on his arm, was attentive to the change in his posture.

"Here is Mr. Martinez, sir, assisting with the prisoners," she said. "May you not leave me with him? Now we are no longer enemies."

Captain Blackwell looked sharply at Mr. Martinez, standing on the gangway and speaking down into the waist where the prisoners were being led. Mercedes would be as safe with him as any of his officers. The man had deserted his own country and service to remain near her. There could be no other reason for Mr. Martinez to throw in his lot with the Royal Navy, which would not let him go now they had him, peace or no peace.

Unknown to Captain Blackwell because he did not have the Spanish, one of Mr. Martinez's shipmates called up to him at that moment. "What do you think, you stupid bugger, eh Martinez? King George's service for you, and liberty for us!"

"*Vaya con Dios, jodido,*" returned Mr. Martinez.

Captain Blackwell approached with Mercedes and a blush rose up Mr. Martinez's neck and reached his ears. It was a most incongruous sight displayed on Mr. Martinez's dark skin and hardened features.

"What plan you to do, girl?" Mr. Martinez asked when Captain Blackwell had walked aft.

"I hardly know."

"You must get off this ship. There is Spain, make your way to your Uncle David. He will not detain you." Mr. Martinez nodded toward the quarterdeck.

"Maybe he would not, but it might suit me to remain with him," Mercedes said. "Long enough to be presented to *Admiral* Gambier."

"Your mother's ambitions need not be your own," Mr. Martinez said. "Nor her vices. Think what it is you want, girl, not what you believe you are expected to do."

"What it is I want I never can have."

She turned a disturbed gaze on a boy, a shadow of the handsome youth who had served her in Captain de Leon y Castillo's cabin, being led out between two sturdy Spanish seamen. This boy was hollow-eyed, very reduced and shaking. Even the Englishmen put their hands out in kindness to steady the boy as he went over the side and into the boat.

"What has happened to Juanito?" Mercedes said. "I asked the doctor to see him. Is it the bloody flux?"

Mr. Martinez's features hardened further.

"I'll tell you what it is, girl, but just you keep your voice down. Do you hear? I'll tell you what it is so you might know what kind of men surround you. It wasn't no bloody flux. It was that bloody minded first lieutenant. Buggered him, buggered Juanito since the first night of our capture."

Mr. Martinez paused as Mercedes gasped and clasped her hands over her heart, whipping round to look at the men in the boats ready to pull away. There, between two seamen, sat the ruin of the boy named Juan Luis Montelongo. When the boats, four boats with twenty or so prisoners each, began to pull away, one of the seamen in the boat with the boy Juanito spoke to Narhilla at the tiller. Narhilla called an order, the boats' oars came up, and at a command in Spanish the departing seamen raised their caps to Mercedes.

Mercedes murmured, "Oh no! Oh no, Tio," as she acknowledged the seamen's salute.

"Master yourself, now, here comes the Captain."

Mr. Martinez backed away as Captain Blackwell came stamping down the gangway to congratulate her on the fine compliment paid her by the Spanish seamen. But after one glance at her face, he said, "Come below with me, ma'am."

Once below, with his cabin door closed, Captain Blackwell turned to her.

"Now what's amiss, Mercy sweetheart. I haven't seen you look this way since ..." He broke off, unwilling to say 'since I captured you' or some such nonsense.

"Did you see the boy, Juanito, sir, that went into the last boat? Did you see how unwell, how terribly ill he appeared?"

Captain Blackwell stared at her. He had remarked the boy, and wondered at the time why the prisoner had not been taken off first with the wounded.

"Is it a fever?" God forbid it, Captain Blackwell thought as he asked.

"A fever? No sir, unless you call inhumanity and cruelty a fever. Your first lieutenant sodomized him."

Captain Blackwell jerked his head back as though she'd slapped him. In the next moment the mask had fallen over his features that he wore when he witnessed punishment at the ship's grating. He knew Mr. Sprague and thought him capable of any wickedness. This was a particularly ugly deed, but what struck Captain Blackwell hardest was at least two of his Marines, men who stood guard at his door and walked sentry on his ship, must have been complicit in this outrage.

"I cannot accuse one of my officers on the evidence of a passenger, and a seaman. I assume it was Mr. Martinez gave you this intelligence?"

"Do you know what rape is, James? I do."

A knock sounded on the door.

"What now?" Captain Blackwell shouted.

"Governor Barnett's compliments, sir, and his barge is alongside."

"Come in, Frank."

Francis walked in to an atmosphere of tension in the cabin.

"I very much regret I am unable to leave the ship at the moment," Captain Blackwell said. Mercedes sank onto the stern lockers at those words. "Pray make my excuses to the Governor and his staff. Pressing business aboard, you understand. I shall order Mr. Sprague to attend these courtesy calls in my stead."

Captain Blackwell bowed to Mercedes and went out of the cabin with his brother in tow.

"Is this wise, Captain?" Francis said. "The man is not your friend and may put about untruths regarding your capture of *La Trinidad.*"

Mr. Sprague's low opinion of Captain Blackwell, as something less than a gentleman, was not a secret among *Inconstant's* officers.

"Aye, Frank, but he has done worse than tell tales, and I must deal with a matter concerning the Marines directly. Without loss of a moment."

The first lieutenant had been informed of his changed duty, and Mr. Sprague came up the after hatchway, handsome and resplendent in full dress uniform.

"Clap a stopper over his capers if you can Frank, ashore. Pass the word for Captain Christensen!"

Captain Blackwell had a long and trying day, first closeted in discussion with Captain Christensen. He required the Marine captain to go over the character of each man: rank, service history, social standing and family connections, all of it. Then Captain Blackwell called the Marines into his cabin in groups, and, he did hope and trust, put the fear of God in them, or at least the fear of himself, which in the ship *Inconstant* amounted to the same thing. He rapped out the penalty for sodomy, for dereliction of duty, for disobedience to orders; death, death, and death.

The marines were to speak to no one when on sentry duty outside his door, except in announcing visitors to the captain.

They were to receive their orders from none but himself and Captain Christensen. This last stretched a point, as Captain Blackwell knew, for they must obey the orders of any superior officer. When he reached this point in his tirade Captain Blackwell brought the small store of subtlety of which he was capable to bear. He did fancy he made an impression. Their faces swam before his mind's eye, most apprehensive and fearful, some confused, and a very few defiant. He would have to know them far better to apprehend which were the offenders. His crew likely knew or had strong suspicions, and the collective opinion is seldom out.

He had made an impression he was certain, and those men would consider before acquiescing again in his first lieutenant's sadistic schemes. If he could only rid himself of Sprague, get him transferred into another vessel, though it wounded his conscience to think of fobbing the man off on another captain. Captain Blackwell was considering whether his diplomat brother might be of use in the case, when Francis was announced and walked in.

"There you are, Frank." Captain Blackwell's voice was nearly gone from the afternoon's exertions. "I was just thinking of you."

He was seated behind his desk, tired and worn. He felt old, and most decidedly unhappy.

"Indeed? I bear an invitation from the Governor," Francis said. "Perhaps you had a presentiment of it. Not everyone is as unmoved by your recent action as the Admiral. Mr. Barnett gives a supper in your honor tonight at Government House."

"Oh, goddamn and blast!"

After his brother left him, Captain Blackwell made his way to the sick berth. Few patients remained, the serious cases had been landed. He inquired of Doctor VanArsdel after his patients ashore. The doctor had a haggard cast to his face; it would have been a wearisome day for him seeing those many wounded men settled in hospital. Of the over one hundred combined wounded initially crowding *Inconstant*'s sick berth, the midshipmen's quarters and even the hold, forty had survived to Gibraltar.

When their discussion of the settling of the invalids concluded, Captain Blackwell said, “Do you recollect a cabin boy from *La Trinidad*, Doctor? Miss Mercedes may have mentioned him, a boy she called Juanito.”

“Yes, I do, sir.” Doctor VanArsdel’s hand came up to rub his temple. “I do remember Miss Mercedes speaking of him. In fact she asked me to attend him in the hold; she said he’d the appearance of the bloody flux. I’m very much ashamed to admit I didn’t. It was the day of the dreadful storm and I had the sick berth full from the battle, and new cases, broken bones and the depressed fracture of the skull that carried off poor Bates. We lost so many those first days. The boy was not brought to me later, sir, but I would very much regret to hear he was indeed unwell.”

Captain Blackwell shook his head. “He went ashore with the rest of the prisoners today. Miss Mercedes merely mentioned the boy to me. Speaking of Miss Mercedes, Doctor, I wonder if you would be so good as to dine with her this evening? I find I must go ashore.”

“Certainly, Captain, it would be my pleasure.” It was the only response Doctor VanArsdel could make.

Captain Blackwell had sent Mercedes on deck during the watch of first Mr. Verson and then Mr. Bransford, while he attended to the wretched business with the Marines. When he gained the deck he saw her on the forecastle, once more amidst the sail maker’s party. He cast a narrowed glance at Mr. Bransford on the quarterdeck. The lieutenant studiously avoided his eye, looking into the ship’s rigging and at the surrounding bay and vessels with careful attention. He’d left her on deck for more than four hours, so he shouldn’t have been surprised to find her employed. Mercedes left the sail maker’s party and met him on the gangway, taking the arm he offered and walking with him as far as the break of the quarterdeck.

“I’ve asked Doctor VanArsdel to sup with you this evening. I must go ashore. I hope this meets with your approval, ma’am?” He heard the cold formality in his tone and regretted it, but he could not change it.

Mercedes had assured him the arrangement did meet with her approval, and then she sat disconsolate at the head of the table in the evening facing Doctor VanArsdel. She'd watched the captain take his leave earlier, looking, to her eyes, very well indeed in his best uniform. As each dish was brought in she glimpsed Mr. Sprague loitering outside the door. Had she not had the confirmation of McMurtry's increasing ill humor as the meal progressed, she would have put the sight of the first lieutenant down to her own morbid fancy.

"I find I must beg your pardon, ma'am, for not attending to the servant boy Juanito — Montelongo was it? — you requested me to see. The Captain spoke of him earlier, and put me in mind of my neglect, my dereliction ..."

The doctor broke off, astonished into silence by the tears that came into Mercedes' eyes.

"Never fear, Doctor," she said at last. "He went ashore today with my countrymen."

Later Mercedes rose with an impatient air and asked the doctor if they might shift their chairs. She turned her back to the cabin door and tried to engage in conversation while they drank their coffee. Then Doctor VanArsdel took his leave; he could not stay with her the evening entire, he said. "Thank you, ma'am, for a most enjoyable evening. I don't know when I have taken such pleasure in sitting quietly alongside someone. You are a most restful person to be in company with."

"You chastise me for my silence, Doctor, and I do beg your pardon. Thank you very much for your company."

Doctor VanArsdel met Mr. Sprague in the passage outside the cabin.

"What business have you here, sir?"

Mr. Sprague neither offered a response nor stepped back from the doctor's path.

Inside the cabin Mercedes tried to read, but she couldn't concentrate on her book. Though she could not see Mr. Sprague she was aware of the man's oppressive presence outside the cabin door. Thoughts of what the boy Juanito had endured while she lay in Captain Blackwell's arms made her feel physically unwell, and she turned her mind away from ugly images again and again.

Mercedes had long been gazing at and studying the weapons hung on the cabin bulkheads. After a time she rose and stepped into Captain Blackwell's sleeping cabin and went through the lockers, pulling them out and pushing them in as quietly as she could until she found a dagger thrown in among brushes and other disused items. She took the dagger and retired to her own sleeping quarters, shutting the door and lying down on her cot without removing her clothes.

Underneath the bolster she rested her head on Mercedes gripped the hilt of the dagger, while thoughts of the ship and the men in her revolved in her mind. They were a good set of men taken together, a very good set except for this one. But the first lieutenant could more than counterbalance the good of those other men, and he could do it uncommon fast. All Mr. Sprague would require were moments alone with her to make her forever undesirable in the captain's eyes.

Late in the evening when Blackwell returned to the ship he was annoyed to find Mr. Sprague skulking in the passage outside the great cabin. The man offered some farrago concerning the watch bill and Blackwell backed him right against the bulkhead and spoke a few words. Threats they were, and he meant them. If ever he was to hear again of an abuse of prisoners or any crew as had reached his ears that day, he would see Mr. Sprague dismissed the service and damn the consequences. Yet since he wouldn't bring Mr. Sprague up on charges he had to work with the man.

Blackwell entered his cabin weary to death of the day and the service, with a faint, a very faint hope of finding a woman in his cot. He wanted to lose himself in physical release with Mercedes. But though he did not fancy himself a man who understood a woman's feelings, he guessed a fellow who would show himself indifferent to a lady's distress, as he had appeared to do, could expect no tenderness. Still he looked into his sleeping cabin, illuminated by a gently swaying dark lantern, full of longing and expectation. When he found she wasn't there he went out and stood before her door.

"Mercedes, sweetheart — "

She flung open her door and fell on his breast. Blackwell took her up in his arms and lifted her off her feet, his heart lightening at once.

"Mercy, sweetheart ... wait. Oh no, sweetheart. Oh, God!"

They had stumbled together into his cabin, where Blackwell struggled out of his uniform jacket and waistcoat. He was bent over trying to remove the buckled shoes when he lost his balance and came down hard on a locker, bringing Mercedes with him. Perhaps believing it was what he wanted, Mercedes sank between his knees, unbuttoned his breeches and touched him with her mouth. Blackwell had a surge of feeling akin to what he had never experienced before except in battle, when he thought he was going to die. With a supreme effort Blackwell pulled Mercedes into his lap and consummated the act holding her around the waist.

He kissed the back of her neck, thinking the encounter had been too hasty, too abrupt by far and could not have brought her much pleasure. Yet when she rose and was going out of his cabin, she put her hand gently on his arm. "That was the only joy in an otherwise wretched day, James."

"I hope I may never have another like it."

Blackwell listened to her moving about behind the closed door of her cabin, his wine-fuddled brain pondering why Mercedes insisted on leaving him immediately after lying with him. She might not care for the sight of a man in the post-coital state. Certainly he was no elegant sight with his clothes half undone, sprawled on the locker and leaning back against the bulkhead. Blackwell heard the sound of water pouring into a basin and realized what Mercedes did. He hauled himself to his feet and leaning over he collected his number one jacket and waistcoat from the deck.

"McMurtry!"

"Sir!"

Blackwell walked out into the passage, handed the steward his clothes, and stripped off the rest as he went." Rig the deck pump!"

One of the afterguard, idling in the waist, considered Captain Blackwell. "Captain looks like one of them special cart horses, hosing down like that, large and muscled for labor. What are them horses called, Bob?"

"How should I know, mate? I ain't no fucking landsman like some I could name. Captain's wishful to wash like a nag you say, "Aye, aye, sir," or he's like to rip you a new arsehole the way he done those lobsters."

Back in his cabin Blackwell tried to dry his large frame with a small towel before a puddle formed at his feet. He waited a few moments after rinsing his face and drinking fresh water, or what passed for such in a frigate, and then bellowed out, "I want a woman in my cot!" It was a far louder cry than he had intended, putting the sentry at the door, McMurtry, and everyone within hearing on the grin.

Mercedes came out of her cabin and into his shaking her head at him, but she took off her dressing gown and climbed dutifully into his cot.

In the afternoon watch Francis returned to *Inconstant*, having spent all day ashore meeting with his chief, Lord Upton of His Majesty's diplomatic service. He had taken rooms at the Crown, from which he could spend the rest of the time necessary for the ship's repairs in Gibraltar conducting his business ashore. As it was the hour when he and Mercedes walked the deck Francis went into the cabin where his brother and Mercedes were sitting comfortably together, the tension of the previous day quite gone. Captain Blackwell was behind his desk, spread with the purser's, carpenter's, and bosun's accounts and innumerable indents. Mercedes sat in a chair by the stern windows, reading the pamphlet Admiral Gambier had given to Captain Blackwell.

"Good day to you, brother," Captain Blackwell said.

"Good day, sir. How do you do, ma'am? Do not get up, I beg," Francis said. "How many days until you are ready for sea, sir, if I may be so bold?"

"Why, day after tomorrow earliest, I should think. The repairs will finish today and tomorrow we could complete our water and provisions if we put our backs into it. Does that suit you, Frank?"

"Certainly. I bespoke rooms at the Crown and I shall sleep ashore for the remainder of our stay, with your leave, sir. Here is an invitation to Government House."

"Mercedes," Captain Blackwell said, after reading the invitation. "Should you like to accompany me to a ball at Government House tomorrow evening? It is a subscription ball sponsored jointly by the British and the Dons — Spanish, pardon me — to benefit the families of service men killed in the late conflict."

"What a question, Captain," she said. "Of course I should like it of all things."

And then Mercedes fell silent, experiencing an inward anguish. She had but recently been on Captain de Leon y Castillo's ship and been his companion. He had a widow and sons in Spain, and she was concerned whether they had learned of his death. The sensibility Mercedes had already remarked in Francis led him to her.

"What make you of that, ma'am?" he asked, indicating the Christian tract in her hand. "It is very much Church of England, and you're Catholic, I collect?"

"No. That is, my mother used to say we were neither fish nor fowl. She was raised in the Catholic faith, and I had a certain amount of religious instruction, but we had a life quite apart. And I was not aware to be called a Christian one must attain the high moral standard demanded here." She laid her hand over the pamphlet.

"I suppose our Protestant, moralistic views are far away from anything necessary to the New World," Francis said, "where freedom and spontaneity must be more the guiding principle. Shall we walk on deck, ma'am? It is past our time."

On deck it was a fine, warm day and Mercedes lowered her eyes against the sun directly in her face as they walked along the gangway to the quarterdeck. They might walk there since the captain remained below toiling over the ship's accounts.

"You need a bonnet, ma'am."

"I do, indeed," Mercedes said. "I need many things at present, which is why I must beg a very great favor of you."

"I am at your service."

"I have a small fortune, a dowry, if you will. But it is in jewels, a little store of jewels my mother passed to me. She was an old-fashioned person. Diamonds and rubies were her preferred currency. So the favor I must ask of you is to change one or two of those gems into the ready. Is that how it is expressed?"

Francis smiled. "It is, Miss Mercedes, among men."

"I beg your pardon, sir. I would not address you on anything so vulgar as money — "

"Not at all, ma'am, I shall undertake the commission with the greatest pleasure. You will need a gown no doubt, for the ball."

"Oh, I have gowns enough, far down in my sea chest. But I do need to step into a modiste's shop there in the town if possible, to see what the styles might be, so that I do not disgrace the Captain. And I need a number of other things ... ladies' things."

"Since we have entered into delicate territory, Miss Mercedes, permit me to tell you something which I would not otherwise dare. Captain Blackwell would supply your wants, were you to ask him, he is the most open-handed man." As Mercedes began to interject, Francis raised his hand to stay her. "Hear me first, if you please, ma'am. He is a generous man, too generous in fact. James paid for my education, I am twelve years his junior, with his blood and hardship in the King's service. But my education, my career in the diplomatic service, is one of the only material benefits he has seen from his many years in the Navy. When I was young James allowed our father the management of his money, his prize money." Francis paused with a grave look. "In short, our father was not a good manager. He is a parson, ma'am. And although James's affairs are now in the hands of Truelove and Wilson, a reputable prize agent, his fortunes have not recovered. Meanwhile we have an uncle on our mother's side, Admiral Hayden, who helped James to his career and left me a handsome competence. He thought that justice. Yet I find myself a man of property while my brother, my very worthy brother, cannot afford a new uniform coat."

"You do me great honor in telling me this, I thank you," Mercedes said. "Perhaps I might be of use to him."

Captain Blackwell was seen coming up to the quarterdeck then and Francis immediately took Mercedes' arm and led her away.

The sight of the two of them, with their heads bowed together, gave Captain Blackwell a queer feeling, a powerfully queer feeling. His brother was the more eligible man, he was aware, and Francis and Mercedes were much of an age. Captain Blackwell considered they had the same intellectual bent, reading whatever was to hand, conversant in multiple languages. None of this inward uncertainty showed in his face, however, as Captain Blackwell took up his station on the quarterdeck. The men there at anchor watch saw the usual stern visage of their commander.

"You say she wants it for clothes, bonnets and the like?" Captain Blackwell asked Francis later that day. "Didn't ask you to take passage for her on some packet or diligence?"

Francis had told Captain Blackwell of Mercedes' commission to him, to convert several gemstones into currency.

"Not a bit of it, sir," Francis said. "Lengths of cloth, bonnets perhaps, and those creams and scents ladies indulge in."

Captain Blackwell threw himself back in his chair, lost for a moment in thoughts of the softness and scent of Mercedes' skin.

"I shall order a boat for you tomorrow after breakfast," Captain Blackwell said. "Oh, I am forgetting, you sleep ashore."

"I will come at any hour you care to name and bring Miss Mercedes into town."

"Much obliged, Frank. She can hardly walk the deck in any case with those ..." Captain Blackwell had been about to say 'brutes', as they were called in Plymouth, but out of delicacy he changed it to "wives coming and going. So I shall be glad of your escorting her into Gib. And I must beg another favor. Take rooms for me if you please at the Crown, a dining parlor, and a bedchamber for Mercedes to dress for the ball. I must give a supper for my officers. I have been quite remiss in having them in to dine. But how could I? She cannot drink the loyal toast. Perhaps she can now with the peace, but in any case she would not be able to sit down with Mr. Sprague. I can barely stomach the idea."

Captain Blackwell looked rather consciously at his brother when he'd concluded.

"Do not thank me, I am only too happy to accompany Miss Mercedes. I do not do it out of duty to you alone, brother — I will see to your other arrangements you may be sure — but for her sake. She is the best, the dearest of women."

Captain Blackwell watched the dear, good woman's final preparations in the cabin before leaving his ship next morning. A portmanteau had been rummaged up from the hold to carry her clothing and toiletries. The Spanish captain's weaponry had long since been wrapped in oiled canvas and put into the jolly boat. Mercedes had on the high-waisted gown she'd worn the day she came aboard *Inconstant*, as well as the sash containing her mother's jewels. The dress was not a fortunate choice where Captain Blackwell was concerned. It increased the odd, uncomfortable feeling her departure gave him.

"Mercedes, I should like to remind you though you go ashore you are still under my protection." He waited for her to respond. "In the Navy we are accustomed to repeat our orders, so there may be no misunderstanding."

Mercedes came over near his chair. "I am to cleave only unto you, sir."

He flushed and brought her onto his lap and laid his head for a moment on her breast.

Chapter 7

At the base of the Rock of Gibraltar was the bustling town. It had been rebuilt after the Great Siege — a siege enduring near four years must be called great — when the French and Spanish had combined in an attempt to throw out the English dog. They had not succeeded, but neither had they gone away, the Dons and the Frenchmen. The streets of Gibraltar were crowded with them and their women. There were besides in this cosmopolitan place blacks from Africa just across the Strait, and Arabs, and Jews sent into exile by Spain in a former age. They became merchants and called the town at the foot of the Rock of Gibraltar the limit of their exile.

Mercedes had not set foot on firm earth nor been in the midst of a populous town since Funchal. She was not a timid woman, yet she was glad of Francis Blackwell's arm and Narhilla following behind. Francis escorted her to the Crown, where he put her into his own rooms. He had a bedchamber with connected sitting and dressing rooms. Francis told her he would sleep in the bedchamber Captain Blackwell had desired him to take. The room for the captain's supper party was bespoken and Francis turned over the ordering of the cuisine to Mercedes. She smiled at the inn-keeper and then proceeded in a flow of Spanish to name the dishes required.

After the landlord had taken his leave Mercedes went to the window and moved aside the curtain. "I should like to climb this Rock one day," she said to Francis. "What a fascinating view it must offer. The Pillars of Hercules."

"And you shall be in the way of seeing both, for Monte Hacho is in Ceuta, where we're bound." It had been agreed in long discussion between Francis and Lord Upton to cast his mission in Ceuta in a purely mercantile light: the British consul promoting trade relations with Oran.

"Captain Blackwell puts me in mind of Hercules. I suppose it is the way the officers stand on the quarterdeck. Do not let me keep you, Mr. Blackwell." She dropped the curtain and turned to Francis. "I know you have pressing business, some of which I have thrust upon you. I'll be very well here until you call for me this afternoon. I'll have a bath, I long for a bath. I think I shall have three! Oh, I am indelicate again."

"Never fear, ma'am." Francis laughed. "We are practically brother and sister, you and I, and it was the first thing I did too directly I came away from *Inconstant*. I will say good day for the present."

Francis bowed and went out of the sitting room. Mercedes took from the portmanteau her mother's letter; too precious to leave behind, it must accompany her wherever she traveled; and sat with it in her hand thinking of Francis's remark. 'We are practically brother and sister.' She was for a time fully taken up in the contemplation of just how much of his brother's heart Francis might know.

Mercedes did not linger over her bath. She dressed quickly and covered her hair and veiled her face with a lace mantilla and slipped out of the Crown. On the streets of Gibraltar, she kept off the Alameda, the main thoroughfare, Mercedes did not feel the lack of a man's arm to lean on. Many women went about singly in the mercantile areas, but when Mercedes reached the quayside she found another scene entirely. Here there were women standing about in clusters, the seamen's wives as Captain Blackwell delicately referred to them, waiting to be taken off to the various men-of-war and merchantmen. There were ladies of good character too walking about, but officers or civilian gentlemen escorted them. A woman alone was subjected to unwelcome and impertinent stares.

She might have asked at the Crown after an abigail, a maid, to attend her; it was what she should have done except for the hurry of spirit she'd felt to look into hiring a boat to the flagship. Tucked into the sash round her waist was her mother's letter, which she was determined to put into Admiral Gambier's hand herself. She called out to the least ill-looking of the boatmen, asking after the charge to row her to *Royal George*.

"Which it's five bob, honey. Reduced to seven shillings if they actually let you aboard, being one way like."

"I am obliged to you, sir."

Mercedes hurried back up the Hard. She paced back and forth. Certainly it would not be impossible to hire a boat to *Royal George*, once she was in possession of the sterling Francis would bring her. But to gain admittance to Admiral Gambier would be altogether more difficult. The ball might offer an opportunity for an introduction, and to meet him socially was to be preferred to brazening her way aboard his ship.

Instead of studying *Royal George*, Mercedes ended by staring over at *Inconstant*. Her gaze softened with affection when she spotted the tallest blue-coated figure on the quarterdeck. *Inconstant's* victory over *La Trinidad*, her taking of the "thumping great treasure" was the talk of Gibraltar, and Mercedes was not alone, at least, among the people on the quayside interested in the frigate. There seemed to be a flurry of activity taking place on her deck.

At last, tearing herself away from the two ships, the two men, captain and admiral, Mercedes turned for the hotel. She was afraid the activity on *Inconstant's* deck was preparation for putting a boat into the water, and perhaps Captain Blackwell was coming ashore early.

Captain Blackwell and Mr. Hammerly were on deck discussing a plan for shifting the ballast in the hold now they were free of prisoners, and before completing their stores. The off watch midshipmen and one or two of the volunteers, boys of twelve and thirteen, were larking about the top masts and rigging. Captain Blackwell didn't like it, nor did Mr. Peakes, the bosun. Mr. Peakes was jealous of the precious new cordage and sailcloth. But skylarking was a tradition in the service, and what was more, Captain Blackwell disliked throwing a damper over high young spirits. Captain Blackwell heard the cry, nothing more than "Ah!" Looking up he saw, for the briefest instant, the surprised countenance of Mr. Knight, the midshipman the captain thought of as 'the squeaker' for his changing voice, before the boy hit the deck.

"Send for the doctor!" Mr. Hammerly cried.

The boy had landed not far from Captain Blackwell and the sailing master, and both men bent over him.

"Belay that order," Captain Blackwell said. Doctor VanArsdel could be seen rushing up from below into the waist of the ship even then. "Pass the word for the sail-maker. He is dead, God rest him."

When the sail-maker's mate Sorenson brought a hammock for Mr. Knight's body Captain Blackwell knelt, lifted the boy and placed him in it. This sort of death was more difficult to bear than those in battle, when one had not a moment to regard the dead as individuals. The youngster was a terrible sight, nearly stripped of semblance to a human being. Captain Blackwell pulled the canvas over the boy's head, the remains of his exploded head, and the sail-maker did his work.

He rose and McMurtry held out a towel for him to wipe his hands. Captain Blackwell squeezed the shoulder of each of Mr. Knight's companions, standing by with tear-stained faces, before going below to write his letter to the boy's parents.

Captain Blackwell's supper for his officers was, almost of necessity, a failure. Under normal circumstances Mr. Bransford, Mr. Verson and Mr. Bowles would have counterbalanced with their good will the ill humor, the froward aspect of Mr. Sprague. But they none of them could be merry after the death and burial of the midshipman. Fortunately the supper dishes Mercedes had caused to be placed before them were of the best quality and preparation Gibraltar offered, and compensated somewhat for the lack of conviviality. Yet most of them had purchased subscriptions to the ball. Mr. Hammerly and Mr. Verson alone returned to the ship, so when they rose from dining they at least had a reason to take leave of one another straight away.

Over their heads in Francis's rooms Mercedes finished the alteration of her ball gown. She had been fairly certain it would be a simple task and so it had proved. After looking in at a dressmaker's, at their latest fashion plates, Mercedes had removed the Brussels lace from an emerald colored gown and added a diaphanous silver overdress.

She had been fortunate to find the elegant material. Mercedes also bought cloth for morning gowns and to make up new shirts for Captain Blackwell, stores for the captain's table, tooth powder and brushes and many feminine items: scented water and soap and skin cream, and sea sponges used both for the monthly cycle and contraception. McMurtry brought her Captain Blackwell's second best coat, largely ruined by the bloodstains from the battle for *La Trinidad*. She had left it with a tailor to be copied. Mercedes didn't undervalue her own skills, but this tailor was particular to the naval trade and could make a jacket uncommon fast. But before the purchase of any of these things, most of which she'd already sent aboard *Inconstant*, she'd given more than half the sum received for her jewels back into Francis's hands.

"Find a way, Mr. Blackwell, if you will." Mercedes refused to take the sterling back from him. "Find a way to make a gift of this to Captain Blackwell, so he may pay his crew the prize money they set their hearts on. It is not unheard of I daresay, for a captain to make up when his government runs short. The ship will be safer for you and I, don't you think, with the crew most willing?"

"What I think, Miss Mercedes, is you must call me Francis. And I shall put your plan in action and contribute to it as well. For I'm sure your judgment is quite sound." Francis did not hide his admiration for her generosity, and he told her of Mr. Knight's fall from the mizzenmast that day in the most confiding tone.

The best part of the evening, Captain Blackwell considered, had already passed. It was when he had taken Mercedes to walk in the gardens of Government House, following the concert that preceded the ball. A woman cellist had closed the concert with Bach's Prelude, from the Unaccompanied Cello Suite Number 1 in G. When he looked at Mercedes as the audience clapped their appreciation he saw tears standing in her eyes. He'd taken her out through the French doors of the music room and into the gardens, which reminded him of England in their conventional arrangement, so unsuited to the wild outcropping of rock on which they grew.

"It was a beautiful piece, to be sure," he said.

"Yes, forgive my weakness, Captain." Mercedes accepted the offer of his handkerchief. "I must tell you how sorry I am for the death of Mr. Knight, a terrible accident." Captain Blackwell bowed to her, and she pursued, "There was a nurse to the children of the governor of California, an English woman with whom in fact I learned the best part of my English. She played the cello beautifully. She played that particular piece to perfection and it put me in mind of her. And of my home in California, of the death of Mr. Knight whose life had barely begun, and so many other sad things I should be ashamed."

He drew her hand to rest on his arm and led her down the rows of neatly arranged flowerbeds and groupings of roses. Captain Blackwell desired her to relate how she was connected to the governor of California.

"My mother was Don Fernando de Santatierra y Ortega's mistress, sir. She knew when she died Don Fernando's good lady would make me feel California couldn't contain us both. She had done so to my mother, but my mother was made of tougher material than Doña Santatierra credited. But in any case my mama didn't wish me to remain and she arranged my passage on *La Trinidad*, and wrote to various connections here to support me. My uncle in Barcelona is one."

"Is Barcelona where you will go now, ma'am?" asked Captain Blackwell, in an even tone. The steadiness of voice he'd gained from six years of covering his emotions on the quarterdeck as a post-captain, but Captain Blackwell was glad the dark as yet moonless night hid his features.

By way of answer Mercedes stopped and turned to him. She put her hands on his arms and clutched him through the heavy blue broadcloth and tilted her lovely face up to his. In a moment he was kissing her, clasping her against him as he did when they were in his cot.

She pulled away from him and spoke into his neck cloth. "I think where I will go is to dance, Captain, if you please."

He had danced with her, of course, but his heavy physique didn't loan itself to the graceful figures of the cotillion and the minuet, and Mercedes soon had other partners a plenty. Captain Blackwell stood at the side of the ballroom watching her as she shone in a ball gown none would have guessed had sailed around the Horn. He didn't wonder she garnered so much attention, particularly from the Spanish officers, for he thought her quite the most beautiful and charming woman in the room. It didn't surprise him either that the Spanish faction had slowly taken her farther and farther away from him down the ballroom; it was what he would have done in their stead. Yet he was beginning to scowl at the group of Dons lavishing their damned Spanish gallantries on Mercedes when a hail interrupted his growing displeasure.

"Jim, old cock, how do you do?"

Captain Enoch Bourne of the *L'Aimable*, a beautiful 32 gun frigate captured from the French in '92, hailed him. They had been together on the *Fortitude* at the Battle of the Dogger Bank. Enoch had helped carry Midshipman Blackwell below, calling to him, "Never fear, Jim, your guts is all where they should be."

"Why Enoch, brother, I'm prime, prime. I didn't know you were in Gib. When did you put in?"

"Just this morning, and had my interview with that parson Admiral Gambier," Enoch said. "Preaching Jemmy. Oh! No disrespect intended."

His friend was a sufficient distraction, as Enoch made him recount the battle for *La Trinidad* in detail, to take his mind away from purely social concerns. Captain Blackwell forgot for the moment he'd been on the point of walking into the midst of the Dons and breaking up their fiesta.

"Look sharp, here comes Jemmy's flag lieutenant," Enoch said.

A handsomely made youth, a scrubbed young man in a smart uniform saluted the two captains, and would Captain Blackwell join the Admiral when he was at leisure? A pitying smile rested on Enoch Bourne's face as Captain Blackwell left the room in the flag lieutenant's wake.

Captain Blackwell found Admiral Gambier in the same foul humor as during their previous meeting. If anything, the Admiral seemed more ill disposed, as though he had swallowed something disagreeable in the extreme. He was not invited to a seat, and Admiral Gambier waited a moment while Captain Blackwell ranged up in front of him before launching his broadside.

"What is this I hear of whoring aboard your ship, Captain Blackwell? Of a woman taken off *La Trinidad* and kept captive in your cabin aboard *Inconstant*."

Captain Blackwell swayed slightly from the blast, but kept his countenance even as it struck him how busy Mr. Sprague had been ashore. He had learned enough from their previous encounter to keep silent until forced to speak, and in truth Admiral Gambier was nowhere near done, and had merely paused to draw breath. "It is written that whoremongers shall not enter heaven," the Admiral intoned. He went on to accuse Captain Blackwell of illiberal, shameful, unlawful and unchristian behavior. But when the Admiral arrived at whoring, ungentleman and unofficer-like, Captain Blackwell's face grew dark.

"She is my intended, sir, the lady aboard *Inconstant*. My fiancée," he interjected.

Admiral Gambier choked and he fell silent, the trembling of his head more pronounced when his haranguing voice was stilled.

"That ... puts another light upon the matter, Captain. I do beg your pardon."

When Captain Blackwell bowed to him, Admiral Gambier, the wind quite gone from his sails, motioned him to a chair.

"Quite a different light, indeed. However, I trust you will make your arrangements and find a good, Christian family to leave her with until your return from Ceuta. You have my permission to sleep ashore if you wish. Should you need a recommendation, the Olsens are a fine family. And I will tell you, Captain Blackwell, I won't have this carrying of mistresses aboard the King's ships. I won't have it in my squadron and so I warn you."

Francis returned to the ballroom from the first floor library of Government House, where he'd been meeting with other political men about the annexation of Ceuta. The peace they'd come together with the Spanish to celebrate was one in which the most able British diplomats did not believe. In spite of Lord Nelson's resounding defeat of Bonaparte's designs in Egypt, the East India Company was still urgent with Government to forestall any French encroachment. A base of operation in North Africa would be most desirable at this juncture, and Ceuta was ideal. An established port that would give the British command of both entrances to the Mediterranean, they would straddle it like Hercules indeed.

Captain Blackwell stood like the mythical hero, legs apart, but with a dark, goddamn you all look on his face that brought Francis immediately to his side when he entered the ballroom. "Why, James, what's amiss? You have a look of hell and damnation."

"Another interview with Admiral Gambier. Accused me of whoring, of keeping a woman aboard *Inconstant* against her will."

"People say unaccountable things, and for reasons we don't understand. There is such a thing as jealousy you are aware, sexual jealousy, even in an Admiral."

Captain Blackwell turned to his brother, startled.

"There is Gambier's admirable lady." Francis bowed to a matron passing by, a decidedly Anglo-Saxon matron with a shelf like bosom. "And there is your lady."

Mercedes was coming up the dance at that moment, with her hand resting lightly on her partner's arm, her eyes shining with pleasure. She gave the brothers a brilliant smile as she passed.

"What a fellow you are, Frank," Captain Blackwell said, smiling and bowing to Mercedes in return. He marveled at his brother's ability to bring him low, or lift his heart with a few brief words. Perhaps here was diplomacy.

But the smile did not last as the dance ended and Mercedes' partner led her away to the large group of Spaniards and their ladies.

"Why do they not bring her to me? They must be aware she came here under my protection," Captain Blackwell broke out. "I could not leave her here unattended even overnight, for any one of those goddamned caballeros might make her an offer."

"Unless you were to forestall them. I fancy your suit would not be unwelcome. No. She seems in fact to tolerate you rather well."

After saying this Francis walked off as cool as might be, eased his way amongst the Spanish, bowing here and conversing there, until he reached Mercedes. At which point he floated back out of the gathering with her on his arm and led her into the set then forming.

"I am so glad you enjoy the evening, Miss Mercedes. I'm sure it must be a great pleasure to speak your own language and be with your countrymen. I wish I could say the same for James. I have seen him look like that when he is about to take his ship into action." Francis nodded toward his brother as they passed him in the dance.

"Oh, Mr. Blackwell – Francis. Do take me to him once the dance is ended."

Francis brought her off the ballroom floor, and with only the slightest hesitation on both their parts, he put her hand onto Captain Blackwell's arm.

"I am quite ready to leave, Captain, if you are," Mercedes said.

Captain Cisneros hurried back into the ballroom with Vice-Admiral de Ávala in tow. Cisneros had retired to seek out Ávala when it had become known among the Spanish officers and nobility that the lovely young woman new to their company, Mercedes de Aragon, had been aboard *La Trinidad*. And further, that she was the daughter of a famous Cadiz courtesan known as La Costeña. Ávala, whose flag flew on the one hundred twenty gun ship of the line *Santa Ana*, had been one of La Costeña's most devoted followers. With the admiral beside him, Captain Cisneros accosted the first officer he came across. "Where is Doña Mercedes, where is the little pet?"

"She is going away with the fat English captain." The officer indicated with a bow where Mercedes and Captain Blackwell were taking leave of their hosts.

"Ah, she is the daughter of La Costeña," Ávala boomed out, in a voice meant to reach across the deck of a first rate.

Mercedes turned, hearing her mother called by a name she didn't care for. She met the eyes of Admiral Gambier, who had entered the ballroom just in time for Vice-Admiral Ávala's declaration. Admiral Gambier was staring at her, but so were many others. When Mercedes looked down and allowed herself to be led away by Captain Blackwell, Admiral Gambier swayed like a mast struck.

"Admiral Gambier, sir, here is a chair!" cried his concerned flag lieutenant. The Admiral's face had gone pale and he trembled in his limbs.

Captain Blackwell did not speak to Mercedes after asking her, "Should you like to stay at the Crown tonight, ma'am? I have permission to sleep out of *Inconstant*." She agreed and he conducted her to a carriage, then up the stairs at the Crown to Francis's rooms. Mercedes was unsure, as she went into the dressing room to remove her gown, if she would find him in the bedchamber when she emerged. She'd felt his displeasure as they came away from the ball, but she couldn't be sure it resulted from what she had told him of her past. Something else might have occurred. He'd been absent from the ballroom during part of the evening, while she was struggling to keep the Spanish from making too great a show of her being La Costeña's daughter.

But she found Blackwell leaning with one hand against the window frame, wearing cotton drawstring trousers that were his nod to on shore modesty. Aboard *Inconstant* he would've been naked, for he disdained the nightshirts worn by nearly everyone. Mercedes went up behind him, peering round his arm to see if it was *Inconstant* he gazed at.

"If I vexed you tonight, Captain, I am sorry for it."

He reached his hand back to her and Mercedes took it, opening her dressing gown so when he drew her arm around his waist, her breasts and bare stomach met his skin.

"I have no elegant address," Blackwell said. "I cannot make pretty speeches, and I'm well aware you should not be with me had I not boarded you in my own smoke."

"James, please. I care only for you. I do not want any other man than you."

He turned so quickly on her, with such a fierce expression of face, Mercedes was afraid of him and she backed against the bedchamber wall. In the next moment he dropped to his knees in front of her, grasping her waist and buttocks.

"But I can do to you what those fine gentlemen never would," he declared, and he began to kiss and to lick her.

"*No me haces esto.*"

"You will bear it, Miss," he said into her sensitive flesh, lifting her leg and placing it over his shoulder. "Just as you made me bear it."

Mercedes had nothing to hold on to and her hands opened and closed convulsively. She was whimpering insensate things neither Spanish nor English, until finally she brought out, "James ... Jim, belay. Oh!"

He picked her up and deposited her on the end of the high bedstead and entered her with her legs clutched against his chest, kissing the inside of her calves. Mercedes' pleasure mounted fiercely with his first thrusts. She covered her face with both her hands as she trembled and shuddered. Blackwell moved her up on the bed so that he could stretch over her, with her legs caught in the crooks of his arms. The strength of his thrusts moved both Mercedes and the bed beneath her.

"Tell me again," Blackwell said.

"You are the only man I want." He released her legs and she immediately wrapped them around his, running her hands down his back and grasping his buttocks. "The only man I want inside me."

Blackwell buried his head in the bolster over her shoulder, but it was still a powerful bellow that escaped him. The walls of the inn were thicker than the deal board out of which ship's cabins were constructed, but Mercedes wondered if their neighbors would think an animal had been slaughtered in their rooms. She didn't rest long with him in the delightful glow of their coupling before swinging her legs out of bed and sitting up. She hesitated in rising, the strength of his attentions had made her weak, and Blackwell reached out his hand to her.

"Do you go to wash my seed from your body? Do you not want children?"

As soon as the words were said Blackwell looked as though he could have cursed himself. Her back stiffened and she looked directly at him.

"It is bastards I do not want, knowing as I do what it is to be one." A little startled at her own temerity, Mercedes' voice softened and she laid her hand on his stomach where the dark hair was damp and clung to his belly. "You are to consider, too, that a child would change our relationship, for I would have to devote myself first to him. That was how I was raised, and I would not know how else to be a mother."

She lay in his arms when she returned to bed for what seemed to her mere moments before Blackwell relaxed, fell asleep, and began to snore. He'd passed a wearisome day; he'd had to bury a boy of thirteen. Mercedes eased away from him to the farthest corner of the mattress longing for her cramped little closet aboard *Inconstant*, where she'd known a measure of security. The absence of the familiar motion of the sea and a tangle of emotions kept her from sleeping until the hours before dawn.

She was not as clever a woman as her mother, nor as beautiful, as the whispers in the ballroom had reminded her. No doubt Arabella de Aragon would have found a way to make herself known to Admiral Gambier, taking the first step along the path of recognition and support. But Mercedes had done little to that end, outside of brave words to Mr. Martinez. In fact she'd done what her mother would deplore. She'd spoken plainly to Captain

Blackwell of her upbringing, and an equal, perhaps greater sin: she'd given him money, however clandestinely.

No, she was not her mother's daughter in many respects. Mercedes found, on reflection, that even had she been able to meet with Admiral Gambier she would not have been willing to act the injured child. She recalled the Christian tract given to Captain Blackwell by the Admiral, and she thought with a sinking heart of Francis's revealing they were the sons of a minister. Her entire upbringing led her toward reticence, and Mercedes could not make a spectacle of herself before the Admiral, insisting upon her due. She would not risk damaging Captain Blackwell's career through mere association with her.

She'd chosen to be forthcoming with Captain Blackwell about her connections. The natural child of a courtesan, not a lady of a respectable Spanish family he could present to English society. It was this question of legitimacy troubled her most deeply, as it must every decent woman. She'd revealed as much to Captain Blackwell in their talk of children. She could do no more now than hope and trust to him, and herein lay the territory of unrest. Mercedes fell asleep at last, murmuring once only, "*Hijo del pastor, oh.*"

Captain Blackwell woke before dawn for the changing of the watch. He put out his arm for Mercedes and though he didn't touch her, he could see her lying there with her back to him as far away on the bed as she could manage. He rose and went to the window and stared at the lanterns of ships swinging to their cables. There was not yet light enough in the sky to distinguish one ship from another, but he knew where *Inconstant* was anchored. Out there the routine of the Navy carried on. The ringing of the ship's bell, the sentinels' cries of "All's well," about the ship, and the changing of the anchor watch. Captain Blackwell alternated between gazing out the window and looking at the woman in the bed, at her dear, child-like form under the bedclothes, while he contemplated the issue of whether all was indeed well.

He didn't know exactly what to make of the events of the day previous, other than to feel matters had gone very ill, from Mr.

Knight's death to the damnable ball with Admiral Gambier's accusations and the Dons clustering round Mercedes. Captain Blackwell would no more leave her in the midst of this company than endanger his own ship now he understood perfectly what life they would lead her.

The very thought made him clench his jaw, the more so as he was aware he could protect her by pursuing the course Admiral Gambier championed. Leave her there in Gibraltar and return to marry her after his cruise was done. Yet Captain Blackwell had told his brother none of this and that fact must be significant. He had reasons for not marrying. He had nothing to offer her except his pay and a pension if he were knocked on the head. But what weighed the stronger in deciding him on his course were considerations certainly stemming from his being a parson's son.

Captain Blackwell went into the dressing room and washed and dressed as quietly as he could, and left the apartments. As he climbed the stairs to the third floor of the inn where his brother slept, Francis's discreet arrangement struck him. Francis had put Mercedes into his own chambers, and if anyone remembered a lady in a gentleman's rooms it would concern Mr. Francis Blackwell, not Captain James Blackwell. Captain Blackwell smiled at his brother's cleverness; pleased with the favor Francis had done him in a port ruled by a blue light admiral.

He sauntered into Francis's bedchamber saying, "Out or down, Frank, we ...". And then Captain Blackwell perceived a fair head stir on his brother's shoulder in the bed. A soft feminine voice said in French, "Monsieur, there is a large man in your room." He bolted back out into the passageway and shut the door.

A moment later Francis joined him, blinking and clad in the black breeches of his evening clothes.

"Frank, I beg your pardon. I didn't know, I didn't think — "

"Another man might want a woman in his cot?"

A laugh burst from Captain Blackwell. He'd been admiring his brother's virtue just moments before and here come to find he was human like the rest. Captain Blackwell loved Francis the more for it. He stifled his mirth out of respect for the other guests of the inn and the early hour. "Pray forgive the intrusion, brother. We weigh at six bells in the forenoon watch. That is eleven o'clock. Look alive!"

Captain Blackwell came up the side of *Inconstant*, saluted the quarterdeck and waited for the remainder of the boat's people to come aboard. The liberty men who had shared the boat came up the side under their captain's sharp eye as smartly as their debauched state allowed. The last out of the boat but one was Mercedes, and Captain Blackwell started when she slipped on one of the rungs. He glowered over the side at Narhilla, who had the unenviable task of looking to Mercedes' safety while touching her as little as possible. Captain Blackwell watched her walk below on his brother's arm, and then repaired to the quarterdeck.

"Good morning, Mr. Verson. How many ashore?"

"The forecastlemen, larboard watch, sir, and five marines," Mr. Verson said. "Mr. Sprague, Mr. Bransford and midshipman Ransom, sir."

"Very well. Run up the blue peter and I'll have a gun. Mr. Peakes! Muster the men to divisions!"

This last was said in a roar that brought the men on deck moving aft.

Francis was invited to dine in the great cabin. Earlier he'd stood at a distance as the mustered crew of *Inconstant* filed by the capstan head, each man receiving directly from the commander's hand a payment in silver. Then Captain Blackwell had taken his ship out into the offing. They met below in the great cabin, where Captain Blackwell and Francis sat down comfortably at table as the soup was brought in.

"Miss Mercedes doesn't join us?" Francis asked.

"She's asleep in her cabin, the poor ..." Captain Blackwell had been about to say 'little dear', but he changed it to "the poor soul. I fancy she did not sleep well ashore." And then he became confounded at what that statement might imply. He hastened on, "I cannot thank you enough, Frank, you and the gentlemen of the foreign service, for giving me the means of paying out the prize money owing my crew. It gave me the very greatest satisfaction."

"And they too, sir, I did quite clearly see," Francis said. "I'm only sorry it could not include your officers."

"No, that would not be fitting. We sea officers must abide by Admiralty decisions, little though we may cherish them."

"What would you have done with your three eighths share, James? Had you received what you deserve."

"Why, that's handsome in you, brother. But I can hardly say what I should have done with thirteen thousand pounds. A tidy sum to be sure. Yet I should not have cared over much for it until just recently. Now I would buy a house in Portsmouth like dear Uncle Hayden's, where I could take her." Captain Blackwell's eye rested on Mercedes' door for a moment. "But it don't signify, what might have been. Can you imagine Mercedes enduring an English winter?"

"I imagine she would endure a great deal besides, for your sake," Francis said.

Captain Blackwell bent his head and addressed his dinner with renewed vigor and a look of satisfaction.

"After he finished throwing out accusations of whore mongering, Admiral Gambier gave me a deuced awkward order I'm to carry out in Ceuta. The brig *Bulldog*, 14, Captain Alexander, was taken by the Dey's cruisers near Algiers five weeks since. I'm ordered to remonstrate with the Dey on this unlawful seizure. Do you know of this, Frank?"

Francis bowed his assent. "The Dey claims he captured *Bulldog* in retaliation for the taking of one of his vessels we seized blockade running."

"Did your chief put it so, *remonstrate* with the Dey? Eh, no? A better head piece no doubt on Lord Upton. He knows better than to order a man who has only ever been used to blow the enemy's brains out, to remonstrate with the Moslems. How I do pity Alexander and his crew. He was a reefer in the old *Leviathan* when I was her premier. Any of us should prefer capture by the French or the Spanish than to be put to row in a galley."

"According to our last report from the region, *Bulldog* carried the Dey to Ceuta, where he resides in spring," Francis said. "I expect Admiral Gambier merely wants the most out of this cruise, ordering you to represent to the Dey the illegality of his actions. Or perhaps he hopes you will remonstrate with the Dey by cutting out *Bulldog*."

"Oh, Frank! You put me in mind of that neat little action of yours last evening," Captain Blackwell said. "When you sailed in among the Dons and brought Mercedes out on the ebb. I am infinitely obliged to you. It was the completest thing I've seen this age."

Chapter 8

Mercedes had awakened alone in Francis Blackwell's rooms at the Crown, wishing she could regain the oblivion of sleep. But she had hardly begun to feel miserable when Captain Blackwell slammed into the bedchamber, crying, "Mercy, sweetheart! Pack your things. We are due at the quay."

She was rowed nodding on Captain Blackwell's shoulder to *Inconstant*. Her fatigue had made her stupid and she missed her footing climbing the ship's side, and been saved from falling by Narhilla clutching her ankle and placing her foot. When she had regained her little cabin below Mercedes told herself she would lie on her cot for just a moment. Then she slept through breakfast and dinner, but she rose when she heard McMurtry come into the cabin to light the lanterns before supper.

Captain Blackwell and McMurtry exchanged a few words but Mercedes couldn't hear what was said. On walking out of her cabin she met McMurtry, who jerked his head significantly at a package tied in paper lying on the stern lockers.

"Supper will be up this directly minute, Miss, and Himself is in the coach."

Captain Blackwell stood up when Mercedes entered. He began to squeeze his frame around the table where maps of the northern coast of Africa were spread.

"Do not get up, Captain Blackwell. I beg your pardon for having slept through two watches." Mercedes was afraid she had reinforced the image of the courtesan lying so long into the day.

"Shore life can be taxing, I always find." Captain Blackwell sank heavily back down into his seat and held out his hand to Mercedes. "Should you like to see our course?"

She sat beside him and they bowed over the charts, their heads almost touching.

"How many days sail to Ceuta, sir?"

"We might be there tonight, winds serving, but I will take this route. Do you see? To look in at these inlets and survey the coast against taking Frank off in a hurry."

Mercedes sat back. She appreciated this confidence Captain Blackwell displayed in her, by revealing his brother's plans. "Francis stops in Ceuta. You think it dangerous?"

"I don't care for the idea of leaving Frank in Ceuta. No. The port is controlled by the Spanish but just outside the city lies the territory of the Dey of Oran. These waters are their corsairs' cruising ground. But Frank has his duty, and I expect he is damn good at it. You have seen him studying the Arabic? But come, sweetheart, let us have our supper." Captain Blackwell rose, urging Mercedes into the great cabin where he always took his meals unless he had four or more guests to dine.

"A boat came alongside at the last moment with that parcel for you," Captain Blackwell said. "A made gown, perhaps."

Mercedes sat down and took the parcel into her lap and unwrapped it. She uncovered fine blue broadcloth, gold lace, and anchor embossed buttons. From leaning near to see what she had purchased Captain Blackwell took a startled step back.

"Shall we see how the tailor has managed the fit?"

"Mercy, sweetheart. What ever gave you the idea I was the type of blackguard as accepts gifts of women?"

But Mercedes rose, ignoring his remark and moved in back of him. She helped him on with the new uniform jacket.

"You need only shift your epaulettes from the jacket that is stained."

Captain Blackwell was reaching for her, and Mercedes felt the familiar pulse of desire the anticipation of his touch provoked, when the drum began to beat to quarters.

"Goddamn, hell and death!"

Captain Blackwell spun around and ripped his sword and belt from the rack on the bulkhead. "Come, ma'am!" He yanked a rapier down and tried to fasten it round Mercedes' waist, uttering oaths when he couldn't make the belt fit her.

"I will do it, James. Go! Go!"

Mr. Bell and his mates rushed into the cabin as Captain Blackwell ran up the companion ladder to the quarterdeck. Every man on deck was turned toward the south south-west. Captain Blackwell looked up at the set of sails and was pleased Mr. Bransford had taken in their topgallants, and shivered the main and foretop sails to bring the ship almost to a halt.

"What is it, Mr. Bransford?" Captain Blackwell inquired.

"Two sail to leeward, sir, right on our beam. Looks to be a brig and a merchantman lashed together," Mr. Bransford reported.

Captain Blackwell took the offered glass and trained it until he had the two ships in the center of the lens. It was exactly as the acting third lieutenant said, a brig and a merchantman lashed head to stern, with the far away crawling figures of men covering the decks of both vessels. A corsair taking a fat prize, bold as brass in the Gut. Captain Blackwell's heart contracted at the sight. They appeared to have many more men than he, blackening the rigging and decks of the two ships lying together.

"Well done, Mr. Bransford. Down your helm! Course west southwest," Captain Blackwell said.

"Aye, aye, sir. Course west southwest."

On the main gun deck the seamen felt the change of the ship's direction as *Inconstant* was worked round to the new heading.

"Shy," Mr. Sprague muttered. "He's altered course away from an engagement. Grown shy now he has his woman aboard."

"He maneuvers for the weather gage, Mr. Sprague," Mr. Verson said in an undertone. Then in a loud bellow that should by duty have been Mr. Sprague's, Mr. Verson called out, "Captain on deck!"

Captain Blackwell strode the length of the gun deck with his whole attention on the readiness of the great guns and the guns' crews. Then he returned amidships. "There is a brig over there that has fallen on a merchantman and is plundering her at this moment. That brig may be *Bulldog*, men, taken by the Oranians from His Majesty's Navy and put to evil purpose. We're going to come up on her tail and rake her. Starboard gun captains! You are to rake the decks of both ships. Double shot them with grape. The crew of the merchantman is in the hold by now, or dead. Run them in and out double quick, and when we are beside her let fly with chain at her rigging. We'll clear those pirates off King George's ship!"

A huzzah broke from the men, but Captain Blackwell held up his hand. "We will hit them hard and fast, and then we will board. Mr. Verson and Mr. Bransford will lead a party across the deck of the brig and take the merchantman. Mr. Sprague and I will board at the brig's waist and forecastle. Mr. Bowles will take command of *Inconstant*. Now hark ye, men, we will do our best to clear the decks of those ships before we board. But if there is a crew left alive over there they will fight like lions. You must be ready for them. And do not, do not I say, let any of those bastards set foot on *Inconstant*."

Three cheers for Captain Blackwell and *Inconstant* rang out from the men at the guns.

Captain Blackwell ran up on deck. "Helmsman! Port your helm. Course south east."

Orders rang round the ship to bring *Inconstant* on her course, bearing down on the locked vessels. The powder monkeys were running past carrying shot to the carronades on the quarterdeck and forecastle. The bosun and his mate were laying out boarding pikes, axes, and cutlasses near the scuppers and securing them under canvas against the order to board. Captain Christensen distributed Marines at the hatchways, and in the tops and on the quarterdeck. Captain Blackwell sent a midshipman for his best glass and carried it forward. He crawled right out onto the bowsprit, wrapped his arm about the shrouds, and brought his glass up to study the enemy.

He'd laid his plan before his crew and Captain Blackwell would carry it through. But what he couldn't express to a soul aboard

Inconstant was his apprehension the brig, the corsair, was laden with men. Not just those he could see through the spyglass, but men crammed in the between decks of the corsair and the merchantman also. Once he got upon the decks of the brig and the merchantman, with three ships lying to in an engagement, any damned unlucky stroke might change the tide of battle. He had confidence in his crew and their gunnery. These were the men who'd taken a 42 gun frigate, but he would not be firing into the hulls of these vessels. If the brig were *Bulldog* he must certainly not sink her, and much less the merchantman. No. He had to board and carry, and it would be an ugly affair.

Captain Blackwell backed down the bowsprit to the deck and found Francis standing there, a rifled carbine in his hand.

"There you are, Frank. How fortunate. I need a word, if you please."

One of the qualities Captain Blackwell most approved in his brother was Francis knew when to speak and when to keep his peace. In this instance, Francis merely bowed.

"It will not change what duty demands, I cannot withhold from a fight," Captain Blackwell said. "But whether she is *Bulldog* or another Oranian vessel, what becomes of your mission? You must give me your assessment of how this will fly at the political level for I cannot fathom it."

"A battle will not change overmuch the matter of Ceuta. This situation of the capture of ships precedes us. Your orders were to remonstrate with the Dey and you are merely doing so more firmly than anyone could have foreseen. If she is *Bulldog* and you're able to send her into Gibraltar, perhaps with prisoners to be exchanged for Captain Alexander and his crew, much to the good. The Admiralty may be grateful to you for several moments together. If she isn't *Bulldog* but another Oranian brig and you take her, we shall tell the Dey we pursue the same game as he. In the Arab world they are great respecters of strength. If we were not to carry the day, however ..."

"We shall not speak of it, brother," Captain Blackwell said. "What do you with that rifle?"

"I want to beg your permission to join the Marines." Francis gestured to the tops where Marines in twos and threes were taking up their battle stations. "I have been up, you know. Narhilla has guided me."

Captain Blackwell looked into his brother's face. He sometimes still glimpsed the boy Francis had been, the little fellow he'd taken fishing and taught to shoot. To allow his brother to remain on deck rather than be confined below as previously tore at Captain Blackwell's heart. But it was a decision he had to take, for Francis had surpassed his instructor long ago. He was an excellent marksman.

"Been up with Narhilla is it." Captain Blackwell threw his arm around Francis's shoulders. "Let us see if you can beat a fat man up to the top. Captain Christensen! Captain Christiansen there!"

They had gained the quarterdeck and Captain Christensen came over and saluted. "Sir!"

"Who is your most reliable man in the tops?"

"That would be Woodrow, sir. Arms like a great ape. Could hold himself and another man and still shoot his piece."

"Very well. In the mizzen?"

"Aye, sir," Captain Christensen said.

Captain Blackwell sent his brother in front of him up the ratlines, placing Francis's feet when he hesitated. Up and up they climbed. The ship's sweeping motion brought them seemingly down to the level of the sea before whipping them back skyward.

There was little time for reflection once they gained the mizzentop. A spyglass was no longer needed to see the brig and merchantman quite clearly, and the men moving on their decks. The enemy was quite probably loading their guns at that moment. Captain Blackwell swarmed up to the topgallant mast crosstree and flew down to the deck on a mizzen backstay. He left Francis in the top a bit pallid, but Captain Blackwell was sure he would overcome his nerves once the firing started. Battle had a tendency to concentrate the mind amazingly.

"Lay us across her stern at pistol shot, Mr. Hammerly," Captain Blackwell called.

Inconstant was an exquisite sight flying down before the wind with topsails set. She tacked and brought the wind abeam drawing near those two ships. Captain Blackwell ordered the colours to be run up, and he shifted into his disreputable jacket. The men aboard *Inconstant* eyed the Union Jack flown upside down beneath a foreign flag on the brig's gaff. Beside the alien ensign in the ship grappled to her, no one had yet lowered the American flag from the merchantman's main topgallant mast.

"Sir! Captain Blackwell, sir, I know that ship!" McMurtry cried, running up to the break of the quarterdeck.

Captain Blackwell went to the rail and looked down inquiringly at McMurtry, who knuckled his forehead.

"She's *Bulldog*, sir, of the Channel Fleet. I was aboard her in Plymouth in '99. My cousin Clark was bosun's mate. She's *Bulldog*, sir. I'm sure of it. Even if them bloody heathens has painted barbaric over her name."

"It means *Hand of God*, or possibly *Finger of God*." Francis Blackwell informed Mr. Woodrow of the Marines, after examining the name painted in Arabic on the brig's stern.

"Then we're going to blow the Finger of God back to Kingdom come, Mr. Blackwell. Hold fast!"

There was a brief parlay, Captain Blackwell calling for surrender and the Oranian managing to fire his stern chaser by way of answer. The starboard guns roared at Captain Blackwell's order. The carnage produced on the decks of those two ships was tremendous. A moment before the blast men were hastening to reload the 6-pounder long gun. Seconds after the two ships were engulfed in a cloud of flying splinters, ropes and blocks, blood and smoke and body parts. *Inconstant* came up alongside the brig and fired into what remained of her masts and rigging.

"Off sheets and tacks!" Captain Blackwell shouted.

Mr. Peakes and his mate were arming the boarding parties, serving out pistols, boarding axes and pikes, while the afterguard under Mr. Sprague grappled the two ships close. Captain Blackwell jumped up on the rail with his party formed behind him and cried, "Boarders away!"

He came down hard on the deck of *Bulldog*, she lying lower in the water than *Inconstant*, with his sword in one hand and a cutlass in the other. Two pistols hung in belts over his chest. There appeared to be no one left alive on the deck covered with torn bodies and gore except the helmsman, who was bleeding from several wounds and was held upright by the wheel.

Mr. Verson ran across the brig's deck at the head of his party and jumped onto the chains of the American. He and Mr. Bransford and their men moved aft once her deck was gained as Captain Blackwell and Mr. Sprague and their parties stepped cautiously among the dead and wounded men toward the brig's quarterdeck.

"It appears our work here is done," declared Mr. Sprague.

Seconds later shots were heard on the American. Men screaming tribal battle cries broke simultaneously from the between decks of the merchantman and the brig. They came pouring up from the hatches, and the decks of both ships filled with bearded, turbaned men swinging their curved swords. Musketry fire rained down from *Inconstant*'s tops, though with the shifting fury of the crowd of men, the Marines' fire had to be expert indeed to hit only enemies in the melee.

Captain Blackwell, hacking his way toward the quarterdeck of the brig, twice faced the upraised arm of an enemy ready to strike him a blow when the man was felled by a shot to the head or chest. Captain Blackwell felt certain it was Frank's steady aim, clearing a path for him, but he made progress aft through the press only with a constant thrust and parry and hack and charge with his weapons. He pulled a pistol from his belt and shot a man throttling Narhilla.

Slipping in the blood covering the deck Captain Blackwell would have crashed down to it next moment but for an iron hard grip that shot out, caught him by the meat of his arm, and hauled him up. It was Mr. Martinez, small and wiry hard. Captain Blackwell knew a fleeting wish he should be so fit for duty when he became a gray beard. He turned in a slow circle, his weapons raised and at the ready, but opposition had ceased. The enemies left on deck were putting down their weapons and clustering together.

"'Vast fighting," Captain Blackwell ordered. Looking forward he saw Mr. Sprague slitting the throat of a man he embraced in his arms.

Captain Blackwell jerked back a step. "Mr. Verson, how fare you?" he shouted. And when the reply came back they were in possession, he called, "Send Mr. Bransford to take possession of *Bulldog*. Mr. Sprague, Mr. Christensen, prisoners across to *Inconstant*. Mr. Bowles, a party of swabbers down here. This is not what is due a King's ship! We'll clean up this goddamn sh — " Captain Blackwell was interrupted when Mr. Verson hailed from the deck of the American.

"Sir! Captain Blackwell, sir! Master of the ship *Lizzie Ann*'s compliments and would Captain Blackwell join him aboard?"

His head cleared the American ship's side and the glare of the setting sun hit him right in the eyes. Captain Blackwell staggered as he gained the deck and acknowledged the salutes of his men working there. They were heaving corpses overboard and preparing to carry the wounded across the decks of three ships.

"We freed the merchantman's people from the hold, sir, and there were a dozen Bulldogs there too, forced to sail the brig," Mr. Verson said. He led Captain Blackwell aft and down to the merchant captain's cabin. "When they recognized *Inconstant* and refused to prepare the guns to fire on us three were killed on the spot, and the rest sent into the hold with the sailors. The master's name is Nelson, sir." Mr. Verson knocked on the cabin door and receiving permission to enter, opened it. "Captain James Blackwell of His Majesty's ship *Inconstant*, Captain Nelson, *Lizzie Ann*." Mr. Verson bowed and backed out the door.

A round-faced young man jumped up from the sofa and came forward to shake Captain Blackwell's hand. Two small children, a boy and girl, rose with their father and stood on either side of him with a hand each clasping his trouser leg. Captain Blackwell took in the children and the homely, comfortable cabin as he received Captain Nelson's effusive thanks, and made his apologies for having savaged the American vessel.

Then the merchant captain came to the real reason for his request to see him. "They took my wife, sir, my Susan. Did you see her, sir? I must go now and look for her."

"No, sir, no," Captain Blackwell said, holding his hand up and almost touching the other man's chest. "I will conduct a search for her. You must not go on deck at the moment, sir, I beg." He couldn't prevent Captain Nelson's taking the deck if he wished to, it was his ship and he might do what he pleased. But Captain Blackwell feared this man's wife was dead, and out of common humanity he wanted to save him the sight of her abused body.

"You did not see her, sir?" Captain Nelson insisted.

"No, sir, nor yet my crew or I should have been made aware of it. I will search for her myself, sir. They took her aboard the brig?"

"Yes. Oh my Susan!"

Captain Blackwell took his leave as quickly as he decently could. The anguish of the young merchant captain and the wide eyes of those children almost made him weep. He was sure he would have to bear the wife and mother's dead body back to them.

"Narhilla!" Captain Blackwell roared when he emerged onto the American's deck.

"Here, sir!" called Narhilla from the deck of the brig.

Captain Blackwell made his way down to his coxswain. "Has anyone taken a party below decks?"

"Mr. Bransford left Mr. Wilson on deck and went down not five minutes ago, sir, with two lobsters and six men."

"No one's been in the cabin?"

"No, sir, not as I know."

"Come with me, Narhilla. Those blackguards brought the merchant captain's wife aboard."

Narhilla's face flushed an angry red and they turned and picked their way through the bodies not yet cleared from *Bulldog*'s deck, attentive for the sight of feminine clothing among the prostrated forms. A mere four steps led down to the brig's cabin. Before descending Captain Blackwell drew his sword, and with his weapon once again poised moved down into the gloom.

He kept his back to the bulkhead once in the cabin and let his eyes adjust to the gloom, taking in the smell of the space, a terrible mixture of blood and sex and fear. Narhilla was beside him and they both saw the crumpled, corpse-like form wedged between a table and several lockers. They moved in opposite directions, stepping cautiously into the sleeping cabin, the tiny map room and pantry, before meeting again near the cabin door.

Captain Blackwell sheathed his sword and went over to the body. When it moved at his approach he started with astonishment, then pressed forward.

"No, please," she said.

The merchant captain's wife must have heard the approach of a man, of two men. Captain Blackwell sat down on his heels and peered at the woman wedged under the table. A fair-skinned woman, clutching the remains of her gown across her bulging flesh stared back at him with wild eyes.

"Mrs. Nelson, I am Captain Blackwell of the Royal Navy — "

"Oh, why did you not come sooner!" Mrs. Nelson cried.

It was the last coherent thing she said, before giving way to sobs and hysterical exclamations. They couldn't persuade her to come out and Captain Blackwell in the end crawled beneath the table and hauled her out. Narhilla was waiting with a blanket that had taken on the odor of the food the Moslems ate. Captain Blackwell began to wrap Mrs. Nelson in the blanket until her shrieking cries stopped him.

"The blanket won't do, sir!" Narhilla said. In a panic he threw his stained black neckerchief over the woman's breasts.

Captain Blackwell hefted her up in his arms and carried her on deck. He could see Captain Nelson leaning over the rail of his ship, too distraught to remain below. He hoped the merchant captain had not allowed the little boy and girl on deck to witness this slaughter. Captain Nelson flew down the side of his ship and came running across the brig's deck.

"She is alive, sir. Alive!" Captain Blackwell put his burden into the husband's arms.

The last of the prisoners were filing down the fore hatchway. Captain Christensen had sent his corporal and privates aft, and Mr. Sprague was bringing along the final man, a man with the air of an officer though wearing no uniform and dressed in the robes customary to the Oranian. The man came level with Captain Christensen, but instead of descending, the Oranian suddenly thrust into the Marine captain with such force both men tumbled to the deck.

The Oranian rolled off Captain Christensen, yanked the captain's sword from its scabbard and in a single fluid movement turned and ran below deck. Captain Christensen jumped to his feet and staggered forward, aiming his musket down the hatchway. But there was Mr. Sprague blocking the entrance. Uttering a cry of frustration Captain Christensen sprang forward, and Mr. Sprague stepped away. From behind the Marine captain came a heavy blow, knocking him headfirst down the hatchway.

He was carried into the sick berth some time later. Captain Christiansen was coherent enough at first to raise the alarm of an enemy below decks and order more men detailed to guard the magazine.

"Captain Christensen!" Mercedes hurried to the Marine captain from where she had been serving out lemonade to the wounded.

"It's nothing, ma'am, merely a broken arm."

Captain Christensen leaned over the edge of the operating table and vomited. Mercedes stepped away from the mess and to make way for Doctor VanArsdel, who came running to them. The canvas curtain screening the sick berth was thrown back and in rushed a young man, clothed in robes to his ankles, and carrying Captain Christensen's sword.

Mercedes backed up, drew her rapier and lunged forward. She pinked him with the first lunge, well in the shoulder above the armpit. She withdrew; regretting her aim at his throat had not been better. Now he was aware his attack would be fierce, and a rapier was not the best weapon against a sword. She had to keep away from him, and maneuver him if she could among the men without his striking out at them. Some of those wounded men would make a supreme effort and help her against their common enemy.

"Sir!" called out Doctor VanArsdel. "You must surrender your sword. Do not fight with that lad."

Unheeding the Oranian slashed at Mercedes. She parried and turned her profile to her opponent, whispering to the doctor, "Try French!"

"Lay down your sword, sir, you must not fight with the lad. If the Captain comes here and finds you fighting with that boy, you will be dead upon the spot."

"Is it his son, his missish son?" returned the Oranian man.

The Oranian attacked and they engaged, with the clash of steel and the deadly concentration of combatants. Then there was a tremendous thud and roar and Captain Blackwell threw back the curtain. Without turning the Oranian flipped his sword in his hand and presented it hilt foremost to Mercedes. She hadn't taken it before Captain Blackwell was there, grasping the sword in one large hand while with his other he gripped the Oranian by the back of the neck. Captain Blackwell looked into the man's face as though trying very hard to see a human.

"Take that man below and clap him in irons!" Captain Blackwell said.

He gave the man a shove toward Lieutenant Hoffinger and Narhilla, and then took Mercedes' elbow. "Just you wait here, Miss," he said in a low voice.

Captain Blackwell went to speak to the doctor. Doctor VanArsdel gave an earnest account of Captain Christensen's wounds, once he had received the nod from his captain to continue addressing the patient. Broken arm and collarbone, a concussion certainly. The doctor was astonished the Marine captain could've been sensible even for a moment after such a tremendous drubbing. And then, as the doctor compelled Captain Blackwell to sit on a locker and have his brow stitched — blood ran down the captain's face, making him a gruesome sight — it was on to the butcher's bill for the battle. Five dead and thirty-three wounded; on the enemy's side, no wounded had been brought to the cockpit.

"That's right, Miss, we was behind you," whispered Sorenson of the sail maker's crew. He swung in a hammock that had given a capital view of the short duel. "He would a copped it if that first stroke of yours were half a foot to starboard."

Captain Blackwell turned and scowled toward Mercedes. Sorenson caught his captain's eye and sank back into the canvas bed. When the surgeon's mate released him Captain Blackwell made a circuit of the wounded men, exchanging a few words with those who were able, and finished with Sorenson.

"You were speaking to Miss de Aragon. To say what? You would have helped her, eh? Eh? I should hope so, indeed, Sorenson. I should hope we all know our duty."

The captain took Mercedes by the arm. He stopped to take leave of the doctor, who pressed a package of lint and a surgical needle into Mercedes' hand. "Attend to the Captain's wounds, he will not sit for us to do it." Captain Blackwell led her out and up to the great cabin at the double. Outside his door, he threw out to the sentry as they passed, "I'm not to be disturbed for any reason for the next half hour," before slamming into the cabin.

He had her clasped hard against him as soon as the door closed, and Mercedes, gasping from the run to the cabin and from the varied terrors of the day, hung on him with her breath painful in her side. The unspeakable fear of losing him, and being left in a ship commanded by Mr. Sprague, had been the foremost of her worries while she listened to the sounds of battle from the cockpit. It had been like listening to the muffled slaughter of hell.

Mercedes recovered and pushed away from Captain Blackwell. In his sleeping cabin she bade him remove his jacket, waistcoat and shirt, and wash his upper body.

Captain Blackwell held still like a patient beast while she further cleaned and dressed the gashes on his torso and arms. None were deep enough that she would have to stitch him, and surprisingly he had no wounds below his waist. She sighed with relief when she had done and put her hand to the hooks of his breeches.

"Sweetheart," he said, drawing her against him. "I don't need that. You don't have to do that. Just let me hold you."

"It is not always for you, James."

Blackwell's body was betraying his words. He found he was hungry for her and grasped her through those men's clothes. He was so excited by her in trousers he wondered if he might suffer a perversion. The thought didn't stop him from pushing the trousers below her hips, and lifting her with a hand under each bare leg to take her against the bulkhead of the cabin.

"Hold onto me, sweetheart," he said. She wrapped her legs tight round him, her arms thrown over his shoulders. Both were careless of the wounds she had just dressed.

There was a knock at the cabin door and a young voice called in, "Mr. Sprague's duty, sir, and — "

"Goddamn it!" Blackwell roared, turning in the direction of the door. Mercedes shuddered in his arms. "I shall be on deck in a moment."

In turning back to her and trying to regain the concentration of his passion he felt a stabbing pain in his lower back. He would've dropped her had he not instead plopped her hastily on her bottom on the edge of the berth.

"Jim," she said, drawing him to her.

She kneaded his lower back by some intuition just where he'd had the sharp, fleeting pain. She whispered to him in Spanish what he imagined were scandalous suggestions, and she put her hand between his active thighs and fondled him so that he exploded inside her.

On deck for the next five hours, working to repair *Bulldog* and the merchant ship, for *Inconstant* had sustained little damage, Blackwell wondered if he was perhaps too old for the woman in his cabin.

He had felt a pain in his chest when Mr. Bowles had called out in his breaking adolescent voice, just after he'd handed that poor woman over to Captain Nelson, "Captain Blackwell, sir! Captain, them buggers is loose below decks *Inconstant*!" Pounding across the deck of *Bulldog* with his heart in his throat, Narhilla behind him, he'd envisioned his good sea boat blowing up as he'd once seen a ship do in a Fleet action. She would take with her young Mr. Bowles and old Mr. Hammerly, and his brother and his lady and his career in the Royal Navy.

Blackwell worked the harder into the night spurred by his need to bury reflection on what might have been by activity. Round about midnight he returned to *Inconstant* and had the deck hose turned on him, and then retired to his cabin feeling aged and done.

He was aware of Mercedes' gaze on him as he dried himself with a small towel. The light of the dark lantern illuminated the pain on his face when he straightened and turned toward her.

"Which troubles you?" she cried, getting up from the cot and pulling on her dressing gown.

"No, it is not these cuts," Blackwell said. "I believe I strained my back doing a damned stupid thing in the name of gallantry."

He saw her abashed and taken aback and he barked out a laugh, then winced and put his hand to his back.

"It was not that, sweetheart. No. As if your little weight could bring this on. It was another matter entirely."

"James, lie down on the cot this way." Mercedes mimicked a body lying face down, arms to the sides.

Blackwell assumed the prone position on the cot, and Mercedes straddled him and began to work his back muscles under her hands, pressing her thumbs either side along the length of his spine and running upward from the bottom of each rib to the top. He emitted grunts like those she was accustomed to hear from him during their intimacy.

"Do you think we did wrong, sweetheart, earlier?"

After a considerable pause, she said, "No, I don't. It's not wrong to have survived and to be glad of it."

Blackwell told her of the action then, unburdening himself in a manner he'd never before been allowed. The commander of a frigate, or any of His Majesty's ships of war, was necessarily a solitary being, living in promiscuity with numbers of men but unable to open his heart to one. Blackwell opened his now to Mercedes, while she rubbed his back and kept silent. He did not describe the gore of the fierce, close fight. But he spoke of his apprehension of facing an overpowering number of the enemy on *Inconstant*'s approach; of the damage he feared doing his brother's career and his own if the action went amiss. Finally he spoke of what had happened to the merchant captain's wife.

"That's how I injured my back, carrying Captain Nelson's wife from below decks on *Bulldog*. A robust woman you might say. Frank warns me never to say fat; it must be stout or robust or generously endowed. However it might be it don't signify, for Captain Nelson seemed passing fond of her. Shall you call on her? I'm quite sure she would welcome the company of another woman."

Mercedes grew still, and smoothing her dressing gown she lay down on top of Blackwell.

"I cannot call on her unless invited. But it would be a kindness if Doctor VanArsdel were to see her."

"What you do to ... to prevent conception, Mercedes?"

"Must be done right away, soon after the act."

"Ah."

"Will he accept her, do you think, Captain Nelson?" Mercedes said. "Some men cannot bring themselves to desire a woman who has been so outraged."

"Who could blame them?" Blackwell said, exhausted. "And even a saint could not accept a child forced on his wife by some villain."

She began to move away from him, but Blackwell put his arm back to stay her. "Do not stir, Mercy sweetheart. You feel like a little piece of heaven."

Chapter 9

The three ships were hove to with several cable's length distance between each vessel. Captain Blackwell had just ordered his gig to take him to *Bulldog,* where sails were being bent to the jury masts. Francis was interviewing the prisoners in *Inconstant's* cabin. The information learned from those Arab men would decide which went to Gibraltar on *Bulldog*, with the remainder to be carried to Ceuta and exchanged, so he and Francis hoped and trusted, for Captain Alexander and his officers and crew.

Mr. Verson stepped over. "Beg your pardon, sir, Captain Nelson putting off from *Lizzie Ann*."

"So he is. Mr. Peakes, prepare to receive a captain aboard," Captain Blackwell said.

For a merchant captain to be received on board a man-of-war with the same protocol accorded to a post-captain of the Royal Navy was an honor. Captain Nelson did not appear insensible of it, but no pleasure showed in his face. There was only a haggard, deeply unhappy look as he bowed to the officers on the quarterdeck and came forward to shake Captain Blackwell's outstretched hand.

"You do me great honor, Captain Blackwell, I thank you," Captain Nelson said. "And I come to presume further on your kindness."

"Step this way, sir, please." Captain Blackwell bowed and motioned for Captain Nelson to join him at the weather rail on the quarterdeck, at the farthest remove from his officers.

"I understand, sir, you have a surgeon," Captain Nelson said in a diffident tone. "I've come to beg he be requested to see my wife, when he has attended all of your wounded first, sir. I collect also you carry a lady, might she come with the doctor?"

Captain Blackwell shouted to the midshipman of the watch to skip below and ask the doctor and Miss Mercedes to join them on the quarterdeck when they were at leisure.

"Thank you, Captain Blackwell, thank you kindly," the merchant captain said. "I confess I don't know how to go on with Susan. I was right relieved when I discovered you'd a surgeon, and you carry your wife. How long has she sailed with you, sir?"

It astonished Captain Blackwell to think it was only a month since the battle for *La Trinidad.* In that short space of time he had grown to feel he could not do without Mercedes. He didn't like to answer Captain Nelson's question and he was almost grateful when the merchant captain seemed not to require a response. Just as most admirals Captain Blackwell had ever known.

"Susan has sailed with me five years, sir. Our first voyage was six weeks after our wedding. Never any trouble like this. No, sir. She's a good wife, is Susan. A good cook and a fond mother, and she keeps a clean cabin. But as to relations shall we say, sir, it has ever been merely a duty to her. I despair of how she may feel about it now."

Captain Blackwell stood with his hands clasped behind him and his head bowed. Mercedes and Doctor VanArsdel climbed the companion ladder to the quarterdeck, and found him flushed about the neck and ears.

"Miss Mercedes, may I present Captain Nelson, *Lizzie Ann,*" Captain Blackwell said. "Captain Nelson, Miss Mercedes de Aragon, and *Inconstant's* surgeon Doctor John VanArsdel."

Bows and handshakes were exchanged all round. Doctor VanArsdel took charge of the party, Mercedes must have told him what business was in hand when they received the summons; he had his case of surgical instruments by him. They would pull to *Lizzie Ann* in Captain Nelson's boat, and Captain Blackwell would collect them in his gig when he quit *Bulldog* later in the day.

"We shall have her ready to sail in the afternoon watch, Captain Nelson, and I see you have nearly completed your repairs," Captain Blackwell said. "You must've had a long night of it, sir. One of my mids, Mr. Bowles, takes *Bulldog* into Gibraltar and you are welcome to join company." He saw the apprehension on the merchant captain's face and guessed at the cause. "*Inconstant* will carry most of the prisoners to Ceuta, sir. The injured and poor hands go to Gibraltar in *Bulldog*."

"I am obliged to you, Captain Blackwell, and I shall be prepared to sail with Mr. Bowles." Captain Nelson bowed and took his leave, descending into his boat.

Captain Blackwell's eye fell on young Jack Verson, who, having been turned away from the cabin, this being his regular hour for lessons with Mercedes, had come out upon the deck and was hovering at the foot of the companion ladder gazing up at them.

"Mr. Verson," Captain Blackwell called. Mr. Verson younger and elder both looked his way. He had recalled the two children on *Lizzie Ann*. "Young Goodman Jack, a word if you please."

"Sir!" the boy said, coming smartly up the ladder.

"Should you like to accompany Miss Mercedes and the Doctor to that ship, the *Lizzie Ann*?" Captain Blackwell said. "Captain Nelson has two children."

"I should like it of all things, sir, to go along of Miss Mercedes."

"You must mind her and stay with the children when she bids you. And if I hear of any disobedience to orders I shall lay you across the cannon in my cabin. Do you know what that means?"

"Yes, sir!" the boy piped. "You shall stripe my arse the way you done Mr. Bowles in Plymouth when he wouldn't put down his wife with the other brutes."

Captain Blackwell was able to suppress his reaction to this pretty speech only because he had years of practice in keeping his countenance. Children, he reflected, absorbed everything. He felt pity for Captain Nelson's children in the midst of these last ghastly days, and with their mother so wounded. Captain Blackwell hoped young Goodman Jack would cheer them, and he grabbed Jack's shoulder and pushed him toward his father. "Go ask your father's leave."

He experienced a tug at his heart watching Mercedes rowed away. He had nearly ordered two Marine privates and midshipman Ransom to go with her. But then he brought himself up; he'd no wish to offend Captain Nelson. Instead Captain Blackwell contented himself with turning and bellowing at his crew to leave off gawping and get back to work.

Lizzie Ann was a merchantman of considerable size. The British seamen had already tagged her variously as 'the great tub' and 'fat *Lizzie*'. The merchant sailors gaped at Mercedes in a manner that would've brought forth Captain Blackwell's darkest looks when she reached the deck a little flushed, with her lips parted from the long climb. Captain Nelson led her and the doctor away from those interested stares and below to his quarters.

The captain's stateroom in *Lizzie Ann* appeared to Mercedes of luxurious proportion, since her experience of sailing was in ships of war. A big suspended bed, swaying slightly with the ship hove to, dominated the space.

"Susan dear," Captain Nelson said. "I've brought Doctor VanArsdel of the ship *Inconstant*, and Miss Mercedes de Aragon." The merchant captain immediately left them.

Doctor VanArsdel commenced by taking a seat on a locker, after motioning Mercedes to the room's only chair, and asking the lady's permission to approach the couch. There were a few stifled sobs, and then Mrs. Nelson said the doctor might examine her if the lady would hold her hand.

Mercedes came forward and took Mrs. Nelson's plump hand in hers and caressed it while Doctor VanArsdel began his examination. It was one of the hardest things she'd ever been called upon to do, keeping her countenance and not weeping at the sight of Mrs. Nelson's bruised flesh. Mercedes had seen far too much of this type of violence, the last instance being Juan Montelongo with his look as though his soul were dead. Her own mother had been victim of the crime of rape, and told Mercedes of it when she was a grown woman solely so she might know the complete account of her birth. But Mrs. Nelson, though wounded and horrified, didn't have the look of despair. Mercedes mastered her tears for the sake of the American woman, so deserving of her compassion.

"You have two broken ribs, ma'am," Doctor VanArsdel said. Both ladies exhaled as one. "Miss Mercedes and I will bind them. You must stay abed today and tomorrow. But on the third day you must rise and attend to as many of your duties as you are able. This is essential, ma'am, for your recovery."

Mrs. Nelson managed a faint, "Thank you, Doctor." But the indignity for her was not done. They had necessarily to put the dressings next her skin, and Mercedes assisted Mrs. Nelson in holding her bosom out of the way so the doctor might bandage her ribs. At last Mercedes was able to put her nightgown back over her head and settle Mrs. Nelson on her pillows. Doctor VanArsdel received again the lady's gratitude. He bowed to the captain's wife and led Mercedes away to the door of the stateroom.

"Listen, my dear," Doctor VanArsdel said. "I will take my leave now but do you stay with her and give her what comfort you can."

"What can I say to her? I have no words of wisdom, particularly for what she has been through. And she is a mother, with two children. I could not presume — "

"She may be older than you, and a mother indeed, but I fancy you are the more mature woman when it comes to the relations of men and women. Pray believe I mean no disrespect to you, Miss Mercedes, in saying so. I honor you for it. And I'm grateful to you, for it would otherwise be my duty to tell Mrs. Nelson how to wash herself and use alum, the vinegar or bicarbonate of soda to prevent conception. As a medical man I know it will likely not help her in this case. The poor woman will have to accept what comes. But I'm certain the knowledge will give her comfort, and perhaps help her feel cleansed of this violence done to her."

Mercedes bowed her head. "I understand, Doctor, and I will do my duty by her."

"You would be a capital surgeon's mate, ma'am."

"No, sir, no. I do not think I could bear it."

Doctor VanArsdel took his leave and Mercedes returned to sit on the big swinging bed. She sat down upon it but was silent, with her head bowed.

Mrs. Nelson took her hand. "Had it not been for your husband's ship coming up, they would have killed me."

"I know they did kill you, ma'am, but you lived through it," Mercedes said.

"Oh! Oh, how did you know?" She threw herself sobbing into Mercedes' arms.

Mercedes held her and let her cry, relieved at last herself by tears. And then, thinking of her own dear mother, she did find a few words of wisdom for Mrs. Nelson, telling her she must choose life, and hold fast to her children and her husband.

"How long have you been married?" Mrs. Nelson asked, lying back against the pillows.

It was obvious to Mercedes that in her distress Mrs. Nelson hadn't heard her presented as 'Miss'. Mercedes sat considering, her eyes on her hands in her lap.

"I'm not married to Captain Blackwell, Mrs. Nelson, I am his mistress. I hope you will not think ill of me ..."

Mercedes used the same plain language her mother had when she told her the practical things she needed to know about sex and men. Although Mrs. Nelson looked somewhat blank, she said, at the end of Mercedes' speech, "I hope you will do me the honor of calling me Susan."

Before putting off for *Lizzie Ann* to fetch Mercedes and the doctor, Captain Blackwell met with Francis to decide the distribution of the prisoners and discuss the departure of *Bulldog*.

"You will not send Mr. Sprague in *Bulldog*?"

"No, indeed," Captain Blackwell said. "I cannot put that man in command, much as I should love to be shut of him. No. I couldn't expose those men on *Bulldog* after what they've been through, to say nothing of *Lizzie Ann*'s people. Poor Mrs. Nelson has seen enough savagery for one lifetime. I shall keep Mr. Sprague with me, under my eye. Mr. Bowles will do very well I'm sure. He must, for I cannot spare Mr. Verson or Mr. Bransford."

"How old is Mr. Bowles, sir?"

"He is seventeen, I believe."

"Your profession demands much of a man at an early age."

Captain Blackwell smiled. He had taken a prize into Port Mahon when he was fifteen. He'd had a hand picked crew of prime seamen sent with him, just such men as he meant to put into *Bulldog*. His brother went on. "I'm sure you do right, sir. And I realize it's a terrible accusation but I believe Mr. Sprague may have had to do with Captain Christensen's injuries, coming so late when the battle was done. They were together at the fore hatchway. I saw the Marine detachment come back that was stationed under Captain Christensen. And not long afterward he was found at the bottom of the hatchway, and raised the hue and cry about the enemy below decks."

The prospect of carrying a Judas on his ship made Captain Blackwell's heart grow cold.

He was happy when Mercedes went directly below into her sleeping cabin when he brought her back aboard *Inconstant*. Earlier Captain Blackwell had given Mr. Bowles his orders and what he hoped was an encouraging yet exacting speech regarding his duty. On deck Captain Blackwell attended to Mr. Sprague's report; the men named to sail *Bulldog* to Gibraltar were aboard her, and the fifteen prisoners had been transferred and were safely in her hold under Marine guard.

"Very well, Mr. Sprague. Send the men to supper. I must see the Doctor, and once the wounded are aboard *Bulldog* she may part company."

He went below to receive Doctor VanArsdel, calling out as he entered his cabin, "McMurtry! A bottle of the Margaux." He motioned the doctor, who followed him in, to a seat at the table.

Captain Blackwell was studying the surgeon's two lists as the wine and glasses were brought in on a tray. The first list contained names of men to be transported on *Bulldog* and the second was of those expected to recover and remaining on *Inconstant*.

"There are certainly more men on the list for *Bulldog* than I could wish, Doctor," Captain Blackwell said. "*Inconstant* shall be short her compliment now forty men. How I regret Captain

Christensen must be one of them. Has he spoken of the circumstances when he was injured?"

"He has not, sir. He rambles through his childhood in Scotland. I am afraid in an action of such ferocity the butcher's bill must necessarily be high."

Captain Blackwell made no remark, but continued to gaze wearily at the lists.

"An action of very great ferocity, sir," Doctor VanArsdel said. "Eighty-five of the enemy killed and thirty prisoners, and civilians involved. Might I suggest, sir, you send Miss Mercedes back to Gibraltar on *Lizzie Ann*? You would oblige both ladies by doing so, and we have just had proof of the dangers of these waters. I do not know if you are aware how much it has distressed Miss Mercedes to witness the events of these last days, sir."

Captain Blackwell wore a look of vexation mixed with another emotion, apprehension or indeed shame, at the doctor's suggestion. But he merely answered, "I shall consider of it, Doctor, thank you." Captain Blackwell stood up to indicate the interview was at an end and went on deck where he gave orders regarding the transport of the wounded.

The invalids were brought up on stretchers and set briefly on the deck before being lowered into the boats and rowed to *Bulldog*, where the procedure took place in reverse order. Captain Blackwell went down on one knee beside the stretcher when Captain Christensen was lying there on the gangway. "We shall meet in Gibraltar, Captain, when I stop for you and our other men. I daresay it is England for us after that."

"It is a date, James. You bring the rods," Captain Christensen said.

"He has a brother James. I believe he mistakes you for him," Doctor VanArsdel murmured to Captain Blackwell. "Is Miss Mercedes ready to remove to *Lizzie Ann,* sir? That's the last boat to *Bulldog*."

"Miss Mercedes stops here!"

The last stretcher was passed below decks and the signal ran up *Bulldog*'s masthead requesting permission to part company.

Inconstant acknowledged and the two ships, the fine, swift sailing brig of war *Bulldog* and the ponderous *Lizzie Ann*, so lately enemies grappled in a mortal clinch, dipped their pennants in compliment to *Inconstant* and sailed away in company. The word was passed the captain's supper was on the table. Captain Blackwell went below, grateful to escape the constrained silence that had followed his declaration about Mercedes.

He had been seated some moments with the plates before him, waiting for Mercedes to appear from her closet. She did not come in, and Captain Blackwell's face grew dark.

"Miss Mercedes!" he called. "I am not accustomed to being made to wait for my supper."

Still she didn't come out and Captain Blackwell scowled down at the tablecloth, until he began to think she might be unwell for she was otherwise a very reliable companion. He jumped up from his seat and knocked on her door. When she did not answer he went in to the sleeping cabin, stopping short when he saw her sitting on the edge of her cot in tears.

Mercedes had been unable to meet him for supper in this blubbered state. She turned away from him, her shoulders shaking with her sobs. She understood now what had troubled him about their coupling when Captain Blackwell brought her into the cabin after the duel in the sick berth. Was she really so low a creature she'd thrown away what she'd essentially been brought up to do — become a gentleman's daughter — her chance to make herself known to Admiral Gambier, for carnal desire. It gave her no comfort, quite the reverse, that she had initiated the encounter that had given even a rough, lusty man like Captain Blackwell pause.

She'd thrown herself into this dangerous life on ships of war, turning her back on respectability, but what she had been witness to earlier had undone her. Mrs. Nelson's tragedy, and then to return to *Inconstant* to hear Doctor VanArsdel recommending she be shipped off with the unhappy couple. Her mind was unsettled and Mercedes wondered at her own judgment. Yet in her heart she did not repent of her decision to stay with Captain Blackwell. He came into her cabin and sat carefully beside her in the small space, and eased his arms around her.

"It is Mrs. Nelson, Susan Nelson has affected me so. She is a decent woman. A woman your gallantry was not wasted upon, sir."

"I should have forbid your going there," Captain Blackwell said.

"What, to protect me? It is impossible even with children. That is what Doctor VanArsdel wishes, to protect me. He is well meaning I'm sure, but he has a mistaken notion of you, Captain. He has somehow conceived the idea you are a brute, and I cannot disabuse him. What would I say, that you are the best lover a woman could wish? I would be so grateful to you if you did not send me away in *Lizzie Ann*."

"Would you, sweetheart?"

Mercedes stood up, wiping her face, knowing what would be the sequel if she did not. "We had best eat our supper. You had none yesterday, and I do not wish to cross McMurtry."

"I shall cross his hawse, by God," Captain Blackwell said. But he gave Mercedes his arm for the few steps to the table, and he told her *Lizzie Ann* and *Bulldog* had sailed.

Later they went on deck and conversed in the clear starlight with Francis for a time, listening to the songs of the forecastle, and passed enough of the evening on deck to take a sighting before retiring below to work out the ship's position. Captain Blackwell regarded their progress with satisfaction. They were running seven knots on a fine northwest breeze, and if the wind held he expected to make his landfall off Oran in three days time.

He rose from the table in the coach where his charts were spread, returned his log to his desk in the great cabin and turned to Mercedes, who sat reading in the armchair under the swaying lantern light. She put down the book when she saw him gazing at her and smiled.

"You are ready for bed?"

His heart thudded in his chest. Such a short time ago he'd wondered if this lovely woman could ever be brought willingly to bed of him. Now he could not seriously entertain for a moment parting from her. Speech failed him he was so moved by the affection in Mercedes' eyes when she looked at him. He unhooked the pewter lantern and ushered her into his sleeping cabin, where he was as tender to her as he knew how to be.

On the morning of the third day Falcon Point was fine on the starboard bow and Captain Blackwell, on deck during the morning watch, called all hands to put the ship about. Mr. Verson had the deck and roared the orders that brought *Inconstant* turning through 12 points of the compass. "Let go and haul," he cried when the ship had passed through the wind. *Inconstant's* foresails were braced round and she settled on the new course, beginning the long beat back up the coast of Africa. Captain Blackwell would not be turned from his plan to survey from Falcon Point to Ceuta. He looked forward in fact to the duty. The evening before he had organized his maps of the region, making them ready for annotation.

Their progress up the coast was necessarily slow, as they sailed close-hauled into the wind that had carried them down with such dispatch. Before noon *Inconstant* hove to at the mouth of the first bay Captain Blackwell intended surveying. He ordered his gig, collected his single remaining midshipman, his instruments and boat's crew, and soon drew away out of sight of his ship.

Captain Blackwell would have dearly loved to take Mercedes with him in the gig. She was as competent at the mathematics as Mr. Ransom, and she wrote a neater hand than the youngster. He had a desire to share his pursuits with her; he made sure she would find this work as fascinating as he did. But Captain Blackwell had a strict sense of what was fitting, and he did not wish it to be said he was idling about those waters with his mistress, rather than prosecuting his duty.

Five days passed with the ship employed running up the coast surveying and making elevations of the shoreline, taking bearings and fixing the position of the few bays and inlets that made suitable anchorages. Captain Blackwell would announce his intention of a closer investigation of an area promising water deep enough for a frigate's draught with "Out boat!" He was gratified by the information he was able to add to his charts, and had set *Inconstant*'s course for Ceuta when the Levanter caught them. A strong wind barreling over the Mediterranean Sea from the direction of those eastern countries known as the Levant.

One emergency succeeded another. The mizzenmast sprung. The crossjack yard carried away and the mizzen topsail split. They were forced out of the Straits, where the ship lay to under bare poles. What should have been an eight hour sail from their last call on the coast of Africa to the Port of Ceuta turned into, as Mr. Sprague put it to the gunroom, "A thirty-six hour fucking nightmare."

Captain Blackwell was on deck for most of those hours, going below only to drink a mug of coffee and eat his biscuit and meat standing up. Once Mercedes found him asleep on the deck outside her sleeping cabin. But he immediately awoke at her approach, took his oilskin cloak from its peg and went on deck again. He was on deck when the wind veered. Captain Blackwell ordered the spare fore topsail yard up in place of the crossjack yard. They bent another mizzen topsail and crawled to the mouth of the Port of Ceuta. *Inconstant* waited for a pilot to put off from shore; it was a long wait. The local pilots were not eager to run out in the driving rain and wind, the storm battered man-of-war be damned.

"There you have her, Frank, Ceuta. A damned forbidding place ain't it?"

Francis had come on deck with his greatcoat clutched round him. "I'm sure it will improve greatly when the weather turns fine."

"Come, gentle Spring!" Captain Blackwell quoted Thomson's 'The Seasons'. He had little time to relish the astonishment on Francis's face. A cutter was putting off from shore and steering for *Inconstant*.

"Here comes our brave hero. Mainsail, foresail halliards let fly! Back fore topsails!" Several moments later Captain Blackwell followed that with, "Clew up, clew up there, goddamnit! Do you not see the fellow standing for us?"

Half an hour later a man of diminutive stature brought his cutter neatly up on *Inconstant*'s lee. Receiving permission to board the pilot sprang onto her deck, his head up and his eyes beneath his southwester keen. The pilot put Captain Blackwell in mind of Mr. Martinez in his tough, weathered appearance. Though he rather thought this man an Arab than a Spaniard, Ceuta teemed with both. He went aft to the quarterdeck to join the pilot and to turn the deck over to Mr. Sprague, who had the watch. Under her first lieutenant's supervision *Inconstant* was brought to anchor in the Port of Ceuta at three bells in the first dogwatch.

"A little nearer the fort than I could wish, Mr. Sprague," Captain Blackwell said. "Pipe the hands to supper, if you please."

And nodding to his brother Captain Blackwell went below and threw himself on his cot.

Mr. Sprague remained on the quarterdeck in earnest conversation with the native pilot, on a portion of the deck at the greatest distance from the other officers.

Blackwell slept through four watches until just before dawn next day when he woke at the end of the morning watch with hunger stirring inside him. He went on deck recalling the work to be taken in hand. *Inconstant* would have a field-day drying the sails, and begin to repair storm damage. Francis no doubt would start the process of settling ashore. There was no satisfaction for Blackwell in this last thought, nor did the aspect of the fortress walls looming over the anchorage, veiled at this hour in mist, offer a view to settle the mind. Under that fortress with her ancient, unserviceable cannon was a prison, a right medieval dungeon where Captain Alexander might well be suffering at this moment.

The thought was too wretchedly sad, and Blackwell stomped heavily below. He met Mercedes emerging from her sleeping cabin, just as he hoped he might. But she had not on her dressing gown with her hair down on her shoulders as Blackwell had envisioned. Instead she was clad in a neat morning gown, with her hair pinned and dressed up.

"What is this, shore going rig?" Blackwell said.

He put his arms round her from behind and brought her close to him, letting her feel his phallus on her backside. She struggled in his enclosing arms, and turned her face away from his as he leaned over her. It struck Blackwell what her being fully dressed at this early hour meant. "Do you mean to refuse me, Miss?" He held her tighter still. "What? Eh?"

She put her hands over his and whispered her reason in his ear. The color rose to his face.

He was not a man easily put out of countenance, and he hugged her and said in a gentle tone, "That don't signify, sweetheart. It is only a week."

Francis Blackwell waited for his brother, with Mercedes on his arm, as they walked up the hill to the house he had taken. The house was in the Moorish style with a covered balcony running all round the second level, where Francis stood smoking a cheroot. On the second floor were the sitting room, a dining parlour, a gallery, and the room he was to use as his office. The first floor was where the bedchambers were situated, kept cooler by the insulation of the rooms above.

The new Vice-consul to Oran had settled in this house during the week that had passed since *Inconstant* came into Ceuta, a week in which the weather had indeed turned fine. The full throated birds and the flowering plants proclaimed spring. Captain Blackwell looked perfectly suited to the day in his second best uniform coat, cocked hat and fine lawn shirt sewn by Mercedes. She wore a muslin gown with a mantilla to cover her hair. She looked very much the elegant Spanish lady, and the pride Captain Blackwell felt in having such a woman on his arm was evident in his bearing, in the way he inclined his head to her when she spoke to him.

Francis had invited Mercedes and Captain Blackwell to dine with him, now he had employed two servants and could entertain guests with decency. He met them at the garden gate. Captain Blackwell and Mercedes walked into a charming walled garden, and Mercedes exclaimed, "Why, this is a little piece of paradise, Francis! We have cypress trees very much like in Monterey.

Perhaps Ceuta is on the same latitude." She wandered away on the garden path, her eyes full of benevolence for the plants reminiscent of the flora of home.

Captain Blackwell stopped on the path, turned to Francis, and waited with his hands behind his back and a look of resignation on his face. His repairs to *Inconstant* were complete, and he was deeply concerned about the prisoners aboard her.

"Well, James, it took a week of petitioning his first minister Abdul Aziz al Hossein, but the Dey has finally consented to an audience. We are invited to a feast, the feast of Sheker Bairam. Where I rather think we are both to be dressed down for the *Bulldog* affair."

"I've had my arse whipped by better than he, brother. I shall not mind it," Captain Blackwell said. "What worries me is the great man may not give a damn for those men in *Inconstant*'s hold. We shall not be able to exchange for Captain Alexander, and in the end I will have to set the Moslems down somewhere. I cannot carry them back to England, so it must be Gibraltar. Admiral Gambier shall cast me loose, I expect."

"The difficulty they have caused in accepting the interview should not be taken as a sign of disinterest. I believe it is rather their nature, this feigning indifference to put us in the weaker position. Leave aside the pace of their culture is distinct from ours. A week for them may be a tearing hurry. Then again it is Ramadan, the start of a new year, and nothing could have been done during the observance of it. They mark the conclusion of Ramadan with the feast and a pyrotechnic display this evening."

"I shall go with you to this supper and bear the Dey's displeasure. Though I hope we may be spared their music and dining while sitting on cushions. I wish you joy of their culture, Frank, yet I do hope and trust my ship may not be much longer a floating prison."

They watched Mercedes, her lower half shielded by greenery, ascending to the top of the wall where it gave onto the sea.

"There are steps there," Francis said.

Captain Blackwell nodded. "On the other hand, do not think I am in a hellfire hurry to return to England. For what awaits me there but being thrown on the beach with hundreds of other half-pay officers clamoring for ships."

"Do you never think of a different life than the Navy? You could command a merchant ship. I'm sure you would make a fine living once your qualities were known to owners, and perhaps be an owner yourself one day. It would be a suitable life for a gentlemen, a less dangerous life."

"I trust, brother, you will not think me one of those bloody minded fellows who live for battle when I tell you commanding a King's ship is all I have ever wanted. But a less dangerous life would not be unwelcome. Come away from the edge, ma'am, if you please," Captain Blackwell called to Mercedes.

Mercedes made for the steps by which she'd ascended the wall, but Captain Blackwell strode over and motioned her to him with his arms upraised. "Come, ma'am, we go in to tea. My brother hints I grow old."

Mercedes jumped and was caught and pressed for just a moment to Captain Blackwell's chest before he set her on her feet.

"You show a shocking want of respect for your elders, Mr. Blackwell?"

"No, indeed, my dear," Francis said, giving Mercedes his arm and leading her back up the garden to the house. Captain Blackwell followed behind smiling. "James and I were discussing felicity, specifically domestic felicity. What think you?"

"Naturally it finds great favor with me," Mercedes said.

"But I fear I must impose upon yours," Francis said. "James and I are to attend a supper this evening given by the Dey. I should be delighted to invite you, but there are no women in attendance at these affairs."

"Except for those who dance in veils for the men's entertainment. Oh, dear!" Mercedes seemed to fear having shocked the parson's sons. But they looked at her amused, and there was laughter that afternoon in Francis's new home.

In the evening, as Captain Blackwell donned his number one dress uniform, he told Mercedes, "It would be best if you did not go on deck in my absence. Mr. Bransford has the second dog watch and I should return during Mr. Verson's watch, well before Mr. Sprague takes the deck." Mercedes made no objection. She was a woman to inspire domestic felicity, and Captain Blackwell thought she would look precious lovely in veils too. "How I despise this mummery," he said, rising after pulling up his silk hose and buttoning his breeches at the knee. He reached for his full dress uniform jacket. "Do not mistake me, I mean no disrespect to the service. No, far from it, but wearing full dress in this weather feels like showing away. I shall be in a muck sweat before we reach the palace."

Mercedes smiled at him in magnificent blue and gold lace with the same tender regard as when he wore working clothes and boots. She came close to him. "When you return, Captain, and take off your finery, I shall show you how handsome I think you are."

McMurtry came in and immediately turned his back to the cabin. "Gig's crew in the boat, your honor, all present and sober."

Captain Blackwell, wiping his mouth before he turned round, walked out of his cabin feigning he hadn't been kissing his woman and pressing her in his arms.

Beside his brother, wearing a sober black suit of clothes with fine linen, Captain Blackwell felt like a peacock, and a peacock weighing fourteen stone cannot be an agreeable sight. But when they were admitted to the palace, where gorgeously attired men came up to make themselves known to the new British Vice-consul to Oran, in a room with cushions upon the floor for seating, Captain Blackwell understood the point of full dress uniform.

In respect of dress he blended rather better than Francis with the Arab men, whose robes were of the finest materials. Several wore gem-studded aigrettes in their turbans, and they all possessed the recognizable, urbane air of wealth. Francis moved in the exotic company with an air of ease, speaking mainly French, some English and a few words of Arabic, which Captain Blackwell took to be of the civil greeting variety.

Francis and Captain Blackwell were invited to seat themselves for the ritual of taking coffee with the Dey's ministers. Captain Blackwell watched with a mixture of admiration and distaste as his brother composed his limbs and plopped down on a cushion. He would have much preferred to remain standing through the ceremony, but he was compelled to sit when Francis turned on him a look akin to what he would have given a midshipman behaving badly on his quarterdeck.

Captain Blackwell enjoyed the coffee, which was strong and heavy but rather to his taste. He tried not to look vacant as conversation in languages he didn't comprehend went on round him. Perhaps it was this incomprehension made him sensitive to the change in the room when the Dey's first minister, Abdul Aziz Al Hossein appeared.

The minister went the round of the room and did the civil, beginning with Captain and Mr. Blackwell. But unless Captain Blackwell very much mistook the matter, the natives behaved as if the Admiral of the Fleet had just walked in. The first minister's appearance seemed to signify a progression to the next phase of the evening, for shortly after he entered Al Hossein invited them to follow him into the palace.

They were led down a long gallery lined with janissaries holding axes on their shoulders. Captain Blackwell, glancing at one man, read in the eyes that met his a warrior's willingness to use his terrible weapon if ordered to do so. Here indeed was a man more like himself, Captain Blackwell acknowledged as he returned the man's insolent scowl, just as those cultured gentlemen with their coffee recognized one of their own in Francis.

The long gallery terminated in a room with a high ceiling where Captain Blackwell and Francis were conducted into the presence of the Dey, who sat cross-legged upon a couch on an elevated platform surrounded by his armed ministers and servants.

After the Englishmen had been brought before him between janissaries and directed to make three salaams to his highness, the Dey demanded, through the English interpretation of Al Hossein, "What brings you here?"

Francis delivered a speech conveying both the compliments of his government and its' remonstrance with his highness regarding the recent taking of vessels. He concluded with a formal and respectful solicitation for an exchange of prisoners. They had aboard the British vessel of war in the Port of Ceuta fifteen prisoners taken in the battle with the ship *Hand of God* and desired an exchange for an equal number of the officers and crew of *Bulldog*.

The Dey flew into a passion when Al Hossein translated Francis's words. His armed retinue shifted and stared at the English visitors as though prepared to fall murderously upon them.

"Remonstrance comes with an ill grace from you, Mr. Vice-consul, British vessels being the greatest pirates in the world, and if I did right," the Dey said, turning on Captain Blackwell, "I should put you and your crew in prison till *Hand of God* is restored; and but for my great respect for the English Government, and my impression that her seizure was unauthorized, you should go there. However, you may go, with a demand from me that the vessel unjustly taken from us shall be immediately restored."

Captain Blackwell believed the matter concluded as he and Francis, with their attendant janissaries, backed out of the Dey's presence. There could be no reasoning with a man who demanded the return of a vessel his cruisers had taken by force mere months before, as though it were his rightful property.

Abdul Aziz Al Hossein directed them into another apartment when they came out of the gallery lined with axe-men. In this spacious dining room were a numerous and lively group. Many familiar faces were there from the coffee reception, and Captain Blackwell and Francis were led to seats of honor.

Having narrowly avoided being cast into prison, Captain Blackwell was bewildered to be treated to a feast. Dozens of dishes of foreign mess, as he thought it, were pressed upon them, along with a clear liquor. Captain Blackwell recognized the drink as ardent spirits and took few glasses.

The passing of this spirit and the appearance of more coffee Captain Blackwell likened to the taking of port after supper, and with the entrance of these refreshments came the entertainment. Musicians walked in, settled in their places and struck up in tones that can only be described as grating to the sensibilities of Englishmen.

Yet Captain Blackwell reflected the dissonance suited the movements of the dancing ladies; for the musicians were followed in by women in costumes not indeed of veils, but of garments revealing the feminine forms beneath. Captain Blackwell's mind was disturbed as to how to behave before this spectacle. He saw the admiration, the unguarded attraction on the faces of the native men. But in his culture a man did not openly admire the ladies of other men, and these lovely creatures must belong to the Dey's harem. Captain Blackwell's principle feeling, when they were invited to rise and move onto the balcony to view the pyrotechnics, was one of relief.

Mercedes sat in the great cabin of *Inconstant* finishing the cuff of a shirt for Captain Blackwell, consulting a pattern she'd copied in Gibraltar after the latest French style. She heard the first explosion and went to the stern windows to see if she might glimpse the display. There was a knock on the cabin door and before she had given permission, young Jack Verson rushed in and grasped her by the hand. "Miss Mercedes! Miss Mercedes!" he cried, as he might have cried, 'Mama! Mama!" had he had one. "You must come see the explosions, you must!"

The boy, tugging her hand, led her along the gun deck, up the fore hatchway companion ladder, and onto the forecastle. Here Jack ran about on his toes for happiness. Mercedes immediately felt she should not have come with young Goodman Jack, as the foremast hands boisterously hailed him.

The hands made a lane for young Jack and the captain's lady, and a spot appeared at the rail for them to stand and watch. Every face was turned skyward. There were exclamations at the beauty of the spectacle, comparisons to Guy Fawkes night, and masculine laughter and talk up and down the deck. Mercedes turned her attention for a moment from the brilliant display, and gazing toward the quarterdeck she met Mr. Verson's eye. Mr. Verson was not looking at the pyrotechnics. He was sweeping his gaze over the deck, into the rigging and alongside the ship, as the officer of the watch is meant to do. When Mr. Verson caught Mercedes' glance he bowed to her, she curtsied, and his eye moved on.

The pyrotechnics lasted half an hour and near the end of this time, when the multiplication of explosions seemed to foretell the end of the display, Mercedes put her hand on the boy's shoulder. "Listen Jack, I must go below. The Captain desired me not to come on deck, and he shall return soon. He may be putting off from the quay this moment."

Her last words were lost in the roar of an explosion next to *Inconstant*. Under cover of the noise and the distraction of the fireworks, a fire ship had been directed against *Inconstant*.The frigate's deck instantly became a chaos of running men, shouted orders, and dangerous swinging objects. Oars and spars, handspikes, the worms of the guns, whatever might be used to fend off the fire ship were rousted out and put into play.

Two additional vessels had come up following the explosion, in the wake of the burning ship. They were gunboats maneuvering to the disengaged side of *Inconstant*. As she went round *Inconstant*'s bow, one of them tossed half a dozen grenades on her deck. A deadly little bomb rolled to a stop by young Jack's feet. Mercedes snatched it up and put out the fuse in her hand. "Run, *chico*, run below!" she said, giving the boy a shove.

The experienced seamen had rigged the fire engine and were directing the jet of water on the sails and rigging. Mr. Verson had a party fending off the fire ship, and he was roaring orders to man the capstan and unmoor ship. The larboard battery under Mr. Bransford was already firing on the gunboats.

Mercedes saw Jack Verson dart down the fore hatchway and she made to follow him, but there were men scrambling in every direction between her and the hatchway and she was pressed back against the rail. She started again to cross the deck and seek safety below when she heard someone shouting in Spanish. All she could make out in the pandemonium was 'Girl!' Looking aft she saw Severino Martinez running toward her with a look of consternation on his face such as she'd never seen there before.

Then she was lifted off her feet and heaved violently over the rail. Mercedes' whole attention focused on controlling her panic, so she wouldn't die as soon as she hit the noxious cold water.

On the balcony of the Dey's palace Captain Blackwell edged closer to Francis until he stood at his elbow. "Frank, may we in decency take our leave? May I at least take my leave? I do not care for the movements of those ships down there, when nothing was stirring but half a glass since."

Francis agreed and they thanked Abdul Aziz Al Hossein and took a discreet departure while the climax of the pyrotechnic display boomed overhead. They regained the street before the palace after winding through half of its interior on their way out, and began the long descent through the town to the quay.

Francis was elaborating his view to Captain Blackwell, his hopeful view regarding the exchange of prisoners in spite of the Dey's admonition, when the fire ship exploded in the port. Captain Blackwell immediately began sprinting for the quay.

"It is either the Dons or the Dey!" he cried to Francis, lagging behind him.

Captain Blackwell's gig was waiting at the jetty with her disciplined, though clearly anxious crew. There were sighs of relief among the men when Captain Blackwell came hurrying up, stepped into her and held his hand out to his brother.

"I do not go with you, sir," Francis said.

Captain Blackwell gave a startled cry and jumped out of the boat and onto the jetty to stand before Francis. "Do you mean to stay among these deceitful barbarians?"

"You have your duty, James, I have mine. Mine dictates I remain. I advise putting the prisoners down at Gibraltar, and God keep you, your ship and her people."

Captain Blackwell clasped his brother's extended hand and yanked him to his breast. He murmured, "Good bye, Frank," and leaped into the boat. His cries of "Stretch out!" and "Pull hearty!" rang out during the gig's transit to *Inconstant*. Amid the confusion of flames and ships, a gunboat and a smaller craft sheered away from *Inconstant* and made for the far end of the port, dedicated to the cruisers of the Dey of Oran.

The fire ship had drifted ahead of *Inconstant* and now lay on her starboard bow, so that the men fending her off were doing so from the starboard gangway and the forecastle. Narhilla brought the captain's gig against the larboard side and Captain Blackwell ran up and into the ship through the entry port. He emerged into the waist where landsmen were running afoul of one another, and as he made his way to the companion ladder he grabbed men by the shoulder, looked into their faces, called them by name and ordered them to their stations.

Captain Blackwell was stepping onto the quarterdeck from the last rung of the ladder when a young body bowled into him. It was Mr. Ransom, running to descend to the waist while looking behind him. The reefer spun away after encountering his solid form. Captain Blackwell caught the midshipman up by the back of his jacket. "That will not do, Mr. Ransom. Mr. Verson, we shall beat to quarters!"

"I gave the order, sir, but there has been no drum," Mr. Verson said. "We were able to fend off the fire ship, the blessed land breeze aided us, and the best-bower is catted, sir."

"Mr. Peakes! Mr. Peakes, beat to quarters!" Captain Blackwell ordered.

"Bosun Peakes copped it, sir, a grenade exploded in an arms' chest," Mr. Bransford said. He was coming up from securing the guns on the main deck. One of the gunboats had been blown to splinters and the other run off.

"Silence fore and aft," roared Captain Blackwell. In the eerie quiet following, when the sizzle and pop of the fire ship could be heard, he called, "All hands to make sail!"

Inconstant's crew jumped to their stations as the drum beat and the pipe of the bosun's mate shrilled. The pumps were clanging, the fire engine manned and the jet turned on the rigging; buckets of water were passed into the tops with whips to wet the royals as they unfurled.

Shouted orders began with, "Man the bars! Heave taut! Off stoppers, and heave around!" until the cable was reported 'Up and down, sir." "Clear away the jib!" and the helm was put to starboard. Moments later the small-bower anchor was catted. The jib was hoisted and as *Inconstant* was paying off she edged nearer the burning vessel until Captain Blackwell called, "Hard a larboard, stations for loosing sail." First the topsail sheets and driver, and then, as the frigate passed the mouth of the bay, the courses flashed out and were sheeted home. Packing on sail after sail as she went, *Inconstant* stood away from the Port of Ceuta.

In the offing Captain Blackwell ordered *Inconstant*'s course shaped for Gibraltar, then turned to Mr. Verson. "Report in my cabin, if you please, Mr. Verson. Pass the word for Mr. Sprague."

Mr. Verson, his face pale and strained beneath the soot, made his report from the time of the explosion of the fire ship to the captain's appearance on the quarterdeck. Captain Blackwell glanced around the cabin with a frown as Mr. Verson concluded. "Could you make out the enemy, Mr. Verson? Was it the Dons or the Dey? What keeps Mr. Sprague?"

Captain Blackwell knocked on the door of Mercedes' cabin, but he knew even as he opened it she wasn't there. The great cabin had a deserted, abandoned air, with the shirt she'd been working draped on the stern locker.

"It was the Dey we believe, sir, turbans were seen in the gunboats. Sir," Mr. Verson said, intercepting Captain Blackwell's circuit of the cabin. "I regret to inform you Miss Mercedes was taken from the ship."

Captain Blackwell stared at his second lieutenant. "What? They did not board us!"

"No sir, and I didn't see the capture, sir," Mr. Verson said. "It happened at the beginning of the attack, when I was occupied with the fending off. Your steward saw what occurred, sir."

McMurtry came hurrying in. He had been waiting for the summons in the passage outside the great cabin, and he jumped only slightly when Captain Blackwell roared for him.

"What's this then, about Miss Mercedes?"

His gaze was fiercely concentrated on McMurtry and might have quelled a man less used to his ways. McMurtry spoke up,

"She come up on the fo'castle after the fireworks started with young Go— she come up to watch the fireworks, like, and we cleared a space at the rail. Then that bitch explodes next us and all hell breaks loose, and them gun boats lobs grenades into us. One lands near Miss's feet. I swear to you, your honor, she picks it up and puts out the slow-match in her delicate little hand. Brave's a lion, our Miss, sir. And she makes for the hatchway but Mr. Sprague comes up behind her, see sir, picks her up and tosses her overboard — "

Captain Blackwell burst out in vehement curses, in oaths that were heard from stern to forepeak.

"Was she alive after she went in the water? Did you see her?" Captain Blackwell demanded.

"Miss were alive, sir, and a rare plucked 'un she is. And she can swim. She struck for the barky three times, us throwing in lines to her, sir, she diving away from them Turks as tried to fish her out. Until the third time she come up too close and bow oar struck her a blow and they hauled her in. She lost her clothes, sir, all but her shift."

During the last of McMurtry's narration Captain Blackwell had sunk into his armchair. For a moment he wore an expression of despair and utter defeat. Captain Blackwell rubbed his hands over his face and managed, "Mr. Sprague?" He expected to hear his officers had him below in irons.

"Missing, sir," Mr. Verson said.

"Missing." Captain Blackwell heaved himself wearily to his feet. He ordered the Marine lieutenant to organize a thorough search for Mr. Sprague. Returning to the coach Captain Blackwell found the charts he needed and summoned Mr. Verson.

"Change course to south, southwest, Mr. Verson. We shall make for this bay here. Now, I wish to view the bosun's body and visit the wounded."

"Aye, aye, sir, course south, southwest. May I say how sorry I am, sir. How very sorry I did not do more for Miss Mercedes."

"Nonsense, you saved the ship, you attended to your duty. No one can say fairer than that. McMurtry! McMurtry, thank you for what you tried to do for the Miss."

While Doctor VanArsdel showed him the bosun's body, Captain Blackwell wondered if his men had scragged the first lieutenant after witnessing him throw Mercedes overboard into the waiting arms of the Dey's men. He nodded to Doctor VanArsdel. "We shall bury Mr. Peakes at eight bells. Pass the word for the sail maker! The butcher's bill, Doctor?"

"One dead, five wounded, sir."

"And one captured," Captain Blackwell muttered as he left the cockpit.

He inspected the ship, going right round her, giving orders for the repair of the damage *Inconstant* had sustained. Captain Blackwell received Mr. Hoffinger's report that Mr. Sprague was not aboard, and his care in ordering the ship was redoubled as he meant to be absent from her. When he was satisfied the necessary work was being attended to he went into his cabin and wrote his report, and his orders for Mr. Verson.

It took some time for Captain Blackwell to complete the task, considering this might be the last report he ever wrote to the Admiralty, and the last orders to an officer under his command. He had also to write personal letters to his father and brother, for if he failed in what he meant to do he might be killed or disgraced, and cast into prison. In the middle of the first watch Captain Blackwell sealed the last document and passed the word for Mr. Verson.

Grim and clad in black frock coat and trousers Captain Blackwell read the burial service over the body of Mr. Peakes. The crew might not have answered the muster for this ceremony, so universally detested and feared was the bosun. But both the watch on deck and the watches below turned up to see their commander put off in the cutter, his destination the coast of Africa from which they'd just escaped.

"Good luck, sir, good luck," the cutter's crew wished Captain Blackwell, when they grounded on the beach.

Narhilla renewed his request to accompany Captain Blackwell back to Ceuta, but Captain Blackwell shook his head and clapped his coxswain on the shoulder. Then he started up the beach at a dog trot with a cutlass and dagger at his waist, and pistols in shoulder belts underneath his greatcoat. Just like a fucking pirate, Captain Blackwell thought. He crested a rocky hill and went down the far side, where the sight of *Inconstant* was lost to his view.

Chapter 10

Mercedes was given a robe when the boat landed and then she was put into a palanquin, which saved her bare feet from becoming wounded as she was taken up under guard through the streets of Ceuta. An African man met the guards at one of the palace's many side entrances. He conducted Mercedes, led between two janissaries, to the upper reaches of the palace where the Dey's women resided. She was shown into a room dominated by a sunken marble bath the size of a bathing pool. The African handed her garments with an admonition in Arabic that Mercedes understood was a command to wash and dress.

She was relieved to be alone. Mercedes had thought for a moment the African, who halted the janissaries at the door, meant to remain in the room while she bathed. She'd signalized her willingness to comply with his direction by immediately stepping into the bath, but as soon as the African left Mercedes fled to the window.

Her head ached from the blow she had received from one of the oarsmen, and her hand throbbed where the grenade's fuse had burnt it. But these were minor considerations compared to the inward distress she experienced as she scanned the Port of Ceuta for *Inconstant*. Visible yet was the fire ship, still burning in the harbor, but no other ships lay near it, and it was too dark to make out more than the lanterns of ships swinging to their cables elsewhere in the anchorage.

Mercedes roused herself from where she leaned against the window embrasure with her eyes shut. She thought she might have fallen asleep, and unable to tell how much time had gone by she hastened into the bath and then dressed herself in the foreign clothes. She had nothing with which to pin her hair and was forced to present herself before the African guard with her wet hair about her shoulders and no shoes on her feet.

She was taken down to the reception rooms and along the gallery lined with axe-men. Mercedes might have trembled more at the sight of those fierce men, and at thoughts of what she might have to do to survive what had befallen her, but there was a lethargy in her body and she felt nearly insensible to her surroundings.

The Dey's frustration at the sight of Mercedes when she was led before him was nearly equal to what he had exhibited when word was brought him of the failure of the fire ship and the gunboats in capturing the English war ship.

"What is this?" the Dey demanded of Abdul Aziz Al Hossein. "This is no Englishwoman. What deception is this? I will not be practiced upon by the likes of an inferior English officer. Withhold his reward! He is to be taken up. I shall sign the firman this moment. Who is this woman?"

Al Hossein translated the king's tirade to Mercedes. "You were taken from the British vessel *Inconstant*. What is your nationality?"

"American, sir. I am from Alta California."

"Where in heaven and earth is that?" the Dey fumed. "She is no Englishwoman, she is a Spaniard by the look of her. What use have I of a Spanish woman? I might have a dozen such women."

"With respect, your Highness," said Al Hossein. "Although I very much regret this woman is not what you had hoped, her capture may yet be turned to account. The British Vice-consul and the British captain value her greatly, if the dog of a lieutenant might still be credited. Your Majesty is to consider, this Spanish woman may prove useful in our dealings with Mr. Blackwell and his government, after we do away with his hawk of a brother. The *rais* is far too skilled at the business of war. The British might be induced to a higher tribute if the woman's release is part of the package, your Excellency."

The Dey regarded Mercedes, whose head had come up at mention of the British Vice-consul's name, but she maintained her eyes properly cast down. It was a severe disappointment to the king she was not the golden haired, blue eyed, pale skinned maid he'd been led to anticipate. The Dey had dark eyed beauties by the score. He did not require another, though such a woman could be useful for those more lubricious acts that a favored wife or concubine did not like to indulge him in. His first minister was a clever man, a man the Dey respected far more than his seemingly offhand response revealed. "Tell me what is in your mind."

Captain Blackwell reached the house Francis had taken in Ceuta before dawn. He went round to the sea side of the wall enclosing Francis's garden, and crouched with his back against the stone. It was quiet in the port with the shipping snugged down for the night. Here and there on the decks of ships Captain Blackwell saw a lantern moving, a watchman doing the rounds. There were no vessels of war, no sentinel's cries of 'All's well.' All was certainly not well with Captain Blackwell. He had been put ashore a little after midnight, and it had taken him the better part of five hours to return to Ceuta on foot. He was fagged out, and he leaned against the stone wall for half an hour before moving to the stairs leading to the top of the wall.

He went over it into the garden, keeping low on the stairs, not standing at the top, and then easing himself over on his belly. Captain Blackwell landed heavily in the shrubbery, but was shielded by the foliage as he stood and observed his surroundings. Nothing stirred save the flutter of birds in the trees now and again, and as he made his way through the garden and around the side of the house where Francis's bedchamber was situated, he surprised a pair of hares — a sure sign dawn would soon be breaking.

Francis had given them a thorough tour of the house the day of their coming to tea, so Captain Blackwell knew exactly which chamber to enter. He opened the shutter over the window with what he thought was a shocking amount of noise and stepped into Francis's bedchamber, expecting to find him sitting up in bed with his rifle pointed at the intruder's head. His brother barely stirred.

He was lying on his back with his hands folded over his breast in the manner of corpses composed for rest. "Bless him," Captain Blackwell murmured, and collapsed into a chair at the end of the bed.

"James! You gave me such a start," Francis cried upon waking. "What do you here?"

"Were I an assassin you would be a dead man, brother," Captain Blackwell could not resist saying. "I've come for Mercedes." And he related to his brother the events transpired since they parted company on the jetty.

Francis was at first too amazed to stir from his bed, but later he rose and dressed in a gray morning suit. He expressed his astonishment at the villainy and disappearance of Mr. Sprague in the strongest terms. Captain Blackwell concluded by begging Francis to use his influence in obtaining Mercedes' release.

"It would be a damned sight easier to demand she be restored to you were she your wife." The words were no sooner said than Francis appeared to regret them extremely. "Forgive me, I didn't mean to intrude in your private affairs."

"No one can be more sensible of the truth of what you say than I. But you will make the demand for her release?"

"Of course. Tell me, what is the disposition of your ship?" And when Captain Blackwell had told him of his orders for the next three days Francis looked grave. "I should think this matter might take far longer than three days. The Dey may be convinced to release dear Mercedes but he will surely demand a tribute in exchange. A ransom, James. I have a few hundred guineas by me but I would have to apply to Gibraltar, or to London for anything above that."

They fell silent, Captain Blackwell thinking what might be happening to his woman in the mean time. He couldn't tolerate such thoughts and jumped to his feet. "I shall go and reconnoiter the palace, and find a way inside and bring her out."

"Stay, James, please. We are not desperate yet. Come, you must lie down. Here is my bed for you. No? Then have a shave at the least, and join me upstairs for breakfast."

After witnessing the anger of the Dey when she was presented to him and the discussion that ensued with his first minister, Mercedes had been dismissed from the exalted presence. She was led back upstairs by the African guard. He put her into a room with several sleepers on the floor, sheltered beneath tents of fine cloth. Waving her to an unoccupied pallet the guard closed the door upon her.

Mercedes went immediately to the window, stepping carefully to avoid disturbing the other ladies. She was relieved to find the window gave a view of the port, and there she waited until dawn. She was convinced Captain Blackwell would come for her. When the sky lightened and she saw the port with no British vessel anchored there her heart misgave her. It was perhaps the most unwelcome sight she'd ever met, and she sank against the wall beside the window unequal to moving the short distance to her pallet.

The first minister chose Hameed Shariff to call upon the British Vice-consul, for Shariff was a clever, cunning fellow with connections to the East India Company, intimate in the ways of the English. Abdul Aziz Al Hossein would not bring word of the fate of the woman captured from the British vessel himself. No, as ever the first minister sought the upper hand before the negotiation had fairly begun, pursuing his strategy to turn everything to do with the British presence in Ceuta to account.

Hameed Shariff had been carefully selected and instructed to call early on the British, to forestall them appearing at the palace. And in execution of his orders Hameed Shariff walked up the street where the British Vice-consul lived and requested an interview just after breakfast time.

Francis's servant brought the name of the Dey's minister waiting downstairs, clad in his European suit of clothes and his air of wealth and influence.

"Wait in the gallery, if you please James, while I receive Mr. Shariff," Francis said. "It seems we may have been given the means of opening negotiations."

"Mr. Blackwell, good day to you, sir," Hameed Shariff said, upon entering Francis's sitting room and while making his bow.

"I can hardly call it good, sir," Francis said. "After His Majesty's ship *Inconstant* was attacked in the harbor yesterday night."

Hameed Shariff's face immediately took on a look of injured innocence, and he expressed how very much he regretted to hear of this attack. He had retired to his residence outside the city after the feast and knew nothing of it; he imagined those explosions were all part of the pyrotechnics marking the end of Ramadan. Had Mr. Blackwell taken the matter up with the Spaniards who controlled the Port of Ceuta?

"Might it not have been in retaliation for the capture of the Spanish vessel *La Trinidad*, sir?" Shariff said. "Your brother was in command of *Inconstant* when that battle took place, I believe."

"Arab crews were seen aboard the gunboats, Mr. Shariff," Francis said. "Furthermore a woman was taken captive during the attack, a young lady by the name of Mercedes de Aragon. Sir, I demand Miss Mercedes de Aragon be restored to me. She was under the protection of Captain Blackwell, and therefore under the protection of my government."

Captain Blackwell, listening from where he stood near the open window, applauded Francis's tactics. Francis was going right at the enemy, just as he would have done in battle. But a disturbing silence followed his brother's declaration that left Captain Blackwell in terrible suspense. He could not see the unspoken tableau played out in the room as Hameed Shariff acted amazed, distressed, murmuring a request for a chair; and the two men seating themselves.

"Of the attack on your brother's ship, sir, I have no knowledge," Shariff said. "But as to this woman, yes, I know of her. She was offered to the Dey by one of your countrymen, a young well-favored officer by the name of Sprague. An ugly name, is it not? So unsuited to the gentleman. The Dey, sir, if you will permit my making so free, has a decided penchant for fair skinned women. His Highness entered into a contract with your lieutenant. Imagine the Dey's consternation when a Spanish woman was presented to him, rather than the Englishwoman he so desired."

"Then there should be no issue with Miss de Aragon's release."

"Alas, sir, that cannot be. So great was his Highness's displeasure, and the woman did not help the case by her conduct, the Dey ordered her put to death."

"Dear God, no!" Francis exclaimed.

Captain Blackwell burst into the room.

"Captain Blackwell!" Hameed Shariff jumped to his feet. "You here? And out of uniform, sir. Were you to be found in this city by the Dey's men you would be instantly taken up."

He could not have chosen better words, words more calculated to bring Captain Blackwell up. Hameed Shariff was quick to seize the halt in Captain Blackwell's charge to close the lid on the coffin. "She died at three o'clock this morning, the woman Mercedes de Aragon."

"I want her body," Captain Blackwell choked out. "Show me her body!"

Francis stepped between Captain Blackwell and Hameed Shariff.

"It is a thousand pities, Captain, that cannot be accommodated. Our religion does not countenance the keeping of corpses. Mr. Blackwell will bear me out. The body was burned immediately after the execution."

"Mr. Shariff, I regret I must bring this interview to an end," Francis said. "Grief is a private matter. A family matter, I am sure you will agree. Do call on me any other time you are at liberty, and I shall be at your service."

Francis hustled Hameed Shariff from the house, but at the garden gate Shariff stood firm.

"You did not allow me to elaborate, Mr. Blackwell, to tell the *rais* if he wishes to revenge his honor on the man who betrayed his lady, he may come to the maidan an hour before sunset."

Francis stared at Shariff in shocked silence. He had not reckoned on the savage nature of the place he'd come to.

"I shall call again in one hour for Captain Blackwell's reply, and to settle the particulars of the meeting," Shariff said. "The Dey will not interfere in this affair, and whomsoever shall be the victor will have safe passage through his territories."

Hameed Shariff bowed and strolled away down the street.

Francis ran back upstairs to Captain Blackwell, muttering, "Will not interfere in the affair, after orchestrating it from start to finish."

Immediately Francis entered the sitting room Captain Blackwell said, "I got her killed, Frank. That beautiful woman, through my arrogance and selfishness."

"You didn't cause this to happen. It was that blackguard Mr. Sprague."

"Yes, Mr. Sprague, who I brought near her when I knew what the man was capable of. I thought I could protect her. Arrogant notion."

Francis gave him Hameed Shariff's challenge; the emissary was to return in a short while.

"You need not accept. There is no disgrace in refusing to play a part in these brutal proceedings," Francis said. "Let Mr. Sprague's fate be on their heads."

Captain Blackwell brooded for some time. "Mad dogs must be put down, Frank. It was my ill judged decisions that brought us all to this disgraceful proceeding, as you say. I shall not try to avoid the consequences now."

"I should warn you they probably won't allow pistols. The sword is more suited to the Arab sense of justice in a matter of honor."

"Then it will be a short contest." Captain Blackwell looked at Francis with weary, grieved eyes.

"What can I do for you, James? Do you wish to practice the sword?"

"No, I thank you, Frank." He shook his head with the ghost of a smile. "If you wish to do something for me then act as my second, and attend to all the particulars of this meeting. Accept whatever conditions are offered. And perhaps it would be wise to engage a competent surgeon to attend us to the meeting place."

They stared at one another; a deep unhappy concern in Francis's gaze, while Captain Blackwell's was resigned, sad, but not lacking in that iron determination that characterized the naval service.

"I shall take that kind offer of your bed, brother, if you please. I do still hope to make old bones."

He felt old as he lay down on Francis's bed, old and stricken of heart. Captain Blackwell was aware his brother thought him an insensitive brute for being capable of sleep, after the news of Mercedes and before this wretched meeting. Yet the fact of having rested a few hours might be the sole advantage he was to have over Mr. Sprague. Captain Blackwell's training as a sea officer served him for he went instantly to sleep; with the anticipation of battle in the immediate future, he knew on an unconscious level he would need the use of all his faculties at full stretch.

Francis had found a renowned Arab physician visiting the port city. Darul Ibn Athur was a *hakim* much respected and esteemed by the community of surgeons in Ceuta, and by fortunate circumstance the physician was sharing the hospitality of the Bedouin's tents just outside the city. The turbaned Ibn Athur was a third in Blackwell's party when at dusk they made their way to the maidan.

The parade ground was three quarters of a mile outside the southeastern gate of Ceuta in a depression, a *wadi*, that looked the ideal spot for a caravan to be fallen upon by raiders, with rising ground on three sides. A festival atmosphere prevailed on the maidan when Blackwell, Francis, and the Arab physician made their way through the crowd. The contest was apparently not to be a private one; there were Arab tribesmen, Persians, Moroccans and Turks, and even a small knot of Europeans — Spaniards and Portuguese — waiting to watch the sword fight. Betting had reached a fever pitch.

A public display was what Blackwell deplored of all things, but he had no control over the circumstances. He reached the center of the gathering and gazed round at turbaned heads and flowing robes, and felt as though he were back in the time of the gladiators or when wars were decided by single combat between opposing commanders. By contrast this was a mere squalid affair, wherein he and Mr. Sprague would try to murder one another.

Mr. Sprague was led forward from the south, the opposite direction from which Blackwell had approached the meeting ground. On either side of the lieutenant were janissaries, and in back of Mr. Sprague walked a captain of cavalry dressed in a uniform of cloth of gold, and carrying before him a wooden case. Mr. Sprague's face was haggard, unshaven, and it was clear he had not enjoyed the hospitality of the Dey's prison beneath the old fortress.

He looked at Blackwell with cold hatred when they were motioned forward to stand either side of the captain of horse. Mr. Sprague's manner had always been that of a man who feels ill used by others. His behavior as they were each offered a curved sword of polished Damascus steel from the box carried by the captain of horse was unrepentant. Mr. Sprague took his sword from the box with a sneer at the captain, who'd offered first selection to Blackwell as the offended party.

Their seconds led them to positions facing one another a few strides apart. Both Blackwell and Mr. Sprague were out of uniform —it could not have been otherwise—and stripped down to shirt and breeches.

The captain of horse in his brilliant uniform stepped forward and held up his arms. "*Inshallah*, as God wills it, do not sheath the sword until honor is redeemed!"

The men round Blackwell and Mr. Sprague pressed eagerly forward. These men of the desert knew a fight with blades between men afoot would be decided quickly, and they did not wish to miss a stroke. Blackwell and Mr. Sprague circled one another, each testing the heft of the unfamiliar saber.

"I should have known you would allow the heathens to lead you to this unholy meeting," Mr. Sprague said. "How did you ever pass for a gentleman?"

"Do you prefer the galley, Mr. Sprague, or it is only boys and women you are willing to meet?"

Mr. Sprague rushed forward. There was the sound of steel whistling through air and then the tremendous clash of blades. Twice more the blades rang together. Mr. Sprague tried different thrusts, demonstrating the agility that had allowed him to best Captain de Leon y Castillo. But when their swords ground together, sliding the length of the blades, their fists meeting at the hilts, it seemed Blackwell must bear Mr. Sprague down with his greater weight. He leaned over Mr. Sprague, but the lieutenant shifted his stance and shoved their locked fists up into Blackwell's face. A gasp from the crowd went up when Blackwell's head jerked back and blood ran from his lip. Shouts followed as Mr. Sprague dealt a downward stroke that opened a gash on Blackwell's left thigh.

Mr. Sprague danced away, a wild excitement on his face. "Your heathen friends killed her, not I."

Blackwell charged him bellowing an inarticulate cry and Mr. Sprague barely parried the blow. Mr. Sprague was forced on the defensive; Blackwell dealing inelegant hacking thrusts and driving him backward as though in a close fight on the quarterdeck. Mr. Sprague seemed to realize he could not continue to give way. A concentrated look came over his features, and he exchanged blows with Blackwell until they were at a stand. The lieutenant had won a second's pause as Blackwell rocked back, his footing off for the blood running into his boot. Mr. Sprague raised his sword over his head for a two handed blow, but Blackwell did not continue backward to avoid the stroke; he stepped forward and brought his sword up under Mr. Sprague's ribs.

The sword fell from Mr. Sprague's upraised hands. Blackwell withdrew his curved blade with a determined yank and stepped away. Mr. Sprague sank to his knees and then collapsed forward, disbelief on his handsome face: a face already draining of color.

"What did I tell you, eh, Martinez?" a Spaniard well back in the crowd said to the man standing at his side. "You should have wagered. A good big one beats a good little one every time."

In a daze Blackwell lurched over and handed his sword to the captain of horse and made his bow, and then Francis had him by the arm. Francis hustled him over to sit on a boulder where the Arab physician attended him.

The gash in his leg Ibn Athur closed with a dozen turns and covered with a field dressing, declaring it would make a pretty scar if he were but to keep it properly dressed. The cut over Blackwell's lip received three neat stitches, and it was while the last was going in that two adolescent boys came up, chattering in excited tones as they bent and took hold of Mr. Sprague's feet.

"'Vast there!" Blackwell called. The Arab physician stepped away from him, leaving the needle and thread dangling from his lip, and shaking his head severely. "Frank, what are those boys up to with Mr. Sprague's body? I'll not have him put on public display, or left exposed in the desert. He was once a King's officer."

Francis spoke to Darul Ibn Athur, who called the two youths to them. Blackwell watched Francis's parlay with the physician, and finally his brother turned to him with a conscious look. "One of the conditions of Doctor Ibn Athur's attendance today was he was to have the body of Mr. Sprague, for investigative, medical purposes. Forgive me, James, but the body of a British sea-officer would be difficult to explain away."

Blackwell hung his head. Francis was awake upon every suit and had planned for the aftermath of this day's work. It entered his mind only briefly to wonder what his brother would have done if it'd been him lying slain, with his life's blood draining into the rocky soil of Africa.

"Tell the doctor with my compliments I will pay for a decent burial, or cremation if burial is not possible, of Mr. Sprague's remains. Whatever remains." Blackwell frowned down at his hands. He felt disordered. "Cut this off me, if you please, Doctor."

While the physician finished the suturing of Blackwell's face the two boys left and then returned with a shroud, into which they bundled Mr. Sprague.

"It is what I should have ordered to begin had I known the *rais* cherished the dead man," Ibn Athur said in Arabic to Francis. "And as for his offer of gold for the rites, I should be paying you for the body. I have longed to examine the vital processes of an Englishman, a pork and beef fed Englishman. You have my word all will be done with proper respect for the deceased."

"Bless you, sir," Francis said. "And as for my brother, it is more the office he cherishes than the man."

Darul Ibn Athur bound Blackwell's wound tighter with additional dressings. His companions the Bedouins, to honor the victor of the contest, and furthermore compensated by the Dey, led forward two beautiful horses. They had selected an intelligent, black-eyed creature for Blackwell, a sleek bay, strong and well up to his weight. The physician looked dubious as the two adolescent boys shoved at Blackwell's backside to heave him into the cloth covered saddle. Even on a well paced mount the wound might open.

But the fleet animals carried Blackwell and Francis to the headland designated for the rendezvous with *Inconstant* well ahead of their time. Blackwell would not hear of returning to Ceuta to recuperate his wounds, and he let himself down from his fine mount having not lost much more blood than during the actual combat.

While Francis tethered the Arabian horses, Blackwell settled against a boulder that still retained the sun's warmth. He was grieved to his soul and he could hardly believe he was living in a world where Mercedes was not; he was never to see her again, never to hear her gentle voice nor press her in his arms. And he'd just murdered a brother officer in an act of revenge. Blackwell thought briefly on self-murder, but his upbringing and all the standards of his life made the idea repugnant, cowardly. Ignoring the throbbing of his wounds, Blackwell brooded over Mr.

Sprague's comment about passing for a gentleman. The remark had struck him hard, for it was his fear of Mercedes not adding to his consequence as a gentleman that had been at the root of his disgraceful treatment of her. He'd always imagined himself marrying an English woman, a gentlewoman of appropriate lineage, connections and marriage portion.

"How I wish I'd listened to you, Frank," Blackwell said, when Francis returned from the horses. "Everyone warned me, Doctor VanArsdel, you, even Admiral Gambier, that I had better let her stop in Gibraltar. Had I heeded I should be returning there now to marry her."

"I never advised any such thing."

"You advised me not to trifle with her. How right you were, brother. In Gibraltar I told Admiral Gambier Mercedes was my intended, so he'd leave off about whoring before I was obliged to call him out, however old and elevated he may be. He clapped a stopper over it straight away, even begged my pardon. But I couldn't make up my mind to marry. Mercedes told me the particulars of her upbringing, and that together with ..." Blackwell left off, his head sank down on his arms resting atop bent knees. "I desired her so much I fancied my attachment must not be serious, not of the sort marriages are based on. I behaved disgracefully toward Mercedes when I should have been overjoyed she would have me. How is that for Protestant, moralistic, Anglo-Saxon folly?"

Francis did not answer, and they waited through the long evening. At last the hour came when Blackwell lit the signal fire. A short while after the sound of oars hitting water with a regular rhythm was heard. The murmur of voices came to them over the water.

The boat was run up and Mr. Ransom jumped out and saluted. Captain Blackwell turned and embraced his brother. Francis seemed ill at ease. "Give my duty to our father," was all he managed to say in parting. Captain Blackwell climbed wet into the boat after it was run out and took his seat in the stern, his broad shoulders bowed.

When the boat could be made out from *Inconstant* word went swiftly round the deck that the captain was returning without the Miss, as the foremast Jacks called Mercedes. After Captain Blackwell came aboard, and the sound of the pipe of the bosun's mate had died away, silence fell on the ship's deck.

Captain Blackwell returned the salutes of his officers and was moving to the quarterdeck when young Jack Verson, leaning over the rail and staring into the unoccupied jolly boat cried out, "Where is she, Pa? You said Captain would bring her back. Where is Miss Mercedes?"

"Hush!" Mr. Verson said to his son.

"Where is she, Pa? Pa? Where is she?"

"The Dey killed her, son, for disobedience to orders," Captain Blackwell said.

There was a collective audible gasp, followed by the cries of young Jack, "No! No, she ain't dead! She's telling the king stories to stay alive."

"Take the boy below," Captain Blackwell ordered, limping onto the quarterdeck.

The kind hands of seamen patted young Jack Verson as he was led below in tears. McMurtry came onto the quarterdeck with Captain Blackwell's uniform jacket, the one Mercedes had ordered made for him in Gibraltar.

Captain Blackwell thanked McMurtry, put on the coat, and took up his station. "Set a course for Gibraltar, Mr. Hammerly."

"Gibraltar sir?"

"Yes Gibraltar! Do you think you can find it?" Captain Blackwell said.

He was grateful for the dark night and the spindrift blown over the side of *Inconstant* as she settled on her course because they hid his tears. He felt ready to sob, just like young Jack.

Chapter 11

Mercedes was conscious of a stench in the room where she lay, and then she became aware the smell started from her. She was grateful to the man and woman who cleaned her and brought water endlessly to her to drink. She was anxious to express her thanks. The African man attending her she remembered; but the olive skinned woman with the dark, lovely eyes was a stranger. Mercedes tried to speak to her, both to thank her and to discover if they had a language in common. But she was so oppressed with illness her speech came out an unintelligible mix of Spanish, English, and French. She suffered pain in her back, her head, and over all else in her vitals. Her guts twisted and tortured her, and her heart ached in her chest.

In this state Mercedes' world shrank to watching the pattern of light change in the room where she lay as day after day went by in a state of complete lethargy. Finally she passed increasingly long intervals robbed of her senses.

The Dey was informed the woman taken from the British vessel was dying. He responded: "Send word to the eunuch guarding her he will be rewarded if he brings her through the cholera. She is of no use to Us dead."

Chapter 12

Inconstant had to call at Gibraltar for her wounded and so her captain could make his report to Admiral Gambier, commander of the Mediterranean Fleet. The great Rock was in sight the day following Captain Blackwell's regaining his ship.

He'd passed most of the night on deck, unwilling to go below to his cabin until he was nearly asleep where he stood. When at last McMurtry had led him below and discovered he was wounded, the steward woke Doctor VanArsdel himself. He brought the surgeon to the cabin declaring, "A great gash in his leg, and one boot nasty with blood, and him on deck the better part of the night." Yet Captain Blackwell was again on deck during the morning watch at the break of dawn, when Mr. Verson stepped over and wished him a good day. He responded with the usual form, but he looked at his first lieutenant with a bloodshot, vacant stare.

"I neglected to inform you, sir, the carpenter's mate Severino Martinez did not answer the muster yesterday. A search didn't turn him up," Mr. Verson said. "I believe he deserted in Ceuta, sir. And I do beg your pardon, Captain Blackwell, for not informing you sooner, that we might have sent a party of Marines into Ceuta to fetch him."

Captain Blackwell stood with his hands clasped behind his back and his head bowed. He imagined Mr. Martinez had seen Mercedes go over the side and he'd followed her. If only he had reached her. Captain Blackwell half suspected Severino Martinez was Mercedes' father, not, as he had claimed, a mere friend of the family. He felt a bond with the man he could now recognize, and acknowledge.

"That is the least disturbing news I've had these several days, Mr. Verson," Captain Blackwell said. "I shall mark the book."

He did not say how he would mark the muster book next Mr. Martinez's name, and when it came to it Captain Blackwell wrote there DD, 'discharged dead'. He wouldn't have the man hounded by the Royal Navy, when Mr. Martinez had done his duty while aboard *Inconstant* and joined the ship solely to watch over Mercedes. What Mr. Martinez's feelings would be when he discovered Mercedes was lost to them, Captain Blackwell knew only too well. It was this sympathy led him to mark the ship's book as he did, and ignore the pricks to both his professional and personal conscience.

The Captain of the Fleet, Captain Hardy, welcomed Captain Blackwell in the cabin of *Royal George* while his report was carried in to Admiral Gambier. Captain Hardy was exceedingly cordial, though they were not previously acquainted. He'd naturally read his reports of the recent battles with *La Trinidad* and *Bulldog,* and he desired Captain Blackwell to relate the encounter with *Bulldog* while she was in the hands of the Arabs. Captain Blackwell could not help the stiff manner in which he responded, it was contrary to what was usual among naval men and he regretted it. It was plain he didn't wish to speak of the action, and Captain Hardy, good man that he was, moved on to other business. The transporting of the prisoners was arranged to be done with all dispatch; pity nothing had been accomplished as yet in the way of exchanging for Captain Alexander and his men; did *Inconstant* require stores, provisions?

The Admiral's secretary entered. "I beg your pardon, sir, the Admiral is ready to meet with Captain Blackwell."

Out of consideration for his wound, Captain Blackwell supposed, he was invited to a chair immediately once inside the admiral's noble apartments. His leg did throb and he was walking with a limp at the moment.

"So you have brought me fifteen more prisoners to eat their heads off in the prison ship, with their special diet, the heathens.

And lost two officers, your premier and your bosun. Mr. Sprague, he was the well-looking young man, was he not?"

Captain Blackwell returned the Admiral a wooden stare. "Yes, sir, that was he."

"Many will congratulate you for the retaking of *Bulldog*, sir. My opinion is, it would have been a discreditable thing had you not taken a brig manned by Moors and Turks with your superior guns. And as to the action in Ceuta itself, and the loss of valuable officers, could you not manage to deposit the Vice-Consul ashore without this sort of cock up?"

"It was an unprovoked attack, sir. They are unaccountable people."

Admiral Gambier was looking at Captain Blackwell as though he did not believe any action he was involved in could be unprovoked. "I wish Mr. Blackwell and the gentlemen of the foreign service joy of them."

There was something new in the way Admiral Gambier was studying him, aside from the general ill will he seemed to bear him, Captain Blackwell read perplexity in his gaze.

Admiral Gambier tapped a sealed document on the desk before him. "Here are your orders, sir, ready writ. I expressly desired these be prepared against your return from Ceuta. In short, you are ordered to the Channel Fleet where *Inconstant* is to be paid off."

Unkind tongues would say Admiral Gambier had cashiered him as an undesirable — most probably for lack of moral fiber.

Captain Blackwell took the orders, put them in his jacket pocket and prepared to make his bow.

Admiral Gambier stood too. "How is your fiancée, if I may inquire? The charming woman on your arm at the subscription ball."

Captain Blackwell swayed on his feet, a pained expression on his face. He answered in less than his usual strong voice, "I don't know who you mean, sir. Good day, sir."

He turned round and his features went slack, he hated the prevarication. He could not even own her. It was the crowning event in a thoroughly dishonorable episode, and Captain Blackwell had to stop and compose himself before he went in to take leave of Captain Hardy.

He wrapped up his business ashore, visiting the hospital and going the round of *Inconstant*'s men with Doctor VanArsdel. Captain Christensen, though in his right senses once more, was not recovered sufficiently to make the journey and would remain in Gibraltar. The only other shore call Captain Blackwell made was to the foreign office, where he went to wait upon Lord Upton and deliver Francis's communications to his chief.

In parting, after an interview as agreeable as the one he'd had with Captain Hardy, Captain Blackwell thanked Lord Upton for the handsome gift made to the crew of *Inconstant*. Lord Upton, shaking Captain Blackwell by the hand, appeared only slightly perplexed but he kept his own council, as those in his profession are wont to do.

"I hope you will not take it ill, your lordship, when I tell you I cannot like leaving Frank amidst that company."

"He shall not be long out of communication with us I assure you," Lord Upton said. "We keep tolerable track of our own. And it is of the first importance to Government he establish a footing in Ceuta. Please do write to him care of the foreign office here, and I will personally undertake to see your letters reach him."

Captain Blackwell retreated to *Inconstant*. He saw those wounded expected to recover brought aboard, took on the last of his water, wood, and stores, and left Gibraltar on the tide. *Inconstant* bore away carrying her grieving commander, a crew happy to be on the homeward passage, and officers uncertain of what lives awaited them in England.

The laughter that had drifted up from the great cabin to the quarterdeck, making the officers there grin in former times, was heard no more. Captain Blackwell, from having the company first of his brother, and then of his brother and his lady, returned to the solitary life of command. He took his meals alone; McMurtry remarking to the cook, "Gone right off his feed, the skipper." And as he could hardly endure the sight of his cabin, Captain Blackwell spent most of his time on deck. It put a not inconsiderable strain upon the crew to be always under their captain's eye, but they had to bear it. Captain Blackwell was on deck at all hours, in heavy weather and fine, appearing to find solace when sailing the ship, with the expanse of sea and sky to absorb his grief.

Both appetite and rest had deserted Blackwell, which was why he was likely to spring up on deck at any hour. When he did sleep he couldn't control his dreams and inevitably they were erotic ones of loving Mercedes, and he would awake frustrated to recall anew his loss. He had recourse to what all military men away from their women did, but it made him feel sadder and lonelier still. One night as he lay in the double berth trying to discipline his mind away from thoughts of Mercedes, he decided he would order a cot slung and leave off sleeping in the fixed berth. He hoped the change would bring relief.

Blackwell swung his legs to the deck and went to Mercedes' sleeping cabin and sat upon her cot. McMurtry had cleared away all trace of her from the great cabin when he saw the pain it gave him to see reminders of her. But tonight he pulled her sea chest from under the cot and opened the lid. On top were the shirt she'd been sewing for him, and the books his brother had given her.

Underneath these things McMurtry had hastily gathered up were her papers; her workings of the ship's position from sights on stars and noon observations; and oddly, the pamphlet given him by Admiral Gambier, and a letter addressed in a feminine hand to Captain Gambier, R.N., *H.M.S. Raleigh*. Blackwell frowned at the letter. The script was old fashioned and flourished, and when he held Mercedes' calculations against the letter, the address appeared to have been written by a different hand.

His eye fell upon one of Mercedes' chemises on the top tray of her sea chest and he put the letter back and took up the delicate undergarment. He held it in his hands and couldn't resist bringing the fine cloth to his face and inhaling her scent, but he paid for indulging himself when his heart contracted. Blackwell hurriedly put back her things, closed the sea chest and kicked it under the cot, before tears gained purchase in his eyes.

The weather had not been kind to *Inconstant* this cruise, and this held true even as they entered the English Channel and were steering for Portsmouth one dark night. It came on to blow a gale from the west south west and *Inconstant*'s fore and main sails parted. Captain Blackwell roared the orders that sent men racing up to cut away the tattered pieces of sail, flapping with the report of guns. The night was dark as pitch and the ship tossed about at the mercy of the waves, many of which were breaking over *Inconstant*'s deck.

Captain Blackwell was amidships peering into the tops when the block came singing down out of the damaged rigging and hit him a glancing blow to the head. He collapsed on the deck. Mr. Bransford, Narhilla and two sturdy seamen were required to carry him below. The doctor reassured his men Captain Blackwell was certainly alive, though he did remark had the block hit him square on the head his troubles in this world would have been over.

The easy motion of the ship told Captain Blackwell *Inconstant* was swinging to her cables when he awoke in his sleeping cabin. He saw Doctor VanArsdel and McMurtry sitting beside his cot. When he asked for a drink, his throat was terribly dry and his voice came out a croak, McMurtry rose with relief writ plain on his face and fetched him a cup of water. While he drank McMurtry went out again to attend to the preparation of a broth the doctor ordered, and Doctor VanArsdel felt his pulse and raised his lids, peering into his eyes. Although Captain Blackwell flinched away at this Doctor VanArsdel seemed satisfied with the patient, but he again settled himself in his chair beside the cot.

A short time of silence elapsed before Doctor VanArsdel said, "I have not expressed to you, sir, how very sorry I am for your loss. I don't believe I ever met a finer woman than Miss Mercedes, and it is evident to me now yours was a love match."

Captain Blackwell didn't know how to answer the doctor's speech or even if he had heard aright, for his head throbbed and his vision was not quite what it should be. Doctor VanArsdel was a circumspect and capable man and he had never spoken to his captain so freely. But perhaps it was in consequence of the end of the commission, indeed the end of the war, and in any case Captain Blackwell murmured, “Thank you, Doctor.”

He took his broth and asked if the men were being paid off, for he could hear an orderly commotion going on over his head. McMurtry answered, “Aye, sir,” ignoring the doctor’s warning glance, and Captain Blackwell insisted on rising and going on deck.

The noise and hustle on deck of the dockyard commissioners calling each man’s name from the muster book; the salutes and acknowledgements to the departing seamen, carrying their wages in their hats and their few possessions in sailcloth bags; and the effort of doing justice to his officers, taxed Captain Blackwell severely. Upon seeing the coins counted out to the last man and boy, and the majority of his officers gone ashore, Captain Blackwell walked to the rail and vomited over the side.

Three days later his nausea had quite passed away, his vision was recovered, and though he was a wretched sight with half his head shaved, Captain Blackwell was preparing to quit *Inconstant* and go into Portsmouth to take lodging.

“What to do with the Miss’s kit, sir?” McMurtry asked.

“Send it along of mine,” Captain Blackwell said, after a moment’s pause.

On deck he met Mr. Verson and young Goodman Jack. They had stayed with the ship as long as possible too, having no home ashore. Under other circumstances Captain Blackwell might have invited his first lieutenant and his son into the country with him, to pay a call on his father. But used as Captain Blackwell was to the sudden deaths of his naval companions — he had been quite attached to Mr. Whittemore, who had met his end in the battle for *La Trinidad* — he could not bring himself to extend the invitation. The sight of young Jack always brought memories of Mercedes fresh and painful to his mind. Her loss Captain Blackwell found difficulty commanding himself to bear: he had never been in love before.

He shook hands with Mr. Verson and with young Jack, who, with the resiliency of youth, seemed to have half forgot the lovely young woman who had given him marmalade and lessons in the great cabin. As for Mr. Verson, Captain Blackwell fancied he comprehended his feelings, and so limited his conversation to other ships and commissions while they watched young Jack capering on the deck. Captain Blackwell took his leave at last and went down the gangway and made his way into the town.

In the taproom of the Goat and Compass he found Captain Enoch Bourne, late of *L'Amable*. "Why Jim, you never was a beauty, but now you're downright hideous."

Whereupon Captain Blackwell narrated *Inconstant*'s weathering of the gale, when he had received his last injury, "Gazing up into the rigging amidships like a proper flat."

Captain Blackwell had removed his hat and tucked the scrapper under his left arm. In the taproom newcomers would glance his way and give comical starts.

"I believe I shall visit the barber and have the rest shaved," Captain Blackwell remarked. "Put me more in ballast."

"Yes, do," Enoch said. "Otherwise I cannot ask you to pay a call upon my mother, and my brothers and sisters, which I mean to do directly I arrive in London. The sight of your phiz might bring on m'mother's next confinement."

Enoch Bourne was among the eldest of sixteen or seventeen, Captain Blackwell had lost count, of Lady Oxford's children. And he may have been one of the few actually belonging to Lord Oxford, whom he strongly resembled. It was rumored various men had fathered Lady Oxford's brood, referred to in society as the Bourne miscellany. Yet Enoch Bourne was far fonder of his mother, and of his notorious brothers and foul-mouthed sisters, than he was of his cold and distant father.

"Shall we go snacks on a chaise, Jim?" Enoch asked, when Captain Blackwell returned from the barber with his pate new shaved. But Captain Blackwell told his friend he could not afford his half, and they took places on the mail coach instead, with their servants on the roof and their sea chests strapped behind.

Once settled in London they did call upon Lady Oxford, who was genuinely rejoiced to see her son. She expressed herself gratified at the conclusion of the war, and she was gracious and welcoming to Captain Blackwell, who dwarfed her delicate drawing room chairs with his bulk. Four of Enoch's sisters and two of his young brothers came in and filled the room with their boisterous chatter and exclamations.

"We mean to find Enoch a bride this season," declared one of his sisters. "Some dear young thing to warm your cot, eh Enoch?"

"And we should be happy to do the same for you, Captain Blackwell," cried another. "But that you have the look of a goddamn monk!"

They all laughed excessively at this witticism. Even Lady Oxford, appearing mildly embarrassed by her outspoken daughters, smiled when it was evident Captain Blackwell didn't mind it. Lady Oxford was known to approve of a man who had an appreciation for the bawdy.

Over the next fortnight the two Navy men went together during the day to petition the Admiralty, and by night to various balls and entertainments. Neither activity yielded satisfactory results, at least for Captain Blackwell. He sat in the Admiralty reception room, after sending his name in to the First Lord's Secretary, among other post-captains, many senior to himself. Never was his name called for an interview toward a possible command, and unlike Enoch Bourne, Captain Blackwell, not being the son of a peer, had no influence to bring to bear.

Neither did he find at the homes of the upper ten thousand, where he went in company with the Bournes, a very warm welcome. That he was a post-captain, the son of a country parson, who had not been fortunate in the way of prize money, was soon known by the *ton*. Society's mamas steered their daughters clear of the grim-faced Captain Blackwell, who looked as though he could break a delicate young lady in two.

Enoch Bourne, whose parentage was so nearly infamous but who possessed a handsome face, and could readily put aside the manner of a rough sea captain, experienced more success with the ladies. Soon there was one in particular, the flame-haired and pert eighteen year old daughter of a country squire, whose connections were willing to overlook much eccentricity for the sake of a viscount's son. Attending a soiree one evening at the home of Lady Bessborough, Enoch had the good fortune to lead the young lady into a quiet alcove and press a kiss on her. Whereupon the bread and butter miss turned into something of the ravening beast. It had taken a great deal of restraint on Enoch's part to save both their dignities.

On leaving the soiree Enoch said, "Shall we end the evening at Mrs. Allen's, Jim? I find myself in need of relief, if you take my meaning."

Captain Blackwell did take his friend's meaning, and he was undressing an hour later upstairs in Mrs. Allen's establishment with an attractive woman waiting for him in the room's ample bed. But the experience wasn't what he craved, though the courtesan he'd chosen opened her legs wide to receive him, she lay beneath him unmoving while he labored over her. There was no tenderness, no passionate whispering of his name, no whimpering little cries or sighs from the woman to delight him. She did not embrace him with her arms and legs, and he couldn't bring her pleasure. Pleasure wasn't in the act for this professional woman, and his own brief release felt sordid for her not joining him in it. And as he pulled on his breeches and laid his money on the room's little table, she went so far as to insult him. "I should charge you double, you weigh as much as two men." Captain Blackwell scowled at her and the woman shut her mouth and turned her face away as though she hadn't spoken.

The doxy's attitude was like England's toward her returning soldiers and sailors; in place of welcome, Captain Blackwell had received both insult and indifference. The Admiralty had taken no notice of him, there were far too many officers desiring appointment to the few peace-time ships in commission. Captain Blackwell decided, as he went out into the London night, to pay his duty to his father. He made his way to the posting office next morning, and took places for himself and McMurtry on the mail coach to Hampshire.

Chapter 13

Mercedes was able to descend to the palace courtyard and walk for an hour with assistance in the gardens there, but she hadn't the strength to climb the staircase back to the women's quarters and the African guard Omar carried her up. Omar had been beside her when she had come to herself some two weeks before, and she had tried to thank him for his attendance.

"He speaks only Arabic and the language of his tribe," said the dark-eyed woman.

"Will you express my thanks to him?" Mercedes said, in French. "I am deeply grateful to you both for your kindness. Do not think I was not aware of your care of me." Her voice wavered in the way of invalids.

"You are not to think of it, Mademoiselle. It gives me great pleasure to speak French once more."

"Are you then a Frenchwoman?"

The lady laughed, an agreeable melodious sound. "No more than you are British, Mademoiselle. I am Persian. My name is Zahraa Albuyeh. These are my children, Farrokh and Miriam." She motioned two beautiful children forward to greet Mercedes.

Mercedes extended her hand to first the boy and then the girl. She'd never seen such long lashes, framing the luminously dark and lively eyes of the children.

"I am Mercedes de Aragon, late of the British ship *Inconstant*."

"Dear Mademoiselle Mercedes," Zahraa said, after she had allowed her children leave to play outside. "You must grow better.

We have all been made answerable for the welfare of the British *hanim*."

"I am astonished. What does that mean?"

"*Hanim*? Why, it means noblewoman."

Mercedes had wished to understand more than a simple translation. "How do you come to be of the king's court, Zahraa. Forgive me if I am impertinent."

"Not at all. I was taken when I was seventeen, from one of my father's merchant ships. His Highness is the father of my children, but after my confinement with Farrokh the Dey seldom sends for me. He prefers his Hungarian woman, and those of his ladies given to more perverse practices."

"How I hope I may not have to ..." Mercedes left off. She could manage no more for the moment.

There is nothing like an illness and a long period of recuperation to concentrate the mind, when the rushing about of ordinary life has necessarily ceased. While Mercedes lay abed, or rather underneath her tent of cloth, far up in the Dey's palace, behind marble columns and fretwork screens, she thought much about Mr. Martinez's advice to her to decide what it was she wanted.

Admiral Gambier did not occupy many of her thoughts; it was those who'd raised her were much in her mind. Spaniards, and Mercedes' mother particularly, had a unique pride in ancestral name, in being part of the *hidalguía*, as it is called, the nobility. And it was a tenet of this pride to despise honest labor. A perverse view, for how could one exist without the other? Mr. Martinez had worked as a shipwright, as a carpenter and master aboard coasting vessels, and even in cattle, the trade in hides, to maintain the three of them in California. When Mercedes reflected on her childish and haughty behavior to Mr. Martinez in return, she felt heartily ashamed.

Another forthright, hard driven man featured in Mercedes' sickbed musings. She justified so much time spent dwelling on the things Captain Blackwell had said to her, his tenderness and his aggressions, by calling it regret at having come so close to marriage to a gentleman. Though Mercedes knew it would not have satisfied her mother's sense of justice, she felt it must be just as well to be a gentleman's wife as a gentleman's daughter.

Mercedes grew stronger, and on their outings together in the courtyards and the gardens of the palace Mercedes and Zahraa strengthened their friendship. Zahraa needed a confidant, for being Persian she did not wear the veil. The other ladies of the harem considered her low and vulgar, nearly as bad as the Hungarian. For Mercedes' part, she was struck by the similarity in their cultures. Persian and Spanish both held family of primary consequence; or perhaps it is only the women who do, Mercedes considered, and for the men it would be their honor.

She had already begun to memorize the layout of the women's quarters and all other areas of the palace she was permitted access to: the locations of windows, balconies, stairways and particularly exit doors. She studied the enclosing walls of the courtyards they paced in, marking the locations of the barred gates that led outside the palace.

"Does the British Vice-consul come to the palace, Zahraa?"

"I don't know, I suppose he must. I saw him once when we ladies danced for the gentlemen, the evening of Sheker Bairam. He and the big, brutish man, his brother."

"He is no brute!" Mercedes cried.

"Forgive me, Mercedes dear, I meant no offence. I thought ... I thought the more cultured man was your Englishman, your James, who you called for so during your illness. Forgive me, indeed, appearances can mean so little. I am not such a child as that."

"Did he never ... His ship never returned here after Ramadan?"

Zahraa sadly shook her head, and Mercedes paced by her side in silence.

Spring had passed into summer and the sun shone gloriously in the palace gardens in Ceuta, where the fresh breezes of the sea moderated the hottest days. The world went about its business regardless of the heartaches of women, and Mercedes reflected that she had survived and was not so terribly situated. She was safe and unmolested, well fed, and she had companions. She would doubtless be given occupation soon, sewing and perhaps teaching the Dey's numerous children. This was what she hoped; she dreaded a summons to the Dey's chamber.

Mercedes had to own her part in what had brought her into this situation, where there was no freedom and no love; she'd forfeited her chance at legitimacy. She had not been wise, but she had no option but to try, for this moment, only to live her meager life.

When she recovered her voice, Mercedes said, "It is I who must beg your pardon. The attachment would seem to have been much more on my side, and that cannot help but wound. I shall recover from it directly, I am sure."

"You must try, dear Mercedes."

"Do they never let us leave the palace? May we write letters? If I could contact Mr. Blackwell, Mr. Francis Blackwell, he should aid us both."

They immediately began to devise ways to have a message carried to Francis. So concentrated was Mercedes on this effort, and on all her contrivances, she very nearly fell ill with fever once more.

The day came when Mercedes was among the group of men and women leaving the palace at mid morning to go to the marketplace. The ladies were covered from head to foot in burqas and the guards wore loose pantaloons with deadly weapons hung over their chests.

A small, hard man dressed in the plain garb of an Arab laborer, a man who had kept a vigil over the various palace entrances until he knew the movements of the Dey's women, waited there outside the palace gate through which the harem exited. Every market day he was there, observing the women. At first he had trailed the ladies through the marketplace until he knew them as individuals in spite of their coverings. After that he merely lounged by the gate and counted the ladies and their guards as they left to market, moving away when he found the group had not changed its composition.

The day Mercedes emerged with the other ladies Severino Martinez counted his females and immediately fell in after the group. He focused his attention on the newcomer, and the ladies had not completed a quarter of their circuit of the market before Mr. Martinez knew Mercedes was one of their number. No garment, no matter how constructed, could conceal the manner of a loved one; the way she held her head, her strong graceful stride, the gestures of her hands. Mr. Martinez offered his silent thanks to the Almighty.

In the months previous when he'd haunted the palace and the market by day, and worked in the coasting trade smuggling all manner of goods by night, Mr. Martinez had crafted a simple plan. He went ahead of the ladies in the marketplace, knowing which stalls they frequented, pulled a letter folded small from his robes and left it on a bolt of English broadcloth. Then he went outside the cloth merchant's tent to await Mercedes' passage. On the outside of the paper appeared one word in Spanish, *Sobrina*. On the other side of the unfolded sheet was a brief letter.

"I will carry word of you to our former shipmates. Pray do not play the fool but recall what *La Trinidad* taught you, and know that I am with you."

Chapter 14

Many aspects of his son's appearance surprised the Reverend Edward Blackwell aside from the purely physical: the hair cropped close and another scar across the head, the loss of weight and a more aged cast of face; yet the deeper change seemed in the character of the man. Reverend Blackwell was used to think of James as a hale, hearty fellow, with his loud voice and seaman's love of the bawdy. These had not entirely deserted him, especially when he was in drink. Yet the elder son who had returned from leaving his brother in Ceuta was a more subdued individual by far than the man who'd embarked on the commission. It was not that James spoke or acted differently; his interest in his brother's affairs, his father's neighbors and his parish, were as keen as ever Reverend Blackwell could wish. But he seemed to have lost his youthful pleasure in living and in private moments he was melancholy, reflective, and silent. He pined, Reverend Blackwell came to believe, for a ship or a woman or both. And while he had no influence to help him to the one, Reverend Blackwell could certainly throw him in the way of the other.

"You remember George Burney, the Reverend George Burney of Ibthorpe?" Reverend Blackwell said. "He has six sons, fortunate fellow."

"Certainly I remember him, sir. Frank and I played cricket with the Burney boys. Two are in the Navy."

The Reverend bowed. "The youngest two. His son Edward sends to invite us to Norbury Park for the shooting. His is a singular case, though I daresay you've heard it already. Taken notice of by rich cousins and adopted, changed his name to Crewe.

Norbury Park has capital sport, I am sure you shall approve of it. Half the Burney family will be there. You remember the girls? No? Well, one or the other is always on hand for Mrs. Edward's next confinement. Dear, good women those Burney girls. And likely Francis and Charles, the Navy men. Then at least you shall have someone who speaks your language."

The change of scene from his father's quiet rectory to a large country house full of company did hearten Blackwell. The shooting and the fine, long tramps through woodland and field formed an agreeable day's occupation. He had the camaraderie of other men, to which he was accustomed, and his appetite sharpened from the exercise. In the evening there was supper with the ladies, who had passed their day sewing Edward Crewe's shirts. The first time Blackwell had seen them at it, coming in mud splattered and just glancing into the drawing room where they sat sewing and chattering away, he wondered why he'd thought Mercedes would not have done in such a setting. She would have suited them to perfection, every bit the gentlewoman just as were Edward Crewe's wife Elizabeth, his sister Jane, and Miss Sharpe, the children's governess.

Mercedes would have been at ease sewing and conversing with the ladies, or she might have gone shooting with him. He imagined a day spent with her in the countryside; teaching her to shoot, standing in back of her and bringing her slender arms up encircled by his to rest the gun against her shoulder. At least shooting was a sport more suited to a female than handling the sword. Blackwell stopped himself for he had begun to pace in the entrance hall in his muddy boots, his hands clasped behind his back and a scowl set on his face.

He determined again to command his mind away from thoughts of Mercedes and as he turned to seek his chamber and change his clothes, he caught the bright eyes of Edward's sister examining him from across the drawing room. Jane had a keen, penetrating gaze, which put Blackwell in mind of his brother, when Francis was about to come out with some singular remark.

The Burney family had formed the habit of reading aloud after supper, when the gentlemen joined the ladies in the drawing room. They favored plays when there was a numerous gathering, but they read selections from novels as well. Henry Burney advised Captain Blackwell as they rose from their port he was to give particular attention to the scene to be read that evening, for the author had produced something quite fine.

Captain Blackwell did try to focus on the reading. Jane's and Henry's voices as the two characters were pleasing, and their performances all very well. The scene, he gathered, concerned a proposal of marriage, the manner of which the woman took exception to and let fly with her full broadside. A deuced awkward passage when passionately spoke by brother and sister. Jane's color had risen and her eyes were alive as she read. Gazing at her, he wondered when he would begin to feel attraction for women of his own class, for a suitable woman. One such as he had been saving himself for when he hesitated to marry Mercedes.

"What do you suppose your gallant captain thinks of when his face takes on that furious aspect?" Miss Sharpe asked Jane after the reading was concluded.

"His last action, no doubt, when he assailed the heathen Turk," Jane said. "And do not call him 'my captain' if you please, he is nothing of the kind. If he were I would make him turn off his servant. Why, if Elizabeth were to come upon that McMurtry unawares the fright might bring her to bed."

Miss Sharp tittered and began to insist the captain did have a *tendré* for Miss Jane, when Captain Blackwell glanced up and caught the ladies' stares. His face instantly softened and he stood up. Though standing across the room from him both women took a step backward, then it became obvious Captain Blackwell stood in consequence of Charles Burney entering the room. He was just come from Portsmouth, and Captain Blackwell was waiting his turn to greet him.

When the two men shook hands, midshipman Burney offered that he had been aboard *Elephant* anchored next to *Inconstant* in Gibraltar. Both men recalled the shout from *Elephant*'s between decks, "You forgot to wipe your arse, *Incontinent*," and suppressed grins.

"What is it about those Navy men, Miss Sharp, that makes them at times look such boys?" Jane said.

But there was no gaiety in the remark Jane addressed later to Charles. "I am so happy you are come Charles, for in a week or so you will be able to see me home. I am concerned for Charlotte, though no one else seems sensible of the depth of her grief. She is not a woman to be persuaded to another, so it is I must marry, if I cannot keep us both by my pen."

Captain Blackwell stepped up, begged pardon for the intrusion, and offered his services as an escort at any time Miss Burney cared to name. His father had told him of the death of Charlotte Burney's fiancé, and as they were to leave next day but one, he and Reverend Blackwell could set her down at Ibthorpe without the least inconvenience. Captain Blackwell had a fine sense of filial loyalty, of what was due to a brother or sister. He esteemed Jane for her devotion to her sister; he meant nothing more by the gesture.

But he had, naturally enough, to accept the invitations to dine that Jane's mother and father pressed upon him by way of thanks for bringing Jane home. And soon the Burneys came to expect to see Captain Blackwell squeezed behind their dining table two or three evenings in a week.

Weeks passed and his father had to give Blackwell a hint, in the form of a straightforward statement of the case as the Reverend saw it, that it would be ungentlemanly to hesitate further. Blackwell was prompted to make his declaration, and he was accepted.

From that point forward Blackwell felt himself in shoal water, and when he stood before the parson he had not had such a feeling of dread since *Inconstant* nearly ran ashore the morning after the tremendous gale. But he couldn't order both watches to wear ship no matter how he longed to turn and flee. In the confusion of his heart he snatched Jane's right hand when it came to the exchanging of rings, and clapped the ring upon the wrong finger. The parson went silent, momentarily stunned, but when Blackwell glowered at him he continued on with the marriage service.

Chapter 15

The Dey had quit Ceuta, taking with him his favored wives and children and his Hungarian mistress, and sailed away with the greater part of his fleet of gunboats and cruisers. He left behind the women, offspring, and servants he could very well do without until spring came again.

Before the Dey departed Mercedes scrutinized every word of Severino Martinez's letter. In the first instance she had been elated, overjoyed she was not alone, her old friend was in the city. Tio Severino had never deserted her and he would carry word of her to the Blackwells. After much thought, she requested Omar to pass the word to the Dey that the woman taken from the British ship knew the navigation and might be employed in map making.

The Dey left for Oran just as the first chills of the end of fall were felt. He had given leave for Mercedes to go under guard, and with a suitable female escort, to the house of the mapmaker Jesus Fernando Rebollazo y Mayer. When she walked into his home the cartographer peered at her through his small, weak eyes. No sooner had Jesus Fernando been presented than he was unceremoniously set aside by Severino Martinez, who stepped forward to embrace Mercedes.

"Tio, how shall I ever thank you," she whispered to him, when he held her in his arms.

"Don't be a fool, girl." He put her from him, joy on his care worn face. "But I see you have not been. You are well?"

Mercedes was giving Mr. Martinez her assurances, and presenting Zahraa and Omar, when Francis Blackwell was shown into the room. There was a confusion of greetings, bows, Mr.

Martinez explaining he hadn't arranged Mercedes' visit alone. In a short while Francis maneuvered Mercedes into the mapmaker's study.

No one moved to check the wishes of the British Vice-consul and immediately after closing the door Francis came over and took both Mercedes' hands. They spoke in excited tones, full of delight in one another, each recounting how they'd hoped and schemed for the meeting.

"I cannot look at you enough," Francis said. "You are so beautiful. I wish you joy of your recovery, and I am only sorry for your suffering. I want to offer you the protection of my home, and I hope you might allow me in future to claim a right to give you all of my protection."

Mercedes looked into Francis's face. He was handsome, full of tact, offering what she'd come to Europe through so much peril and difficulty seeking. If it had been for ambition alone she would have accepted without hesitation. Both Captain Blackwell and Francis were men of consequence; the difference being only one of them seemed to know it. During her illness Mercedes had decided how much was owed to duty. She was sorry for the trouble in Francis's expression. It must have grieved him to make his declaration; he and Captain Blackwell were fond of one another.

"I wish I could express the gratitude I feel for your offer," Mercedes said. "For all you've done in seeking me out and negotiating with the Dey's people. But I can't leave my friends at this moment, I couldn't be the cause of unpleasantness to them, after all they've done for me." She gave Francis a searching look. "If you would help me send a letter to James, I would be more obliged to you still."

Chapter 16

Rectory at Deane

"Dearest Brother Frank,

I hope and trust you are well and your business advances apace despite the obdurate heathen. My father will have told you of my marriage, yet I write to you now a bachelor once more. She ran away from me on the wedding night. In truth, she tolerated me for a fortnight then bolted for the reason that usually causes brides to run."

Captain Blackwell thought back on his disgraceful fourteen day marriage as he wrote his brother. He'd lived with Jane amicably for more than a week, their lives much the same as before, making the same visits to both families every day. It was a time during which Jane's primary concern seemed to be how soon she might bring her sister to live with them. Then one evening when she came to kiss him on the cheek before retiring, he'd asked her to come to his bedchamber. Jane had gone a little rigid and reminded him in a thin voice how he'd said he was indifferent to children. And then she'd acquiesced, as they both knew she must.

He'd waited a precious long time for her, lying in bed naked, making comparisons between women he should not have done. Blackwell knew gentlewomen of Jane's class considered the removal of hair from their bodies a courtesan's trick, associated with the catching of discreditable diseases. Yet he could not think of Mercedes' smooth legs and other areas without excitement, and when he considered what was under most English ladies' skirts he knew which struck him as the more feminine.

Jane had finally come in wearing one of those nightdresses covering her from neck to ankles. Blackwell wondered if she knew how the act was done. But when he had propped himself on his elbow beside her and reached out to her, he found she had brought the nightgown up around her waist. He tried to put his hand underneath her gown to caress her breasts but she had one arm clamped over her bosom. And when he rested his hand on her stomach and moved it lower to touch her intimately, she pushed his hand away.

Blackwell was outraged. He could not believe her behavior, a wife was meant to yield to her husband. He heaved himself over her; if she would not let him make her ready, then it was she must suffer. She did not open her legs to receive him so they were pinched beneath his own. He reached down to pull her thighs apart, and looked right into her face.

In the dim light from a single candle he saw Jane turned from him, her face screwed up in anticipation of pain. Then he sheered off, getting up out of bed with a grunt of displeasure and pulling trousers over his painful erection. He'd come round to her side of the bed and picked her up out of it, bedclothes and all, and carried her to her room. Blackwell couldn't deny he'd been angry. He'd tossed her on her bed. "I do not rape children, Jane. Come to me when you are ready to give up girlhood and be a woman." He'd slammed out of her bedchamber and back to his own, but not before hearing her first sobs.

He had felt like sobbing too as he threw himself on his bed. He immediately began to think of Mercedes, if he'd ever left off. For the first time Blackwell appreciated how brave she'd been, coming to him the way she had done aboard *Inconstant*. He might have been the brute he had just nearly been with Jane.

Captain Blackwell sighed and dipped his pen.

"She did not really like anything about me. Neither the way I speak, the way I smell, nor even my steward McMurtry. It is beyond me why she agreed to marriage. That is not quite candid in me, I do know why she consented. It was to have a home of her own and to be away from her parents. I can perfectly comprehend her reasons and they are not unworthy ones. For my part, I thought there was to be the affection usual between man and wife. But she had understood by a careless remark I threw out, to the effect I did not care if ever I had children, I was not interested in that aspect of marriage. In fact it was the great reason she accepted me to begin.

I am sure the fault is mine. I should not have expected love and tenderness, having had it and not known how to value it. You told me in Gib I had found a woman with a certain toleration, and many men are not so blessed even once in their lives. I should have considered myself fortunate and not sought more. I ran into shoal water, brother, and committed the great sin of marrying where I did not love. But it was she pulled us out, going right off in the dogcart back to her mother and to her sister Charlotte, to whom she is entirely devoted. Her brother came to call with the announcement she seeks an annulment. I shall give it her, of course, and wish her happy.

He brought a letter from Jane, a most handsome letter, and it is much as I had supposed. Her eldest brother James is to take over the living at Ibthorpe upon her father's retirement in December, and in consequence, she, her sister and mother and father are to lose their home. She is mortified to be dependent upon her brothers, as she knows she will be when her father is gone, saving marriage of course. Under such pressures she acted against her better judgment — as I did against mine, I may add — and accepted when I offered. I cannot hold against her the fault of yielding to the expectations of family, when I did likewise. My father intimated it was my duty to offer for her and I went straightaway and did it, though I knew I was on a lee shore.

Jane expressed herself very well indeed. She is an honest and an honorable creature, and I cannot say fairer than that. I am heartily sorry for a fling I made at her in the anger of my heart, respecting her maturity. Some things cannot be done out of duty, or should not be done.

Speaking of duty, brother, I have determined to quit Deane and return to London. I shall have one more run at the Admiralty, and if they cannot give me a ship I shall look out for a merchant command, perhaps the East India service. It gives me pain to contemplate removing from the active service list. I shall never then be an Admiral, but I feel I must put to sea. Nothing has prospered with me, and I am better returning to the element I understand than continuing this disastrous run ashore. Who knows but what I might make a capital living, as you once urged me to do, in a less dangerous profession.

I have taken a house for a twelvemonth and I shall write to Jane and offer it her, and subscribe to her a portion of my pay — my stunning half-pay. I hope I have not given you a disgust of me with this wretched account. I will write you how my affairs stand before ever I sail. I remain,

Your affectionate brother,
Jma. Blackwell"

Chapter 17

Captain Blackwell was much put out he could not simply pack his sea chest and leave Deane. The neighborhood was no longer particularly warm to him; it was in fact decidedly cold, Bluebeard ain't in it, was his private conclusion; and the only callers at his house were his father and Jane's brothers. The post was a distraction. He longed for a letter from Francis, or even — the secret desire of his heart — an Admiralty letter in the official oiled canvas cover. It was a dog's life but he felt obliged to hang on in the country, awaiting the declaration of annulment and the transfer of the house to Jane.

The news came to him in a package under cover of the foreign office. Inside, with the compliments of the British diplomatic service, were three letters. One from the Admiralty, one from Francis, and the third in an unknown hand inscribed to 'James Blackwell, Captain R.N.' exactly as his brother addressed his. Captain Blackwell threw McMurtry, who had brought the package on a tray into the breakfast parlor, a glance and jerked his head at the door.

He reached first for his brother's letter, he could put off reading a few moments longer that blessed letter from the Admiralty. He opened Francis's letter and the hand holding it shook, just slightly. He read, "alive and well in Ceuta ... unmolested ... working toward her release. The poor dear woman has been laboring over her letter to you, James, enclosed with mine. She is in some confusion how to address you, I collect."

Captain Blackwell reached with a hand visibly shaking and opened the second letter.

"My Dear Sir,

Your brother will have informed you I am here in Ceuta, but I am sure he will not have recounted how he has done all for me that kindness could wish and discretion allow. I am very much obliged to him. My situation here is not a desperate one. Thanks to the British consul I am allowed out of the palace and I have the company of Mr. Martinez, by whose good offices Francis became aware of my presence in this city. I have also two kind friends at the palace who have cared for me, for I was ill during a very long time after your departure. You must believe I am quite recovered, and when I tell you no one offers me insult. I have been done no violence of any kind. Yet I cannot be happy without freedom and without love. So I hope and trust James, I do hope and trust to see you again. I desire you will remember me as,

Your obedient and humble servant,

Mercedes de Aragon"

Captain Blackwell was on his feet, having flung back his chair in rising. He snatched up the Admiralty letter and read through the brief note requesting him to present himself for an interview with the First Secretary next day.

"McMurtry! Sea chest packed and second best coat. God bless us all! We are going to sea, one way or the other."

When McMurtry came in; Captain Blackwell needn't have called so loud, for he had been standing the other side of the door waiting to hear what news; Captain Blackwell grasped him by the shoulder and shook him. "She is alive, man. The Miss is alive, there in Ceuta with m'brother!"

"Why, wish you joy, sir," McMurtry said. "Good thing I would not let your honor toss her dunnage."

If a toad-like visage could express joy, McMurtry's did as he helped Captain Blackwell into his number two jacket. Captain Blackwell was off to take leave of his father and the Burneys, and to collect the paper releasing Jane and himself. The annulment was suddenly of the first consequence to him.

"I hope she catches it something cruel," McMurtry said, when Captain Blackwell had mounted a hired hack and ridden off to call on his wife.

They were surprised to see him at Ibthorpe. Mrs. J.B., as Jane referred to her eldest brother's wife, tried to put up some resistance, but Captain Blackwell said, "She would be in the small sitting room this time of day, is she not? No, don't bother to show me, ma'am, I know the way."

Captain Blackwell paused outside the sitting room door; he could hear Jane's voice as though reading coming from inside. He knocked and did not wait for permission to enter. When he walked in Charlotte immediately rose and curtsied to him, Jane was slower to do so.

"I beg your pardon for the intrusion, ladies," Captain Blackwell said. "I am lately called to London and I come to take my leave."

Jane took her seat with a look of relief.

"I want a word with Jane, if you please, Miss Charlotte."

Charlotte curtsied again, and with an anxious glance thrown at Jane she left the sitting room.

"I'm summoned to the Admiralty and I hope to be given a ship, so there is not a moment to be lost. Why have you not returned the annulment paper I sent a fortnight ago? I can put it into the proper channels when I am in London."

Jane stared at him over her desk, she'd pulled a cover over the pages before her. "Mightn't a woman change her mind? A husband away on a foreign station is a much more convenient creature than one near at hand."

"You were waiting for me to be called away?" Captain Blackwell said. "Is it a matter of the settlement?"

"Now you insult me, sir," Jane said. Before Captain Blackwell could say a word, she added, "Why so anxious, Captain? Why this hurry of spirit to undo our union?"

Captain Blackwell took a seat at last, without being invited to one, touching his coat pocket next to his heart where he carried

Mercedes' letter. "You write romantic novels, do you not? All about love and marriage."

Jane opened her mouth and then closed it again, her expression something near contemptuous. "Let us say I do."

Captain Blackwell took a fortifying breath. "I shall tell you my romantic story. During my last commission I formed an attachment to a young lady of many good qualities. I treated her ill, left her unprotected, and when I sailed from Africa I thought she was dead. I just received a letter from Francis, along with the summons from the Admiralty, she is alive and being ransomed from the Arabs."

"Romantic, indeed," Jane said.

"I want to go to her, offer her the protection of my name."

"And you think she will have you? After your prior behavior, and the betrayal of marrying another? You don't know women quite so well as you think."

Captain Blackwell's face darkened. "I told you my private affairs so you might be moved to take pity on me, and release me from our marriage."

"I don't know I'm moved to much of anything," Jane said.

Captain Blackwell was out of patience. He rose and went over close to Jane's chair. "I don't know how it is with gentlemen in books, Jane, and I suppose I ain't much of a gentleman, but men are full-blooded creatures. I'm going to bring that young lady I spoke of back with me, provided she will have me, to live here in this neighborhood, as my wife or otherwise. You can either come home with me now and give me the kind of proper leave taking a sailor expects of his wife, or release me at once."

Captain Blackwell glared at her. He was prepared to insist on his rights, he could lay her out there in the sitting room if he chose.

Jane hesitated a moment then she lifted the desk lid and handed him the annulment paper with her signature already affixed. Captain Blackwell took the paper, folded it and put it into another pocket. He felt like a man who'd bared his soul before an ugly tribunal.

At the door Captain Blackwell turned to Jane, who was uncovering her pages and taking up her pen.

"Good day to you, Jane. I shall be completely out of the house this Saturday, when you might take possession any time that is convenient."

Jane called a distracted farewell, her pen scratching across her paper.

Captain Blackwell felt his ungentlemanly behavior extremely, though it had got him what he'd wanted, he felt it more keenly still when he saw Charlotte and Mrs. J.B. huddled together in the passage outside the sitting room.

"She is writing again." Captain Blackwell nodded to Charlotte. "Good day to you, Mrs. Burney, good day Miss Charlotte."

"Good bye, Captain Blackwell, and God speed you on the King's service," Charlotte said.

Jane's sister was a woman with proper feelings, Captain Blackwell reflected as he left the rectory, but Jane was altogether a different kind of woman. He was sorry to have acted the scrub with her, but he should have done that and more to gain his end. He could not imagine Mercedes writing books instead of living life; all Jane knew of life was Hampshire and Kent.

For Captain Blackwell, Mercedes' letter, his brother's, and the Admiralty note were all the reading material he required. He went on horseback to London, saying he would send McMurtry word when he knew what was afoot at the Admiralty. Captain Blackwell meant once he knew from which port they would sail, for he would put to sea, King's ship or no.

The Secretary to the Admiralty, the honorable Mr. Nepean, admitted Captain Blackwell at the appointed hour. After a few preliminary remarks, greetings, his state of health, the healing of Captain Blackwell's last wounds, Mr. Nepean seated his trim figure in a chair and fixed the Captain with his penetrating brown stare. "It appears we've backed the wrong horse, Captain Blackwell, it is as plain as that. The Dey of Oran, Mr. Ali Khosrow ibn Kodio, two months after returning to the capital city from his Ramadan sojourn in Ceuta, had his palace surrounded and his throat cut by his brother, Mr. Ahmet Khosrow ibn Kodio. It is anticipated when the new Dey should come to Ceuta, probably for the new year celebration, those members of his brother's household and those seen as collaborators with the old regime might be in for some unpleasantness. Lord Upton of the Mediterranean station has specifically requested you for this mission, I understand your brother is involved in the case." The Secretary paused and took breath for a moment, with a significant glance at Captain Blackwell. "It is odd how Fleet commanders are always crying out for more frigates, but when the Admiralty sees fit to send him one Admiral Gambier protests he may just as readily detach one of his own. That is neither here nor there, however; if you choose to accept the commission your orders are to proceed to Ceuta where you will embark the British Vice-consul and his suite, any prisoners whose release has been negotiated or can otherwise be effected, and any of His Majesty's subjects requiring safe conduct to a British port."

Captain Blackwell assented with all his heart to carry out the commission. Mr. Nepean proceeded to the matter of ships. "I cannot let you have a heavy frigate or anything in the way of a ship of the line, though I don't deny your seniority on the list and your service record merits at least a fourth rate. No. It may be peacetime but there are rumblings of a suspicious nature in the French quarter, rumors as yet; however, we must look to every ship not engaged in the protection of trade. In short, I cannot offer you anything greater than a fifth or sixth rate. Your old command *Inconstant* lies at Portsmouth ready to fit out should you choose to take her, or if you prefer to wait a fortnight the ex-French 36-gun *L'Aigle* shall be brought out of dry dock at Plymouth."

"I shall take *Inconstant*, if you please, sir," Captain Blackwell said at once.

The First Secretary handed Captain Blackwell his orders and wished him God's speed.

Captain Blackwell flew down to Portsmouth on hired horses. The ostlers took one look at him and led forward their stoutest animals. He sent word to McMurtry to come down bringing all the old Inconstants he could gather with him. For three weeks Captain

Blackwell made himself the most hated man in the Naval dockyard. Clerks would scatter like grapeshot before him, and the community of bureaucrats and seamen was never so gratified as on the day they saw *Inconstant* standing out to sea.

"There goes Captain Blackwell at last," said the master attendant of the dockyard. "Fucking Tartars ain't in it."

Captain Blackwell left Portsmouth a happy commander with near his full complement of men and fell gratefully into naval routine. The weather was kind and *Inconstant* made her way out of the English Channel without being mauled, but they were headed into the Atlantic in winter and into the Mediterranean in the season of the Tramontane. He did all prudent seamanship required in the way of storm canvas, preventer backstays and double lashings on the guns and boats.

Even with the daily round of noon observation, dinner, sail handling, small arms drill and gun exercises, Captain Blackwell had too much time in which to contemplate Mercedes' and Francis's letters. Mercedes' letter was brief and almost lacking in any pledge of tender feeling. Yet it was like her, so like her he didn't need to compare the handwriting to the papers in her sea chest to be certain. Mercedes truly was an honest and honorable woman whose affection Captain Blackwell hoped he had not entirely lost. He thought of Mercedes with a buoyant, even a hopeful heart; she was quite unlike that cunning creature Jane.

But it was difficult to maintain any pitch of certainly in happiness whatever during the days and weeks of sailing, when Jane's words did weigh on him, and Captain Blackwell grew graver as they entered the Straits of Gibraltar. He had discovered too, in Mercedes' letter, she mentioned Francis three times directly. 'I am very much obliged to him.' He wished she would not be. His brother seemed present throughout her brief letter. Captain Blackwell was sorry she should have been ill, but he imagined her now 'quite recovered' practicing the sword with Francis in that garden she so much admired.

Then too after very much reflection, far too much, Captain Blackwell began to think Francis and Mercedes misled him regarding her not being outraged. What else did it mean to be in the harem? It was inconceivable to Captain Blackwell that the Dey, or any man, being in possession of her would not possess her. He had done it, and he could but judge other men by his own lights.

Neither was Captain Blackwell insensible of the fact Jane had been so kind to point out, that Mercedes might believe herself betrayed when she learned of his marriage. He had written that damnable letter to Francis months ago, right after the marriage had fallen apart, and he made no doubt Francis would show it to Mercedes if it came to him. Francis was, before all else, a gentleman: candid, honorable, upright; and Captain Blackwell was afraid he should not come off the better by comparison now Mercedes had his brother's gallantry constantly before her.

Inconstant raised Ceuta just in time, spiritually speaking, for Captain Blackwell had at last the opportunity of relieving his anxieties with action. He summoned Mr. Verson to his cabin.

"We shall not go into port, Mr. Verson, not for the moment. *Inconstant* will stand off and on, and I shall take the blue cutter in this evening at two bells in the first dog watch. Don't say it, Mr. Verson." Captain Blackwell held up his hand when he saw the protest rising to his first lieutenant's lips. "This time I shall take a file of Marines, if it will ease your mind, though they and the boat's crew are to remain on the quay. We will put into the Spanish side of the harbor, make our presence known, and I will visit the Vice-consul's residence for the latest intelligence. I want ten fathoms line and two grappling hooks put into the cutter in a sailcloth bag, and a boat cloak in Miss Mercedes' size." He allowed himself a tiny smile, gave Mr. Verson a copy of his orders from the Admiralty, and shook him by the hand. "I should be back aboard by midnight, Jack."

At the commencement of the voyage Captain Blackwell had invited his officers and the young gentlemen to dine or breakfast with him in the cabin quite frequently, as though to make up for his lack of hospitality during the previous commission. But as the days had worn on, when he constantly kept the deck, even sleeping on the quarterdeck in a hammock chair lest anyone dare to reduce sail, he had distanced himself from *Inconstant*'s people. Yet "Good luck, sir. Good luck," was heard from the seamen and officers on deck when the appointed hour came and Captain Blackwell went down the side into the cutter.

For the second time there was not a man aboard who did not expect to see the skipper return with a woman under his lee. The old Inconstants had told the new the whole romantic tale. The fire ship attack in Ceuta, with Mercedes extinguishing a grenade in her hand, figured prominent in the seamen's accounts. When they arrived at this juncture the phrase 'a rare plucked 'un' was invariably heard.

Captain Blackwell caused a stir amongst the Dons when he bumped against their jetty and jumped out of the cutter followed by ten Marine privates, their Sergeant and seven seamen. He left the lobsters and the boat's crew and found the Spanish harbormaster's office. Walking in he shook the water from his clothes like a good natured Mastiff. Captain Blackwell gave his name, and stated his business as a call upon the British Vice-consul to Oran.

He'd believed coming into the Spanish side of the harbor a fine strategy, but now he had second thoughts. The cold civility, the almost open hostility he met with in the harbormaster's office made him uneasy. He struggled with whether to ask Francis's advice during the entire long climb to his house. In Captain Blackwell's orders was a phrase no commander of a King's ship could like. 'Defer to the opinion and direction of Mr. Francis Blackwell, His Majesty's Consul to Oran, in all matters civil and political.'

He rang the bell at the gate and was admitted by Francis's aged servant, and as Captain Blackwell followed the old man up the interior stairs, leaving the bag with the ten fathom line and grappling hooks below, his heart began to pound. He heard his brother speaking Spanish, but it was not a feminine voice responding, it was a man's low tone, somehow familiar to Captain Blackwell. The servant knocked on the door and announced him by calling through it, and Captain Blackwell walked in to find his brother on his feet and alone in the room.

Francis came forward and embraced him. "James, James, at last! How do you do?"

And Captain Blackwell, clapping his brother on the back, shaking him by the hand and looking into his shining happy face, wanted to believe his worries about Francis and Mercedes were entirely needless.

"Prime, brother, prime. You must tell me how you do, what are the latest developments here, and dear God, Frank, how is she?"

"Mercedes is very well," Francis said. "Though the worry of whether you would receive our letters and when you would come didn't speed her recovery. She nearly died. That is why we had no word of her for months."

"They were waiting to see if they had a live woman to bargain with, the goddamn — "

"Yes, but she is quite well now. More beautiful than ever, in point of fact. Will you allow me to lay the case before you, the whole of the intelligence I have?"

Francis invited Captain Blackwell to a chair, sent for coffee, and explained the Dey's men were believed to be a week's march from Ceuta. They had no confirmation Ahmet Khosrow ibn Kodio was one of the party; it was assumed he was, and as he did not travel with his women and the usual court entourage it was further assumed he didn't come to Ceuta for a holiday.

"Here is a partial list of the people we are to take off, sir," Francis said. "I will bring the completed, finalized list tomorrow morning to *Inconstant* when we can work out the particulars of embarking them. You will see there are no prisoners from *Bulldog*. I very much regret it, outside of the men you recovered, the survivors were put into galleys and come to this port no more."

Captain Blackwell cast his eye over the sheet; there were few British names among many foreign ones. He stood up.

"You were right not to put Mercedes' name upon that list, for I intend she should come aboard as Mrs. Captain Blackwell, not as a refugee. We had better be about it."

"I wish you joy, brother." Francis rose too, wearily pushing himself from his chair. "But had not you better ask the lady first? I don't mean to be impertinent, James, and I beg your pardon for the intrusion, but many months have passed during which she thought herself abandoned. During which she had to fight for her life. No, no, she has not been mistreated. But she has been most seriously ill, and an illness of long duration can change a person. I do not say she has forgot you, far from it. A braver, truer heart I doubt I've ever met with. But she has lived a life of seclusion these last months, a life in company of women, much as in a convent." Francis paused for a moment, staring back at Captain Blackwell's skeptical expression. "I only say that perhaps she has grown accustomed to a gentler life, to a few luxuries, and might need time to adjust to the notion of shipboard life. Why not write her? Or I can bring her to you Friday and you may lay your suit before her."

Captain Blackwell paced, his hands behind his back. Write her? See her Friday? It was Wednesday evening. Sharp replies rose to his lips but he pushed them down. "It will not do, Frank. Suppose your intelligence is out, or those men have a crack general leading them and they cover the distance of a week in two days. I want her out of harm's way, and I will have her out tonight. With whom were you speaking when I walked in? It was Mr. Martinez, was it not? Mr. Martinez, Mr. Martinez there!"

"He is naturally hesitant to — " Francis began, when Mr. Martinez came in.

Captain Blackwell strode up to him and gave him his hand. "Mr. Martinez, give you joy of the recovery of Mercedes de Aragon, I am forever in your debt. I wish to take her out of the palace tonight. You know the place, inside and out, I would warrant. Will you help me? Can you get a message to her?"

"Aye, sir, I will," Mr. Martinez said, without hesitation or a glance in Francis's direction. "The sooner the better, by my wishes. I can pass the word to her to be in the bath on the third floor where you might get in and find her alone. Meet me by the northwest palace gate, sir. You recall the way? I shall go ahead with your bag. Your bag with the boarding hooks, I looked into it downstairs, sir, I beg your pardon. I will show you the course and how the enemy lies."

It was the most Mr. Martinez had ever spoken in his presence and Captain Blackwell experienced a tremendous fellow feeling toward the Spaniard, and silently wrung his hand.

"In one glass, sir, the northwest entrance," Mr. Martinez said in parting. "You might shift your coat, sir."

Francis brought him a selection of jackets and he threw on a greatcoat, for none of the black frock coats would go over his shoulders. "I beg your pardon, Frank, if I have been ill natured. Call on me tomorrow morning just as planned. And you would oblige me greatly by sending my jacket along to the Spanish quay by a discreet man. It is my second best coat and I have particular cause to cherish it."

He met Mr. Martinez in the lee of a group of commercial buildings across from the palace. They stood well back from the street fronting the palace, waiting for the sentries to pass whose routine Mr. Martinez had memorized. "The girl made a plan of the interior of the place, and I of the outside. It is the sixth window from the back of the building on this northwest side, sir, third floor. They are painting or carrying on some repair, and you can get up the first two floors on that scaffolding. Then swing the hook for the last floor, light along the roof and drop down on her balcony. She will be there, sir, we have a reliable man on the inside. The way out shall be much harder, with her on your back."

"As to that, we shall manage tolerably," Captain Blackwell said. "I have forty minutes, after the sentries pass?"

"Aye, sir."

"Listen now, Mr. Martinez, I mean to offer Miss Mercedes marriage. I wish I had done so all those months ago."

"No doubt the girl will be pleased, sir," Mr. Martinez said. "But I cannot think why you tell it to me before her."

"Why, to ask your permission as it were." Captain Blackwell hoped the older man didn't see him blush. "You are like a father to her. Indeed, I half suspicion you are, for no father could be more devoted to her well being."

"No, sir." Mr. Martinez shook his head. "I told you the case on our first meeting. Mercedes is no relation of mine, though I love her as a daughter. Her mother was dear to me and I thank you for the compliment. As to my blessing it hardly matters, whether she will marry you or no is the girl's affair. I will tell you the right to bestow a father's blessing belongs to an Englishman, who don't deserve the honor. Here are the janissaries, sir, you go into action."

Chapter 18

In some part of his mind, a remote part far below the surface, Captain Blackwell thought it was overly convenient, that scaffolding next the palace, making the ascent of the first two floors nearly as simple as walking up stairs. But he was far too taken up with the effort of stealth and concealment of his fourteen stone to consider of it deeply while climbing with the sailcloth bag on his back.

On the balcony of the second floor, where the lights were out and the shutters closed in this part of the palace, he swung one of the grappling hooks with half the line attached to the castellated roof of the third floor. It did not gain purchase and came flying back at him. Captain Blackwell brought the grapple to him before it rang against the stone façade in its trajectory. He cast again; the hook caught and he tested his weight against the line. Finding it fast he hauled himself up the corner of the building, hand over hand, with his boots thudding against the wall.

He heaved himself over the iron pikes set into the edges of the roof and landed with a thump, just as when boarding the enemy. Captain Blackwell found his grappling hook and brought up the line. He peered over the edge of the roof, bent double so he should not be seen from below, and crept along counting the balconies below him. His heart had been thundering in his chest long since wondering how Mercedes would look, and how she would receive him.

His hands shaking, Captain Blackwell had to command himself to be steady and methodical in making the grappling hook fast. There would be no subterfuge possible to conceal him as he dropped onto her balcony. He would be exposed to the view of the lower balconies of the palace and to the gardens, while he went in and when he brought her out. It was critical there be no failure because his equipment was improperly secured. When he had the hook fast and the coiled line in his hand he crouched near the edge of the roof and studied the balcony below.

A gentle light glowed out from the room, as of a single brace of candles. Captain Blackwell memorized the layout of the balcony and its railing, then he called in a voice meant to carry just below. "On deck there, douse the light."

The lights winked out and Captain Blackwell threw his line to the balcony and lowered away, his heart beating harder now he had confirmation it was his woman in the room. He moved swiftly through the doors she'd opened and saw a form in the shadows. She stood on the other side of an enormous sunken marble bath, quite big enough for two persons or more. Captain Blackwell felt the blood suffuse his face at the idea. She curtsied to him and he was across the distance separating them, and had her enveloped in his arms.

He embraced her hard, crushing her against him, reassuring himself of her substance. Mercedes had clasped her hands to her breast as he rushed upon her, in that characteristic gesture. Captain Blackwell caught her hand lying between his breast and hers, felt the scarred flesh of her palm with his thumb and lifting it to his lips he put a tender kiss on the healed wound. He carried her hand up to his neck and looked into her face. Captain Blackwell couldn't see her expression but he saw she lifted her face to his, he felt her familiar warmth pressed against him and he was surrounded by her clean, lovely scent.

It occurred to him as he bent to kiss her that he, by contrast, had just had a sweaty, anxious climb. She started away from him, her head turned to the corridor outside. Grasping his sleeve Mercedes pulled him toward the balcony. When they were outside and she had softly, firmly shut the door, she examined the rope hanging down from the roof at the corner of the balcony.

"You shall have to get upon my back." He swung the great coat about her shoulders and turning his back on her, he knelt down.

"No sir, I can manage this if you will hold the rope." Mercedes sprang on to the balcony rail, grasped the rope and planted one foot on the building's side.

Captain Blackwell rose with an expression of mixed disappointment and vexation. He had no choice but to hold the rope if he wanted to be away immediately, and he watched her walk up the façade and tumble over the jagged edge. He followed her quickly, coiled the line, took her by the arm and led her to the first grapnel, where he cast the line down to the second floor. Mercedes peered over the edge, keeping low after Captain Blackwell's example.

She shook her head. "Either you must go directly in front of me, or this time on your back, Captain."

"You know which I shall prefer, ma'am." He knelt again in front of her. "Put up the hood, if you please. We shall hope to look like a great, humpbacked ogre from a distance."

They stopped a moment on the second floor balcony while Captain Blackwell lowered her to her feet with a grunt, both their faces flushed for the odd, intimate, primitive maneuver they had just performed. She followed him down the scaffolding with Captain Blackwell placing her feet as he would have done shipboard. No sooner had Mercedes' slippers met the earth than they heard shouts in Arabic. The two janissaries were back far before their time, and Captain Blackwell cursed himself for using the scaffolding.

He drew his sword with a sibilant whoosh. "Stay behind me," he said to Mercedes. "And if you get a chance run for those buildings. Your uncle is there." Captain Blackwell was at the same time hurrying her toward those buildings. They heard feet pounding toward them and saw the glint of light reflected from curved blades.

There was a great bellowing shout in the night. "Fools! May dogs dig up your fathers' graves. That is the *rais* who is meant to take the British *hanim* from the palace."

The pursuing janissaries ran afoul of one another, and Captain Blackwell and Mercedes crossed the road fronting the northwest side of the palace, and ran into the shadows of the shops beyond.

Mr. Martinez stepped from between buildings when they'd come a short way up the street, and he and Mercedes embraced. He put a southwester on her head, and with the great coat still round her shoulders her feminine costume was not ill concealed. Captain Blackwell wished he'd traded his shirt for a seaman's blue tunic; he felt he fairly shone out in his white shirt and waistcoat. But there was no help for it, and with Mercedes leaning on Mr. Martinez's arm they made their way to the Spanish harbor. She did not speak except to ask him, when they were in the neighborhood of his brother's house, "We do not go to Francis?"

"We go to *Inconstant*," he said.

Captain Blackwell caught a conscious look exchanged between Mr. Martinez and Mercedes at his reply. They pressed on, stopping before going into the dockyard where it would be imprudent for Mr. Martinez to enter. His skills as a carpenter and a seaman were too desirable for any navy to resist, and he was cautious of impressment by Spanish, Arabs or English. They were saying goodbye, Mr. Martinez and Mercedes, in low, rapid Spanish, and Captain Blackwell moved away and stood with his hands behind his back waiting for her.

He was anxious for his men down on the jetty, idle this long while, and for what the Dons might have got up to in the meantime. But in a short while Mercedes came and took his arm. He rushed her through the naval yard, nodding with satisfaction to the few officers and seamen about at the late hour as though he'd caught a deserter, and at last he had her at the cutter. The Marines stamped and saluted, someone handed him his jacket. He put the uniform coat on and felt like a complete man once more as he handed her into the boat.

"Welcome aboard, Miss," Narhilla said in an undertone. He took her elbow while she found her seat in the stern. Louder to his captain, Narhilla said, "All present and sober, sir."

"Give way!"

Two dozen hearty pulls and the men set the cutter's sail, Narhilla steering for *Inconstant*. Captain Blackwell wanted to put his arm round Mercedes and bring her against his side. He wished she would rest her head on his shoulder as she'd done when they left Gibraltar. But when he cast a sideways glance at her, she was pressed against the gunwale gazing at the receding shore as though she longed for something left behind.

The motion of the blue cutter was what the seamen termed lively; waves were shipping over the bow and the Marines were bailing. They dashed into *Inconstant*'s lee, the sail came down and Narhilla bumped the craft against the frigate's side.

"Mr. Verson!" Captain Blackwell hailed.

"Sir!"

"I'm sending the lady up first, no ceremony if you please."

"Aye, aye, sir!"

"You are to go up first, ma'am," Captain Blackwell said to Mercedes.

"Yes, sir." She threw off the greatcoat, edged to her feet, and waiting for the cutter to heave up on the swell, she grasped the manropes.

Kind hands were extended to bring her in. "Welcome aboard, Miss. Welcome aboard," the seamen whispered to her from all sides before Captain Blackwell came up. Once on deck Captain Blackwell returned the salutes of the quarterdeck, and ordered, "Eyes out ship!"

Until that moment he'd given Mercedes no indication he thought her indecently dressed. She wore the light pantaloons and close wrapped top that formed the palace ladies' at home attire. Captain Blackwell herded her down the companion ladder before him and into the great cabin.

"Here are your things, ma'am, just as you left them," Captain Blackwell said, opening the door to her sleeping cabin for her.

Mercedes would not meet his eye and a reserve and awkwardness fell upon them.

"McMurtry laundered two of your frocks. They hang on the pegs there, so you need not wear that heathen rig."

"How kind." Mercedes glanced up at him. "But I should like to retire, if you please, Captain."

He instantly became the good host; of course she was fatigued and must rest directly; he bowed to her, wished her good night, and went out the cabin door. Captain Blackwell paused outside, with his hand on the latch and his sentry standing at stiff attention, and listened to Mercedes' hurried step and the sound of her vomiting in the quarter gallery.

His officers gave a decided start when he sprang up on deck. They were clustered together round the skylight, no doubt gossiping about the woman just come on board and listening for what conversation might drift up between their captain and the fair one. The officers scattered at his appearance, and Captain Blackwell began a distracted pacing.

He absolutely longed for the perfect unconstraint of their earlier relationship, when he had done no more than look at her and she'd asked, "You are ready for bed?" But he began to feel, as he paced and reflected, that he had been too hasty by half. He hadn't asked her if she was ready, if she was willing to leave the palace with him. He had meant to do so, but in the excitement of action he'd neglected to make his orders to her clear.

Captain Blackwell fancied he was not unrealistic. He did not suppose they could pick up where they left off; no, he was a gentleman, he would wait. Her indisposition ... And then a thought struck Captain Blackwell that froze him on the deck, and the grunt of dismay escaping him startled Mr. Wilson, the young master's mate and officer of the watch. Suppose she was carrying another man's child? His brother's voice came to him, "Write to her ... I can bring her to you Friday." Had Francis tried, in his diplomatic, subtle fashion to allow Mercedes to make the news easier for him to bear, by being conveyed through a letter?

If it were the case he had of course, in his crude sailor's way, not caught the hint, and had insisted on bringing her out of the palace: like a bull at the charge. Looking back on the evening's adventure Captain Blackwell found he'd handled her roughly, and thrown her into circumstances that might have proved dangerous to a delicate condition. She'd seemed willing to come with him but perhaps it was to shield him; he recollected the janissaries crying off. Captain Blackwell paced, and he thought of her lying ill below.

He'd said to her once, after the retaking of *Bulldog*, a man couldn't be expected to accept a woman and the child forced on her by some vile brute. Captain Blackwell groaned aloud. It was a long, long while before he quit the deck and went into his cabin, where he threw himself, miserable, upon his cot.

Chapter 19

Mercedes did not stir when Captain Blackwell went out of the cabin and on deck for the changing of the watch, but the smell of coffee and the sound of his heavy tread on the planks over her head did waken her. The night before she'd been done up with fatigue. The unaccustomed exertion, the stress of meeting Captain Blackwell, the fear of capture, and then the shout in Arabic that told her it was all for naught. Captain Blackwell might not have understood those words, but Mercedes did. Her release had been effected or perhaps conceded to the British, and Captain Blackwell might have called for her at the palace gate. It made what she'd suffered in reaching *Inconstant*, slammed about in the boat, believing every moment she would be sick into Captain Blackwell's lap, powerfully hard to bear. The nausea had eased when she'd come aboard the larger vessel, but rushed upon her once more in front of Captain Blackwell in the great cabin.

She hoped he did not think she'd become some delicate, pampered harem wench. She struggled out of her cot, most unwilling to give the appearance of the courtesan by sleeping into the morning, and ran out and used the head, then poured water from the kid outside her door into her basin and shut herself in to do her toilette.

She was ready, dressed, her hair up, and exceedingly grateful the smell of breakfast didn't bring nausea with it. The seasickness had passed and been mercifully short. She heard Captain Blackwell's unmistakable pounding of the companion ladder, speaking to someone as he came down.

His voice lowered as he walked into the great cabin. "Hark ye, Frank, there are but three British names on this list, and one of them your own. I'll not carry those goddamn scrubs as kept her from me these many months, wanting to trade her for gold. Causing her to suffer who knows what. Do you hear me? You may be pleased to have dealings with them, I ain't."

"Let's go over this list; allow me to explain," Francis said. "And another thing, sir, Mercedes has been alongside a most noble, admirable woman these months. She has not been in vulgar company. No, far from it!"

"Should you like to give an explanation, indeed? Then tell me why she — "

Mercedes walked out of her sleeping cabin and Captain Blackwell's angry flow was silenced.

"Mercedes, my dear. How do you do?" Francis said.

Mercedes gave Francis both her hands while Captain Blackwell looked on, scowling.

"Good morning, Captain. May I see those?" she said.

He gave the sheets of paper into her outstretched hand. A knock came at the door, and McMurtry and his mate brought in the breakfast dishes. Mercedes considered Captain Blackwell's weary eyes, the lines of care on his face, his generally savage aspect. She knew he would be more human once he'd eaten, and she came to stand beside him and put her hand on his arm as an indication he might lead her in to breakfast.

They sat down and she put the lists with the evacuees' names beside her plate. The three of them ate in an uneasy silence, defying even Francis's diplomatic gifts. But Mercedes hadn't been mistaken in concluding the food and drink would soften him. In a short while Captain Blackwell was pressing dishes on her, but he left off when a wave of discomfort passed over her features.

"With your leave, sir, I have taken all I wish. If you gentlemen will permit me." Mercedes rose, with Captain Blackwell and Francis standing up for her.

She took up the papers and moved away to the captain's desk, pulling toward herself sheets of unmarked parchment, the inkstand and pen.

Captain Blackwell wore a haggard look, he'd sleep but little, and Mercedes was pallid, her head bent over the lists while she wrote on another sheet. In appearance they were the opposite of reunited lovers.

She came back to the table where he'd finished the meal and was determinedly drinking his coffee.

"Here, sir, I sorted the lists," she said. "These are the women, and this list is children. This third on the reverse are the men. You will see there are but three names besides Francis and the other Englishmen. They are most likely older gentlemen, for the Dey's ministers, the active men, would disdain to run. At least to run to the British."

"I see it is quite easy to mistake these foreign names. I thought this lot were men that you've put down as women, ma'am. This Abdul Aziz Al Hossein among the children must be the son of the minister. The cunning chap you had dealings with, eh Frank? I knew I remarked the name and that is what I objected to, carrying such as he. Well, this does change the nature of the case. Don't look so pleased, brother. You will not be when you are swinging in a hammock two deep in the gunroom."

"Speaking of that, sir," Mercedes said. "As you must necessarily give up this cabin to the ladies, may I beg you for a closet, a sleeping space?"

Captain Blackwell stared at her. "You do not stay with the ladies?"

"I have no status among the court women. I must go last up the side if you understand, Captain. And they would not welcome my presence sharing this cabin. I was neither a wife nor a ... I was a supernumerary, sir, no status at all."

Captain Blackwell jumped to his feet and paced the cabin. He wanted to rail, to cry foul against the women that would treat his lady so, and against their country and their tribe for separating her from him. But it relieved his mind to hear her say she was neither wife nor concubine in the Dey's court.

He controlled himself, giving orders she was to have the master's cabin which he had been planning for his own use. Mr. Hammerly had been the single casualty of the voyage from England; he'd died of an apoplexy on the quarterdeck right after the making of noon. Captain Blackwell decided he could sling a hammock or sleep in an elbow chair on deck until they raised Gibraltar.

Francis and Mercedes came on deck at Captain Blackwell's invitation to watch the ship brought into the Port of Ceuta. His spirits were so far recovered that he asked Francis whether the Arab or the Spanish side of the harbor was to be preferred.

All the good will in the world was required to endure the tedium of the next few days as the ladies came aboard in their burqas, throwing them off once in the great cabin and turning it into something resembling an aviary of the tropics in their bright colored dress. Then the children, from babes in arms to youngsters of eight and nine, like Zahraa's children, came aboard; the unhappy, defeated, fault-finding older gentlemen Mercedes had predicted would be in the Oranian contingent.

They came aboard *Inconstant* on a gangway laid down on the Dey's wharf, a strangely deserted place where no bustle of loading and unloading went forward. The Dey's few cruisers and gunboats remaining in the harbor swung to their anchors with a ghost ship, insubstantial air.

Captain Blackwell was alternately contemplating the Dey's vessels with a predatory gaze on Friday, and watching as the last people, possessions, stores and servants came aboard. He realized why Francis had offered to bring Mercedes to him today. She'd said herself she had no status, and yesterday had been the day of embarkation of the important guests. That was when Francis brought to him the admirable woman he'd been pleased to speak of, and her two children. Captain Blackwell was aware Zahraa Albuyeh had done her utmost to do the civil with him in English, as Mercedes and Francis stood by with proud grins on their faces.

The introduction and what he observed after of his brother's behavior to Zahraa quelled somewhat Captain Blackwell's apprehension, his shameful speculation of a fondness between Mercedes and Francis. At the moment Francis was too busy to pay court to any woman as he brought the people on in order of precedence, settled them to their accommodations, and listened to their complaints and demands.

Captain Blackwell was heartily glad it was not his business to deal with them. He could leave that to his brother and his first lieutenant. The unfortunate Mr. Verson, aside from having to share his berth with young Jack and Francis Blackwell, was run off his legs with the accommodation of so many guests. Mr. Verson had also to maintain discipline in the midst of what Captain Blackwell named to himself a fucking Banbury fair.

Down in the waist Mr. Verson cried out, "Put that woman down this moment, McMurtry! And bear a hand with these crates."

McMurtry had been assigned the task of stowing the refugees' possessions and they all came to consult with him, the men and women and the young and old. He was in his glory, and in spite of his disagreeable visage he seemed to be proving his claim of being good with the ladies. Certainly today with what the foremast jacks viewed as the serving wenches coming aboard, McMurtry's gallantry was surpassing fine. In the thick of the commotion Mercedes walked about holding a baby in her arms, having taken charge of the little fellow so his nurse might see to her belongings.

"She looks very well with a babe in her arms, does she not, sir?" Doctor VanArsdel asked, coming upon Captain Blackwell, who stood on the larboard gangway glaring down into the waist.

Captain Blackwell grunted what might have been assent, or something otherwise.

"Tell me, Doctor," Captain Blackwell said. "What are the first indications of a woman being in the increasing way?"

Doctor VanArsdel responded with perfect candor. "The symptoms are different for every woman, as unique as they are themselves, the dear creatures. Yet there are general, recognized indications, fatigue, nausea — some women are prone to vomits throughout the term and during the period of confinement — a changeable mood, tenderness in the breasts and other feminine areas of the body. And the most obvious, the cessation of the monthly cycle."

"Ah," Captain Blackwell said. He raised his voice. "Mr. Verson, let us wrap up our business here. I want to make this evening's tide. Oh, and Mr. Verson, a word when you've a moment." Captain Blackwell bowed to the doctor and went up to the quarterdeck to meet his first lieutenant.

They did indeed glide out on the tide, when Captain Blackwell took a party of men across to the Dey's gunboats and cruisers and spiked the vessels' guns. He had consulted with Francis before acting, proposing to burn the ships to the waterline. Francis was of the opinion the ships should be left unmolested as being the property of Britain's former ally, or at least courted ally, and the property of the present Dey. They had compromised on the destroying of the guns.

Inconstant quit the Port of Ceuta leaving behind her another blaze — one of the gunboats had caught fire — just as on the previous occasion. She collected her boats, their crews, and her captain at the entrance to the harbor as they returned from their work of destruction. The frigate stood out and hove to for the night in the offing at Francis's request. He wished to make sure any persons effected by this last act of the British had a chance to reach *Inconstant* in the morning.

Breakfast was finished next day and *Inconstant* was under easy sail a league out of Ceuta when the lookout at the masthead hailed the deck. "On deck, there. Sir! Sail on a course to cross our stern, bearing north."

The deck was crowded with people staring away over *Inconstant*'s wake at the distant sail. Alongside the watch on deck there were the passengers, those who were not retching and miserable from seasickness in their berths, and a pack of children already running together like hounds and led by young Goodman Jack. Jack, like McMurtry, was exalted among the passengers, for though he might be years younger than the oldest boy, he could lord it over them with his knowledge of the ship and seagoing affairs.

Captain Blackwell focused the spyglass that the midshipman of the watch, Mr. Bowles, handed to him and saw only a fishing scow. Yet the little craft was cracking on for all she was worth. As he gazed the forms of two men became distinct; one in the stern who appeared to both steer and sail, and a black man in the bows.

"Back main sail!" Captain Blackwell bawled out. He had seen, through his glass, what looked like the forms of men lying prone in the boat.

Inconstant lay to and the master of the fishing scow brought his boat round the frigate's lee within the next half glass and stood off from her side.

"Boat ahoy! What boat is that?"

"*Bulldog*!" was the shouted answer. "I have Captain Alexander aboard."

"Come along side at once," Captain Blackwell ordered. "Rig man ropes, ready stretchers. Side boys. Pass the word for the Doctor, Mr. Bowles!"

The whole assemblage watched as the scow was brought smartly up to *Inconstant*, made fast, and the powerful black man in the bow received a stretcher. He loaded the first man onto it without assistance, and positioned him so the waiting seamen could bring him aboard. Three skeletal, sun blistered and parched men were hoisted up from the fishing scow and laid on *Inconstant*'s deck. Captain Blackwell went on one knee beside the stretchers, looking into the gaunt, bearded faces, and at the ragged shreds of clothing. He grasped the hand of one of the men. "Captain Alexander. Edward, Ned old chap, give you joy of your escape! Hang on, brother, we shall attend to you and yours directly."

Captain Blackwell rose and Doctor VanArsdel took his place.

"Boat's crew, permission to board," Captain Blackwell said. "McMurtry, a tot of rum for those men and see what can be found from the galley."

At a nod from Doctor VanArsdel many willing hands stepped forward and lifted the stretchers to bear the three men below to the sick berth.

Captain Blackwell followed behind. "The deck is yours, Mr. Bowles."

When Captain Blackwell's head sunk below the main hatch a sort of pandemonium broke out on deck. Banbury fair, indeed. To the foremast jack there is nothing more stirring than shipwreck and survival. In the case of Captain Alexander, whose actual rank was lieutenant, and his Bulldogs the men speculated stridently on the sequence of events as might have been. Capture, condemned to the galley, shipwreck, escape! The brief glimpses they'd caught of the prostrate forms had shown them men as near to death as a human might be and still breathe; they were amazed.

The few passengers on deck talked over the spectacle just paraded before them, and wished the appearance of the skeletal beings might not incommode them further. In the first amazement after the recovery of the mariners only the children paid any heed to the boat with the two men that had brought them. Miriam and the other little girls leaned over the larboard rail, waving their handkerchiefs at Omar in the boat's bow. Mercedes smiled at the way Omar wiggled his fingers at the girls in reply. She went over the side, with ship's biscuit and a wine bottle filled with three quarter grog in a basket, and dropped into the boat.

"You do not come aboard, Omar?" she asked in the simple Arabic she had learned in her months of captivity. At the same time she extended her hand to Severino Martinez, and would have kissed his cheek but for a wish not to disturb the boat.

"How can you ask it, Miss? Severino tells me those English would put me to another lifetime of slavery. I came out of mercy, out of respect for you." Omar related how he'd come upon the British, captives of the Berber tribesmen, when he'd been three days walking in the Sahara desert. He'd purchased them for two good blankets and carried them to Mr. Martinez.

"I'm going to fend off, girl, before one of the officers smokes me," Mr. Martinez said.

Mercedes expressed her gratitude to Omar on behalf of the British officers, and she pressed into his hand a little pouch with a few gemstones. It had been a sacrifice for Omar to turn back after setting out from Ceuta finally in possession of his freedom and walking cross the continent to his home. Omar did not trust to ships. Mr. Martinez would have willingly landed him anywhere on the African coast, but he was determined having been brought from his tribe over land he must find his way back the same route. Omar sat in the boat's bow uncomfortable, gray beneath his black skin tone, as Mr. Martinez backed and filled his single sail while speaking to Mercedes.

"Shall you come to Gibraltar, Tio?" she said.

"Certainly I will, girl, I would not miss it," Mr. Martinez said. "Am I to wish you happy then?"

"Boat ahoy!" Mr. Bowles called as the scow drifted to leeward. "Return at once! Pass the word for the Captain. The Miss is leaving the ship, the Miss has left the ship."

Captain Blackwell came pounding onto the deck, his eyes red-rimmed, and he rushed to the larboard rail. He roared out the same order as Mr. Bowles, and then in a fury of impatience stripped off his jacket, waistcoat, shirt, breeches and boots and dove over the side from the rail. Several strokes and Mr. Martinez's maneuvering of the scow to intercept him brought him to the boat's side. Omar grasped his upraised arm and hauled him in over the gunwale.

"Goddamn, hell and death, woman! If you want to leave the ship, you need only say so. You need not go off with these ..." Captain Blackwell broke off as the master tipped back his hat to reveal his face. "I beg your pardon, sir."

Mercedes interrupted to present Omar to Captain Blackwell as the preserver of Captain Alexander and his companions. On board *Inconstant* they watched a naked, dripping Captain Blackwell turn and make his bow to the black man and shake him by the hand.

"Do you stay with me, Miss?" Captain Blackwell asked, before turning round again to face Mr. Martinez.

"I do," Mercedes said.

"If you will be so kind as to touch her to *Inconstant* we will part company, sir," Captain Blackwell said to Mr. Martinez. "I must get those men to Gibraltar, there's not a moment to lose."

"A thousand thanks and blessings on you," Mercedes called, in parting from Omar. "In Gibraltar then, Tio?"

"Aye, girl, go."

Captain Blackwell pushed her up the side before him. They gained the deck amid the gaping faces of the passengers, and the shamefaced looks of his officers. Mercedes glanced about with her eyes lowered, working to suppress a smile.

Miriam Albuyeh was staring in horror at Captain Blackwell. Mercedes' first sight of the naked male form jumped into her giddy mind. It was when she was ten years old and passed by her mother's door just as her mother was coming out, talking over her shoulder to Severino Martinez, who had taken off his trousers in her room.

Captain Blackwell turned to Mercedes and grasped her by the elbow. "You are never to quit this ship without you tell me. Do you hear me now? No one is permitted to quit the ship without my permission." He hauled her down the companion ladder.

"Will he?" Farrokh Albuyeh raised his arm in a motion to strike with the back of his hand. He looked an inquiry at Jack Verson.

"I daresay he will seize her to the cannon in his cabin and give her a good half dozen," Jack said.

Captain Blackwell remembered when his hand was on the latch of the great cabin door there were half a dozen ladies in there, in various states of indisposition. He turned to Mercedes; she was on the level of his chest gazing at the scar running down from his right breast, the scar she'd once traced with her fingers. She raised her eyes to his, and at the same time her hand, as though she would lay it on his bare chest. Captain Blackwell saw the amusement on her face and he was on the point of bringing her up for her levity — how could she behave so with poor

Alexander lying below, and after giving him such a start — but he was arrested by the pure, shining love in her eyes. He almost turned round to see at whom she gazed but he stopped himself in time, there was only his sentry behind him.

"Here are your honor's clothes, sir," McMurtry called out, coming aft along the gun deck.

Mercedes slipped inside the cabin as Captain Blackwell took his clothes and turned away, so his men would not see their commander, like any ordinary man, could be aroused by the mere presence of a woman.

The taking off in Gibraltar of Captain Alexander, his servant, and a midshipman who had survived their ordeal in Africa, and the passengers and their belongings, had the air of a battle. More precisely it had the melancholy air of a battle's aftermath. Three basket stretchers were brought onto *Inconstant*'s deck and lowered into the barge bearing the unfortunate men to the hospital. Doctor VanArsdel dropped in last, to attend his patients and hand them over to the doctors ashore. The passengers departed in small groups, in reverse order this time, as the servants went ahead of their masters to make ready what lodgings the British had secured.

Francis had been up since the middle of the morning watch when he went ashore to arrange those accommodations and a host of other details relating to the evacuees' reception. He'd returned to *Inconstant* to escort Zahraa Albuyeh and her children to their lodgings. He asked to speak to the captain before their departure, and Francis was invited to the quarterdeck. Captain Blackwell and Francis were looking down on the crowded scene, after Francis related his arrangements ashore. Zahraa was before them on the larboard gangway, supported by Mercedes on one side and by her son on the other.

"She is very much better, I thank you," Francis said, in response to Captain Blackwell's inquiry after Zahraa's health. "With the prospect of reaching dry land you see she fairly glows. I have requested a leave of absence, so that I can accompany them back to Iran, where I might ask her father for her hand."

"I wish you happy, brother, of the entire enterprise with all my heart," Captain Blackwell said. "I have no doubt you shall carry it off." They fell silent, the question of his own marriage hanging unspoken between them. "Tell me, Frank, how do you come to accept another man's children so readily?"

"Why James, I'm sure it's charming to procreate. I know it is. But children are the same the world over whether one's own or another's. They want the same thing. Love, acceptance, security, and they do so wish to please. We must be willing to endure their little freaks and caprices, but as to blood relation ... consider dear Mercedes and Mr. Martinez. Has he less claim than a father to her duty and devotion? If it had pleased our father to marry again I should have loved a step-mother. I'm ashamed to say I don't remember our mother's face. Do you?"

"I do not. Though I remember ... I remember she used to call me 'darling James'." Captain Blackwell gave his brother a little sideways smile and cleared his throat. "Your lady is going into the boat."

A bosun's chair borrowed from a neighboring third rate had been employed throughout the day. In answer to Zahraa's question whether she and Miriam might travel together in it, one of the seamen replied, with no disrespect whatever intended, "Why, bless you, Miss, heaving you and the little Miss will be as easy as kiss my hand."

"Thank you again for my trousseau," Mercedes said, kissing her friend. Zahraa had organized the donation of linens, soap, scent, and underclothing from the ladies in the cabin to give to Mercedes, who had come away from the palace with nothing but the clothes she stood up in.

"Shall you come ashore?" Zahraa said.

"I believe so, but I cannot say when. Here are Francis and Captain Blackwell."

Captain Blackwell said all that was proper in parting from the exotic woman who might be his sister in future. Francis clasped Mercedes' hands and kissed her cheek and went over the side, followed by Farrokh Albuyeh, who disdained the bosun's chair.

"Give my regards to Gib, mate," cried young Jack Verson, leaning over the taffrail and waving energetically.

"You will dine with me?" Captain Blackwell asked Mercedes. She stood at his side waving at the departing boat with only slightly less energy than young Jack.

Mercedes smiled, and what was rare for her she blushed. "I shall be delighted, sir, thank you."

"If you please, sir, *Royal George* has made our number. The signal is 'Captain repair aboard flag,' sir," piped the duty midshipman.

"Mr. Verson, call away my gig," Captain Blackwell said.

Chapter 20

Mercedes opened the great cabin at McMurtry's insistence the minute the last lady had deserted it for the deck to wait her turn in the boats. McMurtry brought in his mate and they scrubbed, waxed, and polished as though a Mongol horde had occupied the captain's cabin for the last three days rather than six court ladies and their offspring. But when Mercedes walked into the cabin, into the smell of lye soap and beeswax, with the furniture arranged exactly as before, and her own and the captain's sleeping quarters turned out and cleaned, she was grateful for the thoroughness of the seamen.

Captain Blackwell would return soon and they would eat a meal prepared by the captain's cook. Perhaps a not very appetizing meal to Mercedes' taste, but one in the preparation of which she had taken no part. The crew left her few domestic cares. She could sew and do her own wash, which McMurtry might've done if Mercedes were not shy of him handling her small clothes.

She was seated half turned on the stern lockers so out the sweep of windows she could see *Royal George* towering amid the crowd of ships. Yet Mercedes tried to keep her gaze from lingering on the noble vessel where Captain Blackwell was having an interview with Admiral Gambier.

Her mother's letter, once a precious object, neglected in her sea chest this long while weighed on Mercedes' mind. She felt conscious of having been undutiful. Her fingers stilled many times over the stocking she was knitting for Captain Alexander, who had come out of Africa much as she had, with nothing. She had been fortunate in the experience by comparison, and Mercedes compelled herself to her task. She would have plenty of warning of Captain Blackwell's approach. But the drum beat for the officer's dinner, and McMurtry came in and set the table for one.

He brought in her dinner, and took it away again. "Why, you didn't touch your beef, Miss, your good salt horse."

"I did, indeed," Mercedes said. It was Tuesday, and she eyed the lumpish gray brown meat with resentment. She was used to being grateful for the food provided her, but she couldn't give thanks for beef that had been to the West Indies and back in a cask before appearing on her plate.

"You should have to do better than that, Miss, were the Captain here," McMurtry said.

Captain Blackwell returned at five bells in the afternoon watch. "Pull like heroes," Mercedes whispered, looking out the stern windows at his approaching boat. She could not recall from which of the British mariners she'd heard the phrase. Mercedes now had another language, the British seamen's cant.

At Captain Blackwell's urging his boat's crew pulled hard back to *Inconstant* and he came aboard to the usual shrilling of the bosun's pipe, saluted the quarterdeck and ran below to his cabin.

"Mercy, sweetheart, forgive me," he cried, striding toward her. "Captain Hardy asked me to dine. One does not refuse the Captain of the Fleet, lay aside he was uncommon civil to me the last time I was here. I very much regret leaving you alone."

"I do not mind it, James."

It was the first time they had used Christian names since parting months before. Mercedes extended her hand to Captain Blackwell and he took it and sat beside her on the lockers.

"But I do, I mind excessively, and the deuce of it is the Admiral has invited me for supper, and that is more an order, you know, so I must leave again. Mr. Verson will be down in half a glass to go over the watch bills and arrange the men's liberty, and I must call at the hospital and see how Captain Alexander does."

"Oh yes, certainly. Admiral Gambier was not aboard *Royal George*?"

Captain Blackwell studied her. “He was not. He is just appointed Governor of Newfoundland, and was ashore attending to new duties. And old, no doubt, he returns to the flagship this evening and gives a supper for his captains. I’m asked out of courtesy since I happen to be on the station. He cast me out of his squadron back in the Spring.”

“Did he? How very ill-natured.”

Captain Blackwell gave her hand a squeeze. He rose and shouted for McMurtry. When his steward came in Captain Blackwell handed him his uniform jacket and waistcoat.

“Bring tea and some of those Naples biscuits for the Miss. The ones my father sent aboard.”

“Aye, aye, sir,” McMurtry said. “Which she didn’t eat none of her dinner, sir.”

“I shall send McMurtry to buy provisions in Gib tomorrow, so you will have something better than salt beef to dine on. I know it is not fare fit for a lady. If you like to go into town I’ll take you tomorrow. Today I’m so hellfire busy.”

“I would like to, thank you,” Mercedes said. “I was thinking I would step over and visit the Doctor when you leave for supper but I daresay he will be ashore with his patients.”

“Yes, he may be. Listen now, I shouldn’t like you to go about the ship unaccompanied. We’ve been free these last days with those passengers aboard. Now we are a man-of-war again and not a transport, you are to ask one of the mids to accompany you. They are young hounds for the most part, but I fancy they would not cross my hawse and will be true young gentlemen with you. We have no vile brutes aboard like Mr. Sprague. You cannot know how much I regret having allowed that man near you, and I wonder you can ever forgive me such a lapse.”

“I should not have gone on deck when you desired me not to, Mr. Sprague never would have laid hands on me if I’d attended. Your sentry would have protected me. Your men tried to help me even after I’d gone in the water. Need we speak of it?”

“Yes, sweetheart.” He took her hand across the table where they sat with the tea things between them. “We must, otherwise it will hang poisonous between us. I failed to protect you and you suffered for it."

"I know what troubles you. I didn't suffer in that way, I wasn't violated. In the harem I lived with women and children. I was offered no insult just as I told you in my letter. You did receive my letter, when you were living a married man in England? I have always been honest with you. Much to my cost."

Captain Blackwell caressed the scar on the palm of her hand and plunged ahead, though he knew once again he was in shoal water. "I believe you weren't violated, if you say it is so. I am much relieved to hear it, and you must understand I married out of duty and obligation, not love. But Mercedes, tell me, you did not have to make accommodation, you are not with child?"

"Is that what you think, because I was ill?" She yanked her hand from his grasp, and in her haste to get away from him she slammed her leg against the edge of the table. "I haven't been with a man since the last time you and I ... and I wished when we were apart I had allowed myself to conceive your child. You will have to believe me when I say I have kept faith with you, just as I have to believe you when you say you married out of duty."

Captain Blackwell was on the point of reaching for her, to pull her into his lap and tell her he loved her. Not to have done so before now was madness. He'd been given a second chance when he thought he'd lost her, and then stood off and on over trifles like a goddamn fool. The demands of his profession intervened, however; a knock came at the door and the sentry's voice, "Mr. Verson, sir, with the watch bills if you please."

He called to Mr. Verson to walk in, and watched Mercedes curtsey and his lieutenant's acknowledging bow before she ducked into her cabin and shut the door. She contrived not to see him when he returned from the hospital, and before he left for the supper aboard *Royal George*. Resplendent in full dress uniform Captain Blackwell remembered their parting that wretched night in Ceuta, when she'd told him she should show him how handsome she thought he was on his return. The recollection in comparison to their present relations made him very low indeed.

The main dish served at supper was a fine, firm fish. Mercedes didn't know Captain Blackwell had said to McMurtry, before quitting *Inconstant*, "Tell Cook with my compliments if he don't send her something she can eat, he shall answer to me." McMurtry and the one-eyed cook Dickens hailed the passing bumboats throughout the afternoon watches, spending their captain's money on fresh provisions for his lady.

"That turbot ate grateful, did it Miss?" McMurtry asked as he removed the dishes. "Just you tell the Captain so."

"I shall," Mercedes said, rising and clasping her hands in front of her to stop them shaking. "But I shall not need to tell him his order wasn't followed respecting his sleeping cabin, for he will see it directly he returns. Captain Blackwell ordered the double berth restored, and the mattress I made brought up from the hold."

Mercedes waited for McMurtry's reaction, struggling to maintain a matter of fact expression. Captain Blackwell's questioning her constancy earlier had hurt, and she was afraid he might no longer want her, now she'd been in the harem. She was steering a reckless course, in spite of what Mr. Martinez had told her of Captain Blackwell's intentions, but Mercedes had already decided she would follow him right round the world, wife or not.

McMurtry knuckled his forehead to Mercedes. "Right, Miss, carpenter to double the berth and mattress up from the hold."

Her face burned and her knees fairly knocked as she watched McMurtry close the door. Perhaps she was fit only to herd with the beasts. She took her sewing and a lantern into the coach where she could hide from Mr. Bell and his mate. In the event it was Mr. Bell alone who knocked and came in, and went efficiently about his business. Mercedes flushed anew when she thought of Mr. Martinez accompanying the carpenter on the task, when they had been prisoners aboard *Inconstant*.

Yet her Tio Severino had experienced the complications that could arise between a man and woman; and the simplicity on the other hand, of their most basic need of one another. He'd been her mother's lover for years, never acknowledged as the best man

Mercedes' mother had known. She told herself she need not blush for what her uncle or anyone else thought of her. Captain Blackwell would not hear from her of Francis's proposal. Mercedes a little suspected Francis of cunning, of trying her devotion to Captain Blackwell, in his offer. She could not otherwise explain his effortless change in affection to Zahraa. It was not necessity or duty or ambition compelling her; she'd decided what she wanted. She and Captain Blackwell had always understood one another on a certain level. Mercedes pushed any notion of shame in lying with Captain Blackwell, as she hoped to do, firmly to one side.

Admiral Gambier was well known for his evangelical tendencies, but there was nothing abstemious about his table, nor in the excellent wine that flowed quite freely at the supper for his captains. Captain Blackwell found himself seated uncomfortably near the Admiral, on his right hand itself, by custom of the service the place occupied by officers taken prisoner. Admiral Gambier at first directed the conversation, also an immemorial custom of the service, until the puddings were brought in. By this time the empty bottles of 1787 port formed a small tower in the pantry and the talk had become general, boisterous and loud.

"Captain Blackwell, a glass of wine with you, sir." Admiral Gambier raised his glass, looking Captain Blackwell fixedly in the eye. "Will you tell us something of the mission you are recently returned from?"

"We embarked the British Vice-Consul and his suite, sir. Six court ladies, widows of the Dey, and twenty children, infants to about the age of ship's boys. There were four elderly gentlemen and with their servants, *Inconstant* carried a total of forty-six passengers. That is not including poor Captain Alexander, his mid and steward. My brother Francis desires his best respects and gratitude, Admiral Gambier, for the support of the Navy."

Admiral Gambier inclined his head, and Captain Blackwell felt he'd managed the report nicely.

"The Admiralty did not see fit to send anyone but you upon the mission," Admiral Gambier said. "Perhaps they had heard of your experience carrying women."

The smooth old vintage almost caught in Captain Blackwell's throat at the words. Admiral Gambier had chosen his moment well, no one was attending to their conversation.

"I trust this time you will not have mislaid or forgotten any of them."

The Admiral turned away and began talking to his left hand neighbor. Captain Blackwell was struck by how personal the blow had been, as though Admiral Gambier had known all about Mercedes. He was a mum chance heavy companion for the remainder of the evening, right through the drinking of the King's health.

Captain Blackwell came down the side of *Royal George* into his boat five hours after going up. He left behind him a jovial set of fellows, full of wine and superior food, his brother officers chattering away on the flagship's deck. His was one of the first boats to pull away from the flag, and Captain Blackwell stared over at his own ship quite visible in the starlit night.

Lighting in the great cabin would have made her more visible still. She would have shone with greater and greater brilliance as they approached, but it was dark there in the cabin. She has retired, Blackwell thought. When he was piped aboard and heard the merriment rising from the lower deck with the bumboat women aboard Blackwell wondered she could sleep through the clamor. He'd given Mr. Verson and his watch the first liberty ashore, and as Captain Blackwell went below into his own cabin he hoped whoever had young Jack in hand in his father's absence might keep the boy well away from the copulating seamen.

He entered the great cabin, dark except for the lantern light from his sleeping cabin glowing underneath the partitions. Outside Mercedes' door he paused. At least she was with him and he had tomorrow, when he would escort her into town and work on bringing things right between them.

He walked into his sleeping cabin and was staggered by the sight of Mercedes standing next to the restored double berth. She had on a dressing gown, with her hair down round her shoulders. Blackwell recovered from his surprise and went to her and pressed her to his chest. They kissed, and the kiss turned into a hungry, eager embracing.

Blackwell, with a tremendous effort, put her from him. "You are quite sure you want this? You need not, I will wait — "

"Do you mean to refuse me, sir?"

His reply was a muted growl and he had her off her feet at once and put her into the cot. Blackwell leaned over her and kissed her throat. Mercedes opened her dressing gown for him. He passed his hand down her body, caressing her breasts, her stomach, and letting his hand rest over her womb.

He ran his hand under her back, then under her buttocks and lifted her toward him. "I need to wash, sweetheart. I don't want to come to you this time in all my dirt." He wrenched himself away from her and then halted with his hand on the door latch. He didn't like to call McMurtry and his mate away from their pleasure to man the pumps, and to gaze at the evidence of his.

"You might wash here, in front of me," Mercedes said.

When he had washed vigorously he turned to Mercedes and found her kneeling on the edge of the cot. She put her arms around his shoulders and he pulled her close against him. While he ran his hands gently over her, stooping to kiss and suckle her breasts, Blackwell thought what a gift it was to have a woman who wanted him. He cupped her bottom in his hand and then put his fingers between her thighs and applied intimate caress after intimate caress. Mercedes hid her face against his neck and shoulder; she might be mortified he should find her wet and swollen at his first touch. Blackwell was delighted with her warmth. Sweet indeed was the love that comes with willingness. His voice was hoarse in her ear. "You are ready for me, sweetheart?"

She shrugged off the dressing gown, letting it fall to the deck, and lay back in front of him. She was more beautiful than before, just as Francis had said; her curves more pronounced, her lovely skin aglow. It gave Blackwell an odd pang to think, as he covered her, she'd been thinner and stressed when she was under his protection and had filled out and blossomed under the Dey's.

"I love you, Mercedes."

"Show me, James, darling."

She overwhelmed him with that, and with the feel of her body underneath his and clasped around him. He'd meant to penetrate her slowly, in the manner he thought she liked. But a rough and lusty man does not expect to be called tender names and when it happened Blackwell rather lost control, and found himself plunged very deeply in her and moving forcefully over her. He became still and shifted his shoulder the better to see her face by the lantern light. She looked at him with shining love in her eyes, tempered now with passion, and she took one hand from behind his shoulder and touched his face. "Don't stop," she said, and rocked her body beneath his to encourage him.

He felt as though they climbed a summit together, or a mast to the masthead. At the outset he led, but when she gave his shoulder a most prodigious shove he understood her intention.

"James, darling," she said. "I love everything about you. I love the way you taste, I love the way you smell, I love the way you feel."

She moved over him and braced herself up, and touched the length of the scar on his torso. Blackwell gritted his teeth against the pleasure her clenching body caused him, as he'd done their first time together when he'd decided he must always have her. This time he meant to make sure of her.

The feeling of being exaltedly alive experienced in battle and in intimacy washed over him, and Blackwell had been too long in command not to wish to take the helm at the critical moment. He seized her and rolled on top of her.

"Board and carry, Jim," she whispered. "Hard and fast."

He was a powerful man and he became very vigorous at her urging, but there was nothing of roughness in his attentions. He would never mistreat a woman, least of all this lady he loved so well. Blackwell's concentration, his fierce animal spirit was rewarded when he reached a height of pleasure with Mercedes, in the giving and receiving of proofs of love, more exquisite than anything he'd experienced before.

The cabin, filled a moment before with his tiger like growls and grunts and her muted cries, contained only the sound of their labored breathing. When he had sufficiently recovered, Blackwell said, "Lord, sweetheart, I thought my heart would burst."

"I couldn't allow it, Jim. You are to give me such pleasure for many years to come."

"Am I? Yes, I hope so too. You don't know how I missed you." He could tell by the feel of her she was anxious to get up, to go into her cabin and do the needful to prevent his seed taking hold in her womb. He had placed that worry in her heart, and it saddened him as he shifted his weight from her. "And you are not to suppose it was only the pleasure I missed. Though that," he said, clasping her to him, "was quite, quite as wonderful as I remember. No. I missed taking my meals with you, having you here in my cabin to talk to. I wanted to watch you sew, and read."

She smiled at him, putting on her dressing gown. "Your brother told me you suffered."

"Just you come directly back. Do you hear me now, Miss? I have something particular to say to you."

"Aye, aye, sir." She leaned over and kissed his jaw and neck so ardently he began to laugh, a hearty joyful sound reaching the quarterdeck even over the extreme merriment of the men.

Finding he was still awake when she returned to him ten minutes later, Mercedes slid back the window of the dark lantern and blew out the candle. She felt her way into the cot and into Blackwell's arms.

"I am all yours."

"You had better believe you are, sweetheart. Listen now. I know I've done a damned poor job of keeping you in my lee, of protecting you. No, do not protest my innocence," he said, turning to silence her with his kisses. "I mean to do better. If you will have me, I want to give you the protection of my name. Will you do me the honor of becoming my wife, Mercedes?"

"Oh, with all my heart! I should be delighted to be Mrs. Blackwell."

"Mrs. Blackwell shall be Frank's wife, your friend Zahraa if he has his way. No, you will be Mrs. Captain Blackwell, if you please.

And I shall expect you to love, honor and obey or answer the contrary at your peril."

Mercedes accepted the commission and they lay happily silent, her body half over his.

"Oh James! You should have told me before I ... it will be my duty now to bear you children."

Blackwell flushed in the dark cabin. "As to that, sweetheart, I know I am a selfish brute but I wish to keep you by me, and was you to become in the increasing way I would have to put you ashore. If we might wait, a year or two." Or five, Blackwell thought, for he would be over forty then and perhaps carnal satisfaction would be of less importance to his future self. "Why, then I would try to reconcile myself to being second, or third in your affections."

"I should not have told you — "

"What kind of mother you intend to be?" Blackwell said. "You were honest, and I wish you would not stop being so now. I know all women want babies."

"I'll do what you ask. But you must be aware these measures often fail, and not blame me should that happen."

"No, any child you have shall be yours and mine and most heartily welcome. But I will not have you bear a child a year as ..." he had been about to say 'as in Jane's family' but he brought out instead, "as these are modern times. Perhaps there is something I can do. I shall speak to the Doctor." Blackwell felt rather proud of his composure.

"Shall I tell you of my fortune and birth?" Mercedes said. "So you may know the contract you are making?"

"Please do."

Mercedes told him of her store of jewels, sewn into the sash she had come aboard from *La Trinidad* wearing round her waist. "I do not know exactly how to value the stones, but I believe they will bring several thousand pounds."

"To think I've been carrying an heiress all this time," Blackwell said.

"No, not an heiress. The natural child of a prominent man, I find. Did you see a letter in my sea chest while we were parted? A letter directed to Captain Gambier."

"I did. I beg your pardon for looking into your things, I — "

"Should you like to read it? You will have a perfect right once we are wed."

"What gives you the notion I'm the type of scrub as reads another man's letter, eh Miss? Eh?" Blackwell gave her a gentle shake.

"I shall tell you what is in it. My mother wrote it and showed it me before she sealed it. She assures him again, Captain Gambier, I am his child and begs him to do what he can for me now she would not be able to care for me herself. I was one and twenty at the time. Can you imagine the tenderness of a mother to be concerned so for a grown woman? I said 'again' for she'd given him to understand I was his at the time of conception, but he would not believe it. My mother," Mercedes' voice wavered, "my mother was violated by a vile brute as you say, just such as Mr. Sprague. Afterward Captain Gambier could not accept her. Nor credit when she told him I was their child. She had been taken aboard *HMS Raleigh* after the Spanish ship she was on met with accident in St. Helena. My mother formed an attachment to Captain Gambier, and he to her. But after this unfortunate, tragic attack he put her down in Alta California."

"Left her in the New World, by God!"

"It was my Tio Severino took care of us then, took care of her, he was the only father I knew until I was twelve. Then my mother began a relationship with Don Andreas Santatierra y Ortega, the Governor of Alta California."

Mercedes paused, he heard an unhappy sigh, and she continued, "It took my mother some time to recover from the savagery done her. All of this I know only from what Tio, and she herself told me later. I had a perfectly happy childhood. When my mother recovered and was able to think of men again, she was not one for loyalty. If she ever had been."

She fell silent, and Blackwell tightened his arms round her. He was frankly stunned, and absolutely convinced Admiral Gambier would not like him for a son-in-law. He cleared his throat after a time. “Should you like me to deliver her letter to the Admiral?”

“No, I thank you. I’ve thought about this a great deal. It was my mother’s plan, she very much wished me to demand Admiral Gambier’s notice. But when we came to Gibraltar and I learned he was here, a man in a position of authority, and you brought that tract he gave into your hand ... no. What good could it do? He would never own me, and what if our association were to damage your career?”

“You are not to make that a consideration, Mercedes.”

“Do not protest my innocence, if you please, sir. I am a bastard and he would never recognize me, the sort of man he is, and I felt no need of his support when we first came to Gibraltar. I had quite enough in Tio Severino’s, and in what I believed I had of your own. And I most certainly don’t need it now when I have a family in you, and in Francis. No, bringing myself to the notice of Admiral Gambier would serve no good.”

“You must not forget my father,” Blackwell said after a moment, his voice heavy with emotion. “You might turn to the Reverend Blackwell as to your own father, to Mr. Martinez, I mean to say, once we are as one. I believe he’ll be proud to have such a lovely, brave woman to call daughter.”

Mercedes made no answer, and he turned and kissed her.

“Come, sweetheart, none of that,” Blackwell said, tasting her tears.

And he led her into maneuvers that would not have done if they’d been at sea. Maneuvers that might’ve pitched them both out of the berth and onto the deck, but for *Inconstant* being anchored head and stern and the exceptionally calm night.

Chapter 21

In the dark of the pre-dawn hours Mercedes woke up and heard rather than saw Captain Blackwell moving about in the sleeping cabin. She discovered he was dressing; tying his stock, buttoning his waistcoat and taking up his jacket.

"Jim?"

"Do not stir, sweetheart," Captain Blackwell said. "I go to check on the anchor watch. The youngsters are never very attentive, and with Mr. Verson out of the ship ... I thought I should desire young Jack to give us the pleasure of his company at breakfast. Keep him off the lower deck."

"Yes, do."

He came and bent over her in the cot before he left the cabin. "Pray remember, you are everything to me."

Mercedes sat down to breakfast with two glowing males; the captain was new shaved, washed, and had on clean linen, and young Goodman Jack came in pink and scrubbed. The steady, middle-aged quartermaster in whose care Mr. Verson had left Jack had done the gunroom credit when he brought the boy to the great cabin washed, dressed, and punctual to the minute. No one cared to make the captain wait for his breakfast.

The contrast between the boy's bright, fresh young face and the tanned, battle scarred one of Captain Blackwell could not help but strike Mercedes. Yet the similarity in their expressions of delight over the beefsteaks and eggs, and the happiness and vigor shining from them made Mercedes wish to take first one face in her hands and then the other, and kiss them thoroughly.

She restrained herself, though perhaps the more passionate side of her nature, her mother's Spanish blood, would not always be subsumed to the decorous English half. But at the present time Mercedes felt Captain Blackwell needed that side of her to be his private domain. Outwardly she was dressed the English lady in what the captain would have called shore going rig. As soon as he came into the cabin after the changing of the watch, he'd said, "We go into Gib at five bells, if you please, ma'am."

When Jack learned they were to pull into Gibraltar he asked if he might go too.

"You may not. What were your father's orders, eh?" Captain Blackwell said.

The boy's face took on a look of pained concentration. It was the same considering expression that came over the faces of the midshipmen when they were trying to recall the exact wording of the orders of a superior officer.

"Mind quartermaster Joe," Jack said. "And stay off the berth deck unless I want a half dozen over the cannon in your cabin, sir."

"There you have it. There is no going to Gib in those orders, Mr. Verson. You may see us off from the quarterdeck. Ma'am, may I help you to another egg? Jack! That coffee ain't for you."

On deck they watched the captain's gig lowered over the side. Narhilla ran down into it, and Captain Blackwell had just turned to Mercedes. "Should you like the bosun's chair?" She was on the point of declining when Captain Blackwell's head came up sharply and he stared in the direction of the forecastle. "Go in the boat, ma'am, if you please." Mercedes went over the side, and Captain Blackwell strode forward off the quarterdeck and onto the larboard gangway.

"Mr. Bowles!" Captain Blackwell cried out. "Take that woman below, goddamn your eyes! This is a King's ship, not a floating bawdy house. Do you need to be taught the difference, Mr. Bowles?"

Mercedes was so startled by the captain's bellowing out she lost her hold on the manropes and dropped into the gig. Narhilla caught her in a feat of gallantry so fine he blushed for it, but all eyes were turned on the spectacle aboard *Inconstant*. The shouting receded and then flowed back redoubled. The gig's crew flew into the boat, followed at last by Captain Blackwell who dropped heavy and scowling into the gig.

Mr. Bowles began the climb to the masthead; they watched him ascend after Captain Blackwell gave the order to pull away. The boat's crew kept their eyes turned carefully away from their skipper as they stretched out; it was easy to imagine their sympathy with the little woman at their captain's side, who could no more escape his company than they could. Captain Blackwell looked as though he were ready to damn all their eyes.

"Lay on your oars!" Captain Blackwell ordered. A boat pulling in the opposite direction carried Mr. Verson and the larbowlines returning to *Inconstant*.

"Mr. Verson!"

"Sir!"

"All present and accounted for?"

The captain did not ask if they were sober. Some of the men lay in the bottom of the boat, and those sitting up were a frowsy, dissipated, disreputable sight.

"Yes, sir."

"Very well. You will dine with me tonight?"

"With pleasure, sir. Thank you, sir."

"Bring young Jack! Carry on, Mr. Verson."

The conversation had taken place in a roar across two cables distance. The gig bore up for the hard, where Captain Blackwell jumped out and helped Mercedes ashore.

"You gave me such a look when I came into the boat," Captain Blackwell said, pressing her hand to his arm as they walked up Waterport Street. "It was hard to keep my countenance I will tell you, Miss. I know it seems hypocritical but there is a difference between what happens in the captain's quarters, and parading a wench on the forecastle before the hands."

"I was merely startled by your blowing up poor Mr. Bowles so," Mercedes said. "Is there anything left of him?"

"Don't trouble yourself for that young Lothario. I shall invite him to supper, to show I ain't such a hard horse. Mr. Bowles comes of a fine naval family. He is a good seaman and has shown he can keep his head in a crisis, but he must learn what is due a King's ship. There! There is the look of disapprobation."

"I will make no comment on the workings of the Royal Navy, Captain, and what it calls fitting."

"Very proper in a captain's relation. An admiral's too."

He made the comment in the happiness of his heart, meaning he himself might be an admiral one day — if he lived long enough. He had not meant to imply her attitude suited an admiral's daughter. Captain Blackwell couldn't help but wish she should be acknowledged as a gentleman's daughter. Yet he certainly did not want, nor would he permit, any obstruction to be thrown in their path. But he believed Admiral Gambier missed a great deal by not knowing her. Perhaps another chance to decide for himself whether he wished to was due the Admiral.

They continued on to the Crown to call on Francis, talking with the natural, unrestrained confidence Captain Blackwell valued so highly, and he decided he must allow Mercedes to order what were essentially her own family affairs. He put the Admiral out of his mind, and in perfectly restored high spirits Captain Blackwell walked into his brother's sitting room at the Crown, beaming all over his face.

"Frank, you must wish me ..."

He was arrested by the fact Francis was not alone. Zahraa and her children were there in the sitting room. Captain Blackwell's countenance took on its professional character.

Francis stepped forward. "Wish you happy, brother? With all my heart!" He embraced Captain Blackwell, who began to smile again, especially as Francis turned to Mercedes next. "Mercedes, dear, I've waited long enough to call you sister. Give you joy." Francis gave Mercedes a hearty kiss.

They had then to receive the congratulations of everyone in the room. A short while later Mercedes followed Miriam out of the room, Zahraa began to speak in Farsi to Farrokh, and Captain Blackwell took his brother's arm.

He steered him onto the balcony for a private conference. "I have particular reasons for wishing to marry straight away, Frank. Do you have the acquaintance of the Rector of Gibraltar? No? Well, it don't signify. I shall flush the fellow out and request a parlay. May I beg you to allow Mercedes to stay with you while I call upon the rector? I don't like to take her in case I have to persuade the parson to forego the calling of the banns. And the ladies might like to go a shopping."

Captain Blackwell gave his brother a wide smile, while Francis assured him Mercedes might stop with him as long as need be.

"Do you know she brings me both fortune and influence?"

Francis seemed taken aback. "You refer to the jewels her mother left her? What she calls her dowry."

"Just so," Captain Blackwell said. He wasn't above feeling a certain satisfaction in being alone in Mercedes' confidence, and as he did not wish to pursue the matter further, he changed the subject. "You must sup aboard with me tonight, Frank, bring Miss Albuyeh. It is to be a party. I am having my officers in too. Mercedes, ma'am, if you please!"

"She is just gone into the other room with Miriam, sir," said Farrokh, who possessed the most English of his family. "I shall go fetch her, shall I?"

It had fallen out that Miriam was frightened for Mercedes. And when her marriage had been announced she'd asked Mercedes into Francis's bedchamber and said, "Mademoiselle, are you quite sure you wish to marry that man? Mama says I'm not to be impertinent, but she also said if I am so concerned I must ask you myself. Must you do it? Might you not live with us, or with Mr. Blackwell?"

Mercedes sat down in one of the armchairs near the foot of the bed. "You are quite right to be concerned, and it is very dear of you. We ladies must choose carefully in the matter of a husband. I read recently 'the heart is what we women should judge by in the choice we make, as the best security for the party's good behavior in every relation of life.' Captain Blackwell is a good man, with a very good heart. Pray don't think what you see of people on the outside is all there is — "

Captain Blackwell called out for her then and Miriam jumped. Mercedes stood up and put her arms around her. "He is honorable and kind. He is a gentleman, and he would never, ever lay a hand on me in anger. If young Goodman Jack told you he did, it was nothing but boys' ill tricks."

Farrokh walked in grinning with a message from the captain, just like a real midshipman. The sight of him seemed to strengthen Mercedes' last declaration in his sister's eyes, for Miriam went out of the room looking rather more cheerful than when she'd walked in.

In the afternoon the Reverend George Turnbull received a call from Captain James Blackwell, *H.M.S. Inconstant.* The visit began cordially with Captain Blackwell declaring himself the son of the rector of Deane, the estimable Reverend Edward Blackwell. The captain then presumed upon this thinnest of connections to insist Reverend Turnbull marry him next day, foregoing the traditional publishing of the banns. The lady, Captain Blackwell explained, had no relations but one to support her; she was from the Americas. Reverend Turnbull, used as he was to the freakish ways of sailors, who would marry the most unsuitable creatures, had yet not heard this particular sally. He imagined the future Mrs. Captain Blackwell as a Red Indian, and he had a great curiosity to see her. The Reverend therefore became persuaded to Captain Blackwell's plan, without loss of blood on either side.

Captain Blackwell walked out of the rectory and across the street with a light step, an enchanted smile resting incongruous on his habitually stern face.

"Why there you are, Mr. Martinez!" Captain Blackwell called out, far too loudly in his good humor.

He ducked his head when he realized his indiscretion. "Come along of me, sir. I shall take you to Mercedes." When they were winding their way to the Crown through back alleys, Captain Blackwell explained. "She is with my brother. She will be pleased to see you, much to discuss I believe. How came you here, sir? You knew I would appeal to the rector and you cut across my stern, eh? Wish I had you back aboard, Mr. Martinez, man with your abilities, prime seaman. But that's not to be, however, I marked you dead on the ship's book. I am sorry for it. For what that does to your name in this and every British port. It is a hard service."

"I had rather be dead than deserted, sir," Mr. Martinez said. "I go back to Ceuta when our business is done. I have a woman there and a living. All a man needs, Captain. We are better herding with our own kind. Mercedes will do very well with you, sir, she is half Anglo."

Severino Martinez could not be invited to the jolly party forming in the great cabin of *Inconstant* for supper in the evening, but he had been told the hour next day when he would be called upon to give Mercedes' hand to Captain Blackwell in church. This was the reason he had brought with him a good black suit of clothes.

The civilians in their fine black frock coats came first into *Inconstant*'s cabin at the hour appointed for supper. Francis and his companion had been received by Captain Blackwell on the quarterdeck and sent below. When they walked into the great cabin Mercedes went first to Francis and then to Captain Christensen and gave him her hand. "Captain Christiansen! How glad I am to see you."

"How do you do, ma'am? I am a captain no longer as you see," Mr. Christiansen said. "A mere civilian, survived, and sold out."

"Francis is to be congratulated for finding you out, sir, and bringing you to dine with old friends," Mercedes said.

"It was Captain Blackwell, ma'am, I ran across him in town and he invited me aboard. I am delighted to see old shipmates again, to show them I ain't dead."

Just then Mr. Verson and Jack, Mr. Bransford and Mr. Bowles walked in, and in the greetings of the former captain of Marines and general uproar, Mr. Bowles quite lost his look of apprehension over facing his captain after the public humiliation of the morning. Yet his captain was nowhere in sight; he remained on deck. Soon the drum would beat for the officer's supper, and it would be very odd if Captain Blackwell were not in his cabin with his guests at the first stroke.

Mercedes took Francis aside. "Zahraa does not come. Captain Blackwell invited her, did he not?"

"He did indeed, Mercedes. Zahraa sends her regrets," Francis said. "She stops at home because Farrokh is indisposed, and she herself fears coming aboard ship. No, do not be concerned, I beg. The boy got into an ill humor when he learned he is to go home to Iran in a packet ship, not Captain Blackwell's frigate. He has made something of a hero of James, a British Xerxes."

"Has he, indeed? So have I. I wonder what keeps Captain Blackwell. We are missing only the Doctor, and these naval fellows turn peckish if they are not fed on time. I fear them."

Mercedes' laughter met Captain Blackwell as he threw open the door of the cabin and walked in with Doctor VanArsdel behind him. Everyone in the room turned to him, and he strode directly up to Mercedes and went down on one knee before her.

"Miss Mercedes de Aragon, would you do me the very great honor of becoming my wife?" Captain Blackwell had been concerned about the manner of his proposal to her, and his anxiety to do her justice was the motive of the public declaration, an act that would normally have been repugnant to him.

Mercedes resembled in no small measure the woman he'd taken off *La Trinidad*; she stood in front of him shocked, brave, and self contained. She replied in a clear voice, "Yes, with pleasure, sir, thank you, sir," as though he'd invited her to supper. She leaned over him and whispered, "Belay this, Jim. Pray get up."

Captain Blackwell sprang to his feet like a boy, and the cabin erupted in the sounds of compliments and best wishes.

"Well done, James, very well done indeed," Francis said.

He was the first to shake Captain Blackwell by the hand, and the only one, saving the Doctor and young Jack, to kiss Mercedes. Captain Blackwell led Mercedes to sit beside him at the table. After tomorrow, as his wife, she would sit at the opposite end of the table when his officers dined with him. Tonight he wanted to hold her hand under the cloth. They took their seats just as the drum beat 'Roast Beef of Old England' for the officers' supper. McMurtry and his mate carried in the first dishes, and in spite of the sentimental scene just passed order was restored to the naval world as the men fell upon their supper.

It was a meal such as *Inconstant* had not seen during Captain Blackwell's command; a fine supper thanks to the bullocks and sheep brought aboard *Inconstant* earlier that afternoon, wedding gifts from the captain's brother; a jolly gathering with everyone willing to be pleased. But there was a specter at the table, that of Mr. Sprague, at least for Captain Blackwell. They had all survived him well enough, with the exception of the cabin boy from *La Trinidad*. Captain Blackwell determined to ask Mr. Martinez to locate the young man in order to offer what support he could.

Mercedes looked questioningly at him; he had dropped out of the conversation. Captain Blackwell called out, "Doctor! The bottle stands by you, sir," and smiled at her. He admired her extremely. Her natural, unaffected manners put his officers at ease and she even joked with them in a mild way. When they were receiving the congratulations of the company Captain Blackwell heard Mr. Verson say to her, "Pray forgive me, ma'am, for not doing more to aid you that wretched night." "Nonsense, Mr. Verson, you saved the ship," Mercedes had replied. Captain Blackwell was struck by the similarity in the exchange to the one he'd had with Mr. Verson the night Mercedes was taken from him. He felt fortunate in securing to himself this particular woman, who was so much of one mind with him. It went without saying he wished to be of one flesh with her as often as might be. Captain Blackwell squeezed her hand, and pressed his heavy, booted leg proprietarily against hers. He would dwell no more on the misfortunes of the past.

As if capturing his brother's sentiment Francis proposed a toast to Captain Blackwell and the future Mrs. Captain Blackwell. His speech was full of compliments and a happy future with no reference to the troubles of the past, and he threw out at the end only the barest hint to his brother respecting a less dangerous profession. The pudding came and went, a great, quivering figgy-dowdy, and toast after toast followed Francis's. Mr. Bowles cried out, "Wives and sweethearts!" and Mercedes, reaching awkwardly for her glass with her left hand — Captain Blackwell had her right captive under the table — was forestalled by young Jack snatching up her glass to drink the toast.

"That is not for you, sir!" Mercedes said.

She took the glass out of the boy's hand, not before he'd slurped down a finger's worth of wine, and handed it back to McMurtry standing behind the captain's chair. McMurtry tossed off the contents and nodded to her, and Mercedes brought the same hand down and gave Jack a sharp rap.

"Three cheers for Miss Mercedes!" the normally sober Mr. Verson cried out.

Young Goodman Jack joined in the huzzah. Mercedes hadn't struck him hard and even at five a boy does not like his father, nor the exalted company he found himself in, to think him a scrub. When the uproar and hilarity died down Captain Blackwell judged the moment right, and he stood. "Gentlemen, ma'am, I give you the King!"

They were all on their feet. McMurtry handed Mercedes a fresh wine glass and she drank King George's health. Tomorrow she would marry an Englishman and become a British subject thereby; today she could drink the King's health with perfect equanimity.

"Captain Blackwell, gentlemen, thank you for a very pleasant evening. Goodnight."

The drinking of the loyal toast was also a signal for ladies to retire, and Mercedes curtsied to the room after taking her leave and went into her sleeping cabin. She could hear the men perfectly well; their party was by no means at an end. It was customary at supper in a captain's cabin that one spoke only in response to the captain's direct question. But the talk had long since become general at this particular supper, and Mercedes listened to a jumble of conversation. She heard Captain Blackwell's response of, "Now there is a plum," after Mr. Bransford finished describing a ship called *Assurance*, 44, rumored to be fitting out for hydrographical work and the protection of trade in the Pacific.

Mercedes was on the edge of sleep when they started singing. And they did not sing in low church-going voices, no, the seamen bawled out the words. Several had fine voices, making it a not unpleasing performance.

> Now let every man toss off a full bumper,
> Now let every man toss off a full bowl,
> For we will be jolly and drown melancholy
> In a health to each jovial and true-hearted soul.

Mercedes heard young Jack's boyish pipe amid the men's deep voices. In ten years, perhaps less, the boy might be a midshipman. Where would ten years take her and Captain Blackwell? The songs, the sounds of the men carousing, the clink of glasses, made no disagreeable background to Mercedes' reflections on the future. But she had taken off her gown and gone to sleep in her cot before the party finally broke up.

Captain Blackwell sent two reliable forecastle hands in the boat to see Francis and Mr. Christiansen to their lodgings.

He had drunk a great quantity of wine, but Captain Blackwell saw his guests safely away before he allowed Narhilla and McMurtry to lead him down the companion ladder. "Us not wishing the skipper should stove in his head before ever he's a bridegroom," McMurtry would later say.

The bridegroom came awake near the end of the morning watch tolerably well, though he remembered nothing after giving the order for two hands to accompany his brother and Mr. Christiansen ashore. Blackwell felt beside him in the berth, naturally Mercedes was not there and he was glad of it. He had been far too drunk to attend to her properly. As though in confirmation of the fact Blackwell's hands passed over the cloth of the nightshirt covering him. He recognized McMurtry's humor, putting a nightshirt on his half conscious captain and tucking him into his berth like a maiden. Blackwell rose with barely a wince, pulled his breeches on over the nightshirt, and immediately he was outside the cabin door he began shouting for his steward and the gig's crew to row him out past the filth of the collected shipping for a morning swim.

Chapter 22

Levity there might have been the evening before and a great deal of it, but the marriage ceremony was to be a serious and solemn proceeding. It was also to be quite a private affair. Captain Blackwell had a great respect for the Anglican service, though some might assert otherwise; he could not help being his father's son. When he returned from his swim and had breakfasted, he donned his best full dress uniform, buckled on his sword, and he and Mercedes went into Gibraltar. Mercedes' finery waited at the inn, purchased the day before. They proceeded to the Crown where Mercedes shifted into a flowing crepe gown and they took up Francis, Zahraa, and Mr. Martinez — waiting in a side alley. Captain Blackwell conducted the entire party to King's Chapel, proud as the flagship first in the line of battle.

On walking into the chapel Captain Blackwell felt something akin to the sensations experienced before an action; a sharpening of the senses, a calm, grave expectation. When Mr. Martinez was asked who gave the lady away in marriage, he answered in accented English, "Her mother and I do." Captain Blackwell did not mistake which finger to put the ring upon and he spoke his vows in his strong quarterdeck voice, the better to hide the fact he was deeply moved. Like many battles Captain Blackwell had been in, the momentous action was over in fifteen minutes.

Mr. Martinez would not attend the wedding breakfast at the Crown, and Francis took Captain Blackwell aside after they came out of the chapel and had walked into the convent garden next door. "Listen, James, I will fetch a carriage and take Zahraa to the

Crown to await you. I can hardly bear to be out in this glaring sun, but we must let Mercedes take a proper leave of her uncle."

"Certainly, Frank. I had noticed you look a little peaked."

Francis shook his head, and then he went over and spoke to the ladies and Mr. Martinez, afterwards walking away with Zahraa on his arm. Captain Blackwell stood with his hands behind his back and his feet planted apart, watching Mercedes stroll through the garden on Mr. Martinez's arm.

Captain Blackwell was not anxious this time for Mercedes to hurry her leave taking of Mr. Martinez. He was prepared to wait as long as she wished to pay her duty to the man who had concerned himself so actively in her welfare. They had besides, when they left Mr. Martinez, merely to step over to the Crown for the wedding breakfast with Zahraa and Francis before repairing back aboard *Inconstant*. Captain Blackwell didn't have leave to sleep out of his ship, and there was to be no wedding trip while he daily expected to receive new orders. He was content for the moment to smoke one of the cigars his officers had given him and watch Mercedes, watch the play of emotion over her much cherished face, as she alternately laughed and cried with the only father she knew.

The Reverend Turnbull passed Captain Blackwell in the convent garden, he was pacing and smoking a cigar no doubt given him as a groom's gift; they bowed and the Reverend moved on. At supper the same evening at Government House the Reverend said to his neighbor, "Admiral Gambier, sir, I had the honor of performing the marriage service for one of your captains today."

"Eh? Which one?"

"Captain James Blackwell, son of the Rector of Deane, the Reverend Edward Blackwell. His bride is a Spanish lady of the romantic name Mercedes de Aragon."

Reverend Turnbull had been disappointed of the sight of a Red Indian, Captain Blackwell's bride being merely a lady wearing an elegant silver colored gown and a mantilla after the Spanish fashion. It was something of a solace to the Reverend when he later learned the lady on the arm of Mr. Francis Blackwell that morning was one of the wives, or rather widows of the former Dey of Oran. He didn't remark Admiral Gambier's face wore quite a different expression than when they had begun their interchange. It was a look that would have warned the Admiral's subordinates not to cross his hawse, but Reverend Turnbull, unaware, went on. "Captain Blackwell tells me his lady is from America, and she certainly had no one at all to support her other than a villainous uncle. Neither mother nor father."

He was sitting at his desk with the ship's books before him but for the last ten minutes Captain Blackwell had stopped working and been watching Mercedes move about the cabin. Today was a wash and mend day, and she was stowing her clothes and his. She had taken the cover from their bed and laundered it, and as it was not dry she'd laid material out in preparation of making another covering. Captain Blackwell was deeply gratified Mercedes seemed content to live by the Navy's routine, but he was uneasy in his mind about the immediate future.

The most likely event was *Inconstant* should be ordered back to England and laid up in ordinary. He would be on the beach, a half pay officer once more, with no recourse but to live on his wife's money. If such were the case it might be most fitting he should request leave and take Mercedes to Barcelona; providing she wanted to make herself known to her relations there; or indeed he might take her anywhere she wished to go. He could not guess where she would want to travel were he to make the offer — what if it were to far away Alta California — but from the great distance of being two days a married man Captain Blackwell thought he comprehended one thing: Mercedes was a complicated creature.

He by contrast was not. Captain Blackwell knew two great desires, though with a sailor's superstition he did his best not to wish too fervently lest he kill his own wind. He wanted another sea-going command and to keep his lady by him. And with a ship under his command he would have his profession, full pay, and a home to offer her. In any case he could acknowledge himself a fortunate man. If the Royal Navy were not to employ him, he could picture living ashore with her while he looked about for a merchant command.

Captain Blackwell became lost for a moment, imagining himself alone with Mercedes in a snug cottage, where they might make as much noise in their love making as they wished without two hundred men surrounding them in a wooden ship. His needs were simple, but Captain Blackwell recognized Mercedes' desires, at least the motives behind her passion, were less so.

She'd always been able to meet him in the purely carnal aspect of their relationship, indeed she had at times overreached him, but she had done so seeking more than pleasure. She had gone to bed of him in the first instance to secure his protection: they both knew it. Later she'd turned to him when she was distressed or overwhelmed, as though his solid body over hers offered her protection of a not quite physical kind. Now she lay with him as an act of love and it was what Captain Blackwell had wanted all along, without being able to name it.

Captain Blackwell shook off these reflections, he was growing heated, amorous. There was light left in the sky, supper was over, and there was something he meant to show his bride.

"Mercedes!" Captain Blackwell called in rather a hoarse croak. "Put on your midshipman's rig, we are — "

He left off and cocked an ear to the sounds of commotion on the quarterdeck; shouted orders and running feet.

"We are what? Do we practice *la espada*?" Mercedes said.

Captain Blackwell didn't answer for he heard a rapid tread coming down the quarterdeck companion ladder, then there was a great, resounding crash. He strode to the cabin door and flung it open. There sprawled Mr. Hogan, an awkward fourteen year old midshipman new to *Inconstant* this commission. He hauled the boy to his feet by the back of his jacket.

"Are you hurt, son?"

"No, sir. Well, yes sir, perhaps a little," the youngster said. "Mr. Verson's duty, sir, and the Admiral's barge shall be alongside in five minutes."

He glanced around for Mercedes, who had run into her sleeping cabin and was emerging with a towel. Captain Blackwell took it from her and squeezed her hand.

"Very well, Mr. Hogan, I shall be on deck directly." He handed the young man the towel to put over his bleeding lip. "Do not bleed here, son, cut along and have the Doctor see to that."

McMurtry stepped in with his coat and Captain Blackwell hadn't time to say a private word to Mercedes before running on deck. They exchanged a glance; she didn't seem terribly put about, and he went to receive Admiral Gambier aboard. Mr. Verson had everything prepared on deck: sideboys in white gloves, the bosun and his mate ready with their calls, the Marines lining the quarterdeck. And it was thanks to Mr. Verson the Admiral would not find the lower deck full of women. Mr. Verson had put the sailor's wives ashore the morning of Captain Blackwell's wedding, out of respect for the captain's legitimate wife coming aboard.

The men didn't take it too ill; the first lieutenant and the captain were allowing small parties of liberty men in Gibraltar, and they had hopes the skipper would share the largess he was receiving, the gifts of livestock, with the lower deck. The Inconstants satisfied even their exacting first lieutenant's expectations in their reception of Admiral Gambier. The full-throated wailing of the bosun's pipes was just dying away as Captain Blackwell stepped forward, saluted, and welcomed Admiral Gambier aboard.

"Captain Blackwell, how do you do? I heard from the Reverend Turnbull you were married on Thursday, and I've come to offer my congratulations. Please accept these," the Admiral waved his hand toward the store ship coming alongside with its cargo of lowing cattle, "as a small token of my heartfelt best wishes."

"Thank you very much indeed, sir, you are too kind," Captain Blackwell said. "May I present my officers, Admiral Gambier?"

After the introductions Captain Blackwell considered it wise to move on to the real reason for Admiral Gambier's visit with the utmost dispatch. "Would you care to step below, sir?" he asked, and dismissed the men standing at attention on the quarterdeck. Before following the Admiral below, Captain Blackwell said, in a quick aside to Mr. Verson, "Slaughter two of the beeves for the men's dinner tomorrow, Jack." If no one else, the hands would emerge happy from this meeting.

Captain Blackwell opened the cabin door and let Admiral Gambier pass in before him. Mercedes was standing by the exactly arranged sofa and armchair, looking every bit the English lady in a white muslin gown, her hair neatly dressed and her hands clasped in front of her. She'd stowed the sheet she was making for their bed in the time he'd been on deck, and Captain Blackwell eased around the Admiral to present her radiating happiness. Pride formed a large part of his happiness; what he'd felt that afternoon when he gave Captain Alexander a package of linen and stockings with the declaration, "My wife made them"; and now, as he presented her, his lovely bride with her unmistakable air of a gentlewoman. Only he knew she had once come to bed of him after a battle, with the fresh blood seeping through bandages she'd just put on him. She suited him perfectly.

"Mercedes, may I present Admiral Gambier. Admiral Gambier, my wife."

Mercedes curtsied, gave the venerable man her hand, and stepped back to Captain Blackwell's side. The Admiral made a decent show of his best wishes to the newly wedded couple. Then Admiral Gambier, giving evidence why some in the service called him 'Preaching Jemmy', fell into the sanctity of marriage – which Mercedes and Captain Blackwell bore with identical patient expressions.

The Admiral ended rather feebly, as McMurtry left the cabin after bringing in the wine and cake. "Has Mrs. Blackwell told you, sir, we have an, ah, acquaintance in common?"

"Yes, sir, I believe she may have mentioned that," Captain Blackwell said.

"Then you will not think it so very queer, Captain, if I beg a few moments discourse alone with Mrs. Blackwell?"

"You will permit me, sir, if you please."

Captain Blackwell led Mercedes to the door of the cabin, where in a hushed voice he asked her, "Shall you be alone with him, sweetheart?"

"You know I didn't wish to seek him out," Mercedes said. "But now he is here perhaps I owe him the letter, if no more."

"Just you send for me if he offers you insult, do you hear me now? Or gives you the least discomfort, and I shall serve him out. Admiral or no."

Mercedes twice started to speak but left off each time. At last she brought out, "Why, James, you know me. He is not a young man and I could knock him on his beam ends if I chose. Have no fear of me."

Captain Blackwell turned his back full to the Admiral long enough to say to her, "Don't make me kiss you, woman, right here in front of the Admiral." He turned round and bowed. "Sir!" he said, and withdrew from the cabin.

Admiral Gambier had been covertly watching the couple. He couldn't comprehend what a comely young woman like that saw in a man like Blackwell, who was scowling down at her as they spoke. She so resembled her mother, yet with a fairer skin and the Roman nose characteristic of his family. Obviously she was ladylike and well brought up, whereas Blackwell was scarred, knocked about, a fighting man.

In Admiral Gambier's opinion Blackwell was a man far more representative of the hard drinking licentious century just past than he was himself, who belonged more to it in respect of age. But the Admiral could not miss the pure love in Mercedes' eyes as she looked at Blackwell, nor the way she raised her hand and touched his chest right before he bowed and left the cabin. Neither could the Admiral avoid the pang to his heart the sight caused him. It recalled so vividly to his mind when this woman's mother had looked at him just so.

Mercedes decided, as the door closed behind Captain Blackwell, to take the great Vice-Admiral Lord Nelson's advice she'd heard so often repeated by the naval men and go straight at them.

She turned on Admiral Gambier. "An acquaintance, sir? Is that how you name my mother? If you will permit me, sir." Mercedes took up a letter from the captain's desk, and gave it to the Admiral. "My mother wrote that you in December of 1800, a month before she died. I am sorry not to have delivered it sooner. When you read it you may understand my hesitation. I will leave you to your letter."

She curtsied, the Admiral bowed, and Mercedes withdrew into the captain's sleeping quarters. There she waited ten, then fifteen minutes before Admiral Gambier called, "Mrs. Blackwell, if you please." Mercedes was concerned for the Admiral when she came into the great cabin; the hand holding the letter trembled, and the Admiral was slumped back in the captain's desk chair.

She refreshed his wine and brought the glass to the Admiral, but thought to ask, "Should you like a cup of tea, sir?"

"Yes, ma'am, I would be grateful."

Mercedes ran to the cabin door. "Pass the word for McMurtry, and he is to bring tea for the Admiral."

Admiral Gambier drank his tea and recovered. "I understand your hesitation in giving me the letter, as you know its content. Your mother is very blunt, she always was so. Will you tell me about her?"

When Mercedes considered what this man had caused her mother to suffer in spirit, she strongly felt Admiral Gambier had no right to question her, nor to details of the woman he'd abandoned. Then, though the case was much different Mercedes remembered how dearly she would have loved to hear of Captain Blackwell during their separation.

"She was beautiful, and full of spirit, until the last months," Mercedes said, "when the illness consumed her. She never forgot you. My mother desired me to present you her letter, to force myself on your notice if need be."

"Why did you not?"

"She would have known how to do it, I did not. And by that time I'd met Captain Blackwell, and I could not do anything to risk his good opinion. My mother's insistence, sir, on my reclaiming against you was but a reflection of her very strong affection for you."

Admiral Gambier appeared self-conscious and cleared his throat several times. "Nor did I ever forget her, but I hadn't the courage for such a wife, and by the time I began to feel differently she was half a world away. I chose my career over ... and I often wonder if there would be more of joy and less of duty in my life had I chosen differently."

"We cause ourselves much ill not knowing what we want," Mercedes said.

The Admiral gazed sternly at her. "I wish you will have less reason to regret your choices, ma'am. Your mother begs me to give you my support, but I don't know I am inclined to do it. I must first comprehend what is in your best interests."

Somehow they'd moved from a conversation wholly human and personal to one of interest, and Mercedes gripped her teacup, pressing her lips together to hold back making the Admiral an impertinent reply. If Severino Martinez had given her into the care of Captain Blackwell, need anyone know more of her interest?

Yet Admiral Gambier went on, with the confidence of a man who expects to be attended to. "It is not usual for a captain, and a captain with Blackwell's reputation least of all, to carry a wife. You're aware, ma'am, he must have Admiralty permission to do so. Or at minimum leave from his commander in chief. Allow me to enlighten you further, this peace will not last. We shall be at war with France again hammer and tongs within the twelvemonth, and fighting captains like your husband will be required to engage the enemy. Don't tell me living aboard a man-of-war in wartime is in a lady's best interest."

"Sir, whether Captain Blackwell carries me to sea with him or sets me down in port is his decision," Mercedes said. "As his wife I will do what he requires of me. And Captain Blackwell, I make no doubt, sir, will do what the service requires of him."

Admiral Gambier smiled, he could not help it, she was a clever woman and he felt something akin to paternal pride. Mercedes had silenced him at a stroke with reference to her duty, and her husband's. Admiral Gambier sipped his tea while considering the woman next to him, a captain's wife and an admiral's daughter.

"Before I take up my duties as Governor of Newfoundland it lies in my power as commander in chief to make certain promotions and appointments. If your interest lay in that direction, ma'am, I would, out of the great esteem I bore your mother, consider of any request from you most seriously."

Mercedes was silent a moment. "I cannot make any request in Captain Blackwell's name, sir, he would not like it. Perhaps you wouldn't think so to look at him, but Captain Blackwell is not a belligerent man. He meets England's enemies when he must but he has no love of bloodshed. I never saw him happier in his work than when he surveyed the coast of North Africa."

She was confessing to having been aboard Captain Blackwell's ship before she'd been his wife, but Admiral Gambier chose to be charitable. Even he could see it served no purpose to harangue Mercedes over past sins, though he didn't go so far as to recognize he should be the last person to do so in any case.

The interview between Admiral Gambier and his daughter had been civil and odd, yet strangely comfortable, though the Admiral admitted no parentage and scarcely dropped his air of command. He did not, at least, until Captain Blackwell had been sent for and he was taking his leave of Mercedes in the cabin. He bowed over her hand. "It is an honor to have met you, Mrs. Blackwell. Arabella de Aragon was the great love of my life." Admiral Gambier went out the door and met Captain Blackwell on the companion ladder.

For Mercedes the Admiral's behavior was much of a piece with what she had experienced from other quarters of the Royal Navy.

It was the dark of the moon and difficult to make out anything beyond the frigate's deck. Captain Blackwell had to lean far over the rail to be sure the Admiral's barge was secure to *Inconstant*'s main chains. He thanked Admiral Gambier again for his handsome gifts, and told him his barge was alongside and ready to receive him.

Admiral Gambier's voice came out of the dark. "Good luck to you, Captain Blackwell, you shall need it. Mrs. Blackwell is exactly like her mother, a lady I knew intimately well. Never afraid to heave to and fire her full broadside."

The Admiral went over the side, leaving Captain Blackwell on the quarterdeck wondering, greatly curious to discover what had passed between Admiral Gambier and his wife.

Curiosity brought Captain Blackwell below to his cabin a short time later where he found Mercedes waiting, dressed in trousers and the Spanish midshipman's jacket. He was taken aback, having forgot what he'd been about before the great man came to call. Captain Blackwell knew a moment of relief the Admiral's visit hadn't been made after Mercedes had changed into these clothes and they'd been doing what he had then in mind.

She rushed to him and pressed herself to his breast, the way she'd last done when he'd told her of the manner of Mr. Sprague's death. Her arms were between his jacket and waistcoat and then she insinuated a hand beneath the band of his breeches, right where his back sometimes still gave him a cruel twinge. Captain Blackwell wanted to hear exactly what Gambier had said to her, and what she'd done to provoke that comment of the Admiral, but he found he desired even more urgently to remove Mercedes' trousers. "Come, sweetheart, you shall tell me all about it in a moment." He hustled her into his sleeping cabin.

Mercedes was living with a deeply happy man, the present commander of His Majesty's Ship *Inconstant* and the future one of His Majesty's Ship *Assurance*. And as the appointment was to begin next day when Captain Blackwell would go aboard *Assurance* and read himself in, he was also a very busy man. "Bees ain't in it," McMurtry said to Narhilla, after Captain Blackwell had downed his breakfast in what, even for the skipper, was record time.

In the second dog watch Captain Blackwell put his head into the cabin and called out, "Mercedes! Midshipman's rig in half a glass." She was not sure she cared for being bawled at like one of his officers, but Captain Blackwell had been in tearing high spirits since his orders had come. Mercedes was ready to forgive him if he momentarily forgot she was not one of his crew.

Though perhaps she was; for she sat there in the jacket, shirt, breeches, stockings and boots of a Spanish midshipman, awaiting further orders. Mercedes stroked Miriam Albuyeh's wedding gift to her, resting on her lap, and wondered if Captain Blackwell had ordered her into these clothes so he could take them off her again. She pulled her legs up under herself in the armchair and smiled, both at the thought and the recollection of Captain Blackwell's expression of delight with this new command. "A forty-four gun frigate! We shall have room and to spare, sweetheart, and a broadside weight of metal of 467 pounds."

No one could deny *Assurance* was an old vessel, Captain Blackwell had told her, but he was prepared to love her and the commission to take her into the Pacific suited him admirably. She had at last been some use to him, yet Mercedes and Captain Blackwell had not spoken of the interest behind this stroke of good fortune, the awarding of this plum command.

"What is that?" Captain Blackwell walked into the cabin and was arrested by the sight of Mercedes.

"It's Miriam Albuyeh's wedding gift to me. A cat, James, surely you have seen one before?"

"Not like that feral beast. It has more the look of a fox."

"She is quite domesticated, and has been with us these three days. She was frightened and has only just come out, so I beg you will not alarm her."

"She, eh? God help us."

"Miriam gave her me so I should have something to love," Mercedes said. "She cannot credit that I love you."

"I hardly can myself." Captain Blackwell pursed his lips, looking down at Mercedes with the tawny cat in her lap; the cat returned his gaze out of insolent yellow eyes. "I'm sorry the child should have seen me mother naked, a man's body is an unlovely thing." Captain Blackwell leaned over Mercedes, and taking the cat gently from her lap he set it on the deck. "Come with me, Miss, if you please."

He led her onto the quarterdeck. There was a bare sliver of a moon but the stars were numerous in the sky.

"Good evening Mr. Bransford," Captain Blackwell said. "I'm taking Mrs. Blackwell up to the maintop. A whip to be prepared in case of trouble on the descent."

"Aye, aye, sir, a whip to be made ready. Good evening, Mrs. Blackwell, ma'am."

Captain Blackwell took Mercedes' arm and led her to the mainmast ratlines and pointed up. "Away aloft, ma'am, I shall place your feet."

He didn't need to, except once or twice, and the third and fourth times he touched her calves or ankles, Mercedes felt sure it was because he liked doing so. They reached the platform and Mercedes stood up in the precarious space.

"Are you frightened, sweetheart?"

The evening was dark, so much so the deck below was made tangible only by the points of light from the hanging lanterns. Overhead was the most spectacular array of stars, the night sky a brilliant, pierced dome. Mercedes was afraid of being at this height above the fragile wooden vessel in the same way she feared rounding Cape Horn again, with its terrible storms and ice islands. She answered Captain Blackwell, "No, this is stunning, thank you for bringing me. What must it be like here when the ship is in motion! You sailors are a fearless lot. Or is that why midshipmen are sent to the masthead as punishment, to play upon and conquer their fears?"

She heard him chuckle as he passed a line about her waist so she might feel more secure, though he also put one arm round her shoulders.

"It is not much of a punishment, more symbolic if you will. Most young fellows don't mind it, I never did. And it's a damned sight better than being seized to the gun in the captain's cabin and given a dozen strokes."

"Unless you like that sort of thing."

"Lord bless you, sweetheart, don't provoke me. This ain't the place."

Mercedes suspected Captain Blackwell blushed, remembering he had in fact seized her to the cannon in his cabin when last she had on her midshipman's attire.

He cleared his throat. "I thought this would be a fitting place to tell you, the most fortunate day of my life was the one *La Trinidad* hove into view. You are my greatest prize, Mercedes. I hope that don't offend you. You've brought me fortune, influence — an admiral's daughter, sweetheart! — and more love and tenderness than any man was ever blessed with. You are even in my orders. I shall read them to you when we go below."

"Wish you joy of your prize, Jim." When she could better command her voice, Mercedes said, "We have been fortunate. Only look at my mother and poor Admiral Gambier. There is not much romance in life. It is more often a hard service as I've heard you say of the Navy. Yet we were given our share of romance and good fortune."

"For which I am heartily grateful. Long may it last! Do not think I'm insensible either to the likeness of Gambier's and your dear mother's affair to ours. That must have been difficult for you to bear."

"But ours is to have a much happier issue," Mercedes said.

"Amen to that, sweetheart."

About the Author

—

V.E.Ulett

A long time resident of California, V.E.Ulett is an avid reader as well as a writer of historical fiction.

V.E is a member of the National Books Critics Circle and an active member and reviewer for the Historical Novel Society.

Eighteenth and nineteenth century journals and letters inspired the writing of CAPTAIN BLACKWELL'S PRIZE. The sequel takes Captain Blackwell and Mercedes to the far side of the world, on a new personal and cultural adventure.

About Old Salt Press

Old Salt Press is an independent press catering to those who love books about ships and the sea. We are an association of writers working together to produce the very best of nautical and maritime fiction and non-fiction. We invite you to join us as we go down to the sea in books.

More Great Reading from Old Salt Press

A fifth Wiki Coffin mystery

"Combining historical and nautical accuracy with a fast paced mystery thriller has produced a marvelous book which is highly recommended." — David Hayes, Historic Naval Fiction

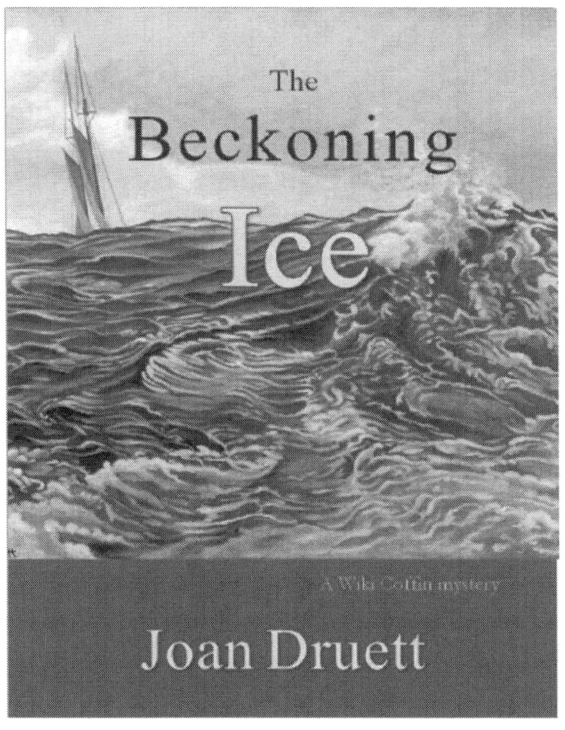

The Beckoning Ice finds the U. S. Exploring Expedition off Cape Horn, a grim outpost made still more threatening by the report of a corpse on a drifting iceberg, closely followed by a gruesome death on board. Was it suicide, or a particularly brutal murder? Wiki investigates, only to find himself fighting desperately for his own life.

Thrilling yarn
from the last days of the square-riggers

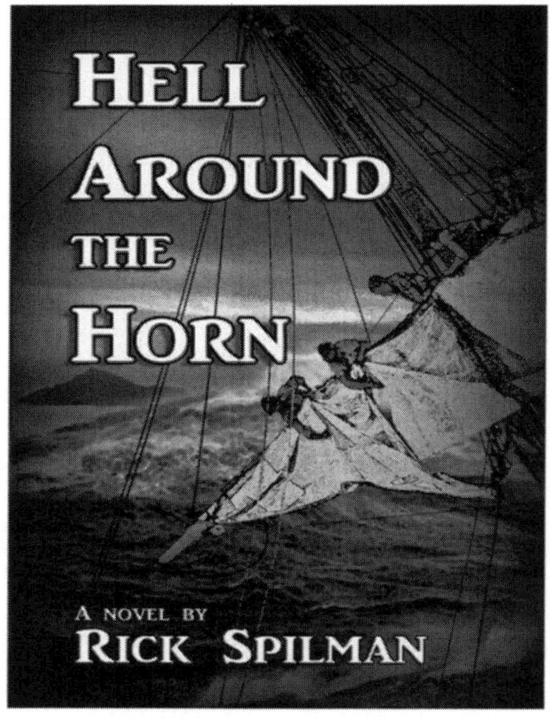

In 1905, a young ship's captain and his family set sail on the windjammer, Lady Rebecca, from Cardiff, Wales with a cargo of coal bound for Chile, by way of Cape Horn. Before they reach the Southern Ocean, the cargo catches fire, the mate threatens mutiny and one of the crew may be going mad. The greatest challenge, however, will prove to be surviving the vicious westerly winds and mountainous seas of the worst Cape Horn winter in memory. Told from the perspective of the Captain, his wife, a first year apprentice and an American sailor before the mast, *Hell Around the Horn* is a story of survival and the human spirit in the last days of the great age of sail.

Another gripping saga from the author of the Fighting Sail series

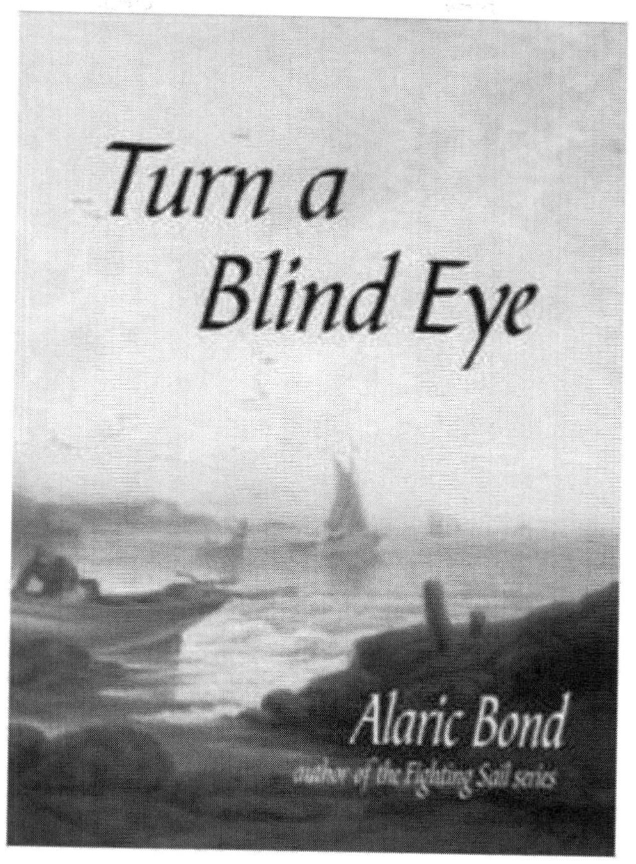

Newly appointed to the local revenue cutter, Commander Griffin is determined to make his mark, and defeat a major gang of smugglers. But the country is still at war with France and it is an unequal struggle; can he depend on support from the local community, or are they yet another enemy for him to fight? With dramatic action on land and at sea, *Turn a Blind Eye* exposes the private war against the treasury with gripping fact and fascinating detail.

Made in the USA
San Bernardino, CA
14 January 2015